TO HIS NEW WIFE

BOOKS BY WILLOW ROSE

STANDALONES
My Husband's Mistress
The Woman He Married

DETECTIVE BILLIE ANN WILDE SERIES
Don't Let Her Go
Then She's Gone
In Her Grave
Find My Girl

EMMA FROST MYSTERIES
Itsy Bitsy Spider
Miss Polly Had a Dolly
Run, Run, as Fast as You Can
Cross Your Heart and Hope to Die
Peek a Boo, I See You
Tweedledum and Tweedledee
Easy as One, Two, Three
There's No Place Like Home
Needles and Pins
Where the Wild Roses Grow
Waltzing Matilda
Drip Drop Dead
Black Frost

TO HIS NEW WIFE

WILLOW ROSE

Bookouture

Published by Bookouture in 2026

An imprint of Storyfire Ltd.
Carmelite House
50 Victoria Embankment
London EC4Y 0DZ

www.bookouture.com

The authorised representative in the EEA is Hachette Ireland
8 Castlecourt Centre
Dublin 15 D15 XTP3
Ireland
(email: info@hbgi.ie)

Copyright © Willow Rose, 2026

Willow Rose has asserted her right to be identified as the author of this work.

All rights reserved. No part of this publication may be reproduced, stored in any retrieval system, or transmitted, in any form or by any means, electronic, mechanical, photocopying, recording or otherwise, without the prior written permission of the publishers.

ISBN: 978-1-80550-583-9
eBook ISBN: 978-1-80550-582-2

This book is a work of fiction. Names, characters, businesses, organizations, places and events other than those clearly in the public domain, are either the product of the author's imagination or are used fictitiously. Any resemblance to actual persons, living or dead, events or locales is entirely coincidental.

PROLOGUE

The pasta water boils over, hissing as if it's trying to warn me that I'm about to be arrested. Right before they enter the house, I lunge for the pot with my left hand, burning my fingers as I grab the handle, a cutting knife still in my right.

Heavy footsteps thud across the marble foyer. Not Benjamin's familiar stride. These are heavier. Multiple sets. They sound purposeful. Benjamin comes up from the basement. We were having a fight. That's why I had forgotten about the pasta.

The kitchen doorway suddenly fills with bodies. Two uniformed officers, their badges catching the amber pendant light, faces set in stone. Behind them, more footsteps. More people.

"Emma?" The tallest officer asks, though it's not really a question.

"Yes," I say, and my hands tremble.

Detective Lucas Ramirez steps forward, and I recognize him immediately—Benjamin's friend, the man I've shared dinner with, whose salt-and-pepper hair always looks slightly disheveled by the end of the evening. His eyes won't meet mine.

Bad sign. In advertising, we call this body language "distancing from the toxic brand." He's separating himself from me.

Gone is the man who laughed until he cried at our dinner table last month when Lily's science project volcano erupted prematurely, sending red foam cascading across the table and onto Ben's pristine white shirt.

Gone is the man who brought a bottle of my favorite cabernet and told stories about his rookie days on the force. This is Detective Ramirez now, hand hovering near his radio, eyebrows rising as he spots what's in my hands. "I need you to put the knife down."

I glance at my hand in surprise and put the knife on the counter, slowly, carefully. The pasta water is still boiling violently, overflowing again. I reach to turn it off.

"Keep your hands where I can see them," snaps one of the uniforms.

I freeze, and my heart starts hammering against my ribs.

Lucas takes a step forward. His muddy shoes leave light footprints on the tiles. Evidence contamination, my mind notes absurdly. "Emma Stone, you are under arrest for the murder of Alice Stone."

Alice? Benjamin's ex-wife?

"Me? No. That's—that's impossible." My voice rises, thin and desperate. "You have the wrong person. It's not me you want to arrest."

BEFORE

ONE

I stare at my reflection, barely recognizing the woman looking back at me. The makeup artist has worked miracles, transforming my usual tired eyes into something luminous and wide-awake. My hands shake as I touch my face—is this really happening? In three hours, I'll be Mrs. Benjamin Stone. The thought sends a fresh wave of butterflies through my stomach, wings beating against my ribs like tiny prisoners desperate for escape.

"Don't touch," the makeup artist scolds, gently batting my hand away. "You'll smudge."

"Sorry," I whisper, but I can't stop staring. Can't stop wondering if this is all a dream I'll wake from, alone in my condo.

The bridal suite sprawls around me, all cream and gold with floor-to-ceiling windows framing the Gulf. Sunlight dances across the water, casting fractured light patterns on the ceiling. My wedding dress hangs on a padded hanger near the bathroom —an ivory silk column that cost more than my first car. Robert— my soon-to-be father-in-law—insisted on paying. "My only son's wedding should be perfect," he'd said, pen already moving across the check before I could object.

Perfect. The word lodges in my throat. What if I'm not perfect enough? What if Benjamin realizes I'm still the awkward account executive who used to stammer when he visited his father's agency?

"You're fidgeting again," says the hairstylist, bobby pins clenched between her teeth. "Deep breaths."

I nod, inhale deeply. The air smells of hairspray and expensive perfume—Chanel N°5, my splurge for today. My "something new" alongside borrowed pearl earrings from my soon-to-be mother-in-law, Margaret, who'd presented them with a warm smile.

Five years. That's how long I've watched Benjamin Stone from across conference rooms and holiday parties at Stone Advertising, while I was working for his parents. Five years of cataloging the way his hands move when he speaks, the precise angle of his jawline, the rare laugh that transforms his serious face into something boyish and unguarded. Five years of listening to office gossip about the brilliant pediatric surgeon married to the art curator who died tragically in a car accident. They were the perfect couple according to what people said. The perfect family.

I never spoke to him beyond polite hellos. Never imagined he would notice me. For years, the grief was too heavy for him.

It was a Tuesday when he first really saw me. I was presenting a campaign for a children's hospital—his hospital. He stayed after the meeting, asked questions about my research. Thanked me for understanding what parents of sick children need to hear.

"Would you like to get coffee sometime?" he'd asked, and I'd nearly choked on my own surprise.

After coffee came dinners. Dinner became weekend plans. His hand found mine across restaurant tables, tentative at first, then certain. When he kissed me the first time, on my doorstep after our third date, I felt dizzy with disbelief. Benjamin Stone was kissing me. Me.

"Almost done," the hairstylist murmurs, inserting one final pin into my updo. "You look beautiful, Ms. Caldwell."

The door clicks open without a knock. I turn, expecting my mother with her worried eyes and nervous hands—she'd been as surprised as I was to learn that a man like Benjamin had wanted to marry me. "He's so established, Emma," she'd whispered. "And you're so... young." But instead of her soft, apologetic face, I find Benjamin's daughter, Lily Stone, standing in the doorway.

She's already dressed in her bridesmaid gown—pale blue silk that emphasizes her willowy height. At seventeen, she looks startlingly like the photos I've seen of Alice—same straight black hair, same penetrating eyes.

"Lily," I say, surprised. "I thought you were getting ready with the other bridesmaids." The four girls I'd chosen—my best friend from work, Jen; my college roommate, Jessica; my two cousins—they were supposed to be keeping her occupied.

"I finished early." Her voice is neutral, polite. Her eyes scan the room, taking in the scattered makeup, my dress, the champagne cooling in an ice bucket. "They're all talking about boring stuff. Jessica keeps showing everyone pictures of her new *hunk* of a boyfriend, and Megan won't shut up about the new house she bought at a low interest rate. Boring."

The makeup artist and hairstylist exchange glances, pack up their things with practiced efficiency. "We'll check on you before the ceremony," the makeup artist says, squeezing my shoulder before they slip out, leaving us alone.

Lily glides across the room. She's nothing like a typical teenager; not awkward in her body. "Your veil's crooked," she says, reaching for the delicate lace confection pinned atop my head.

"Oh—thank you." I sit perfectly still as her cool fingers

adjust the pins, hyperaware of how close she stands. And I feel... uncomfortable. Something about Lily has always unnerved me. Perhaps it's just how much she looks like her mother.

"Mom wore a cathedral-length veil," Lily says conversationally, fingers still working. "Twenty feet long. Dad said it was like watching an angel float down the aisle."

My stomach clenches. Of course, Lily would think of her mother today. Of course, this is hard for her. "That sounds beautiful," I say carefully. I've seen the photos myself.

"It was perfect. Their whole wedding was perfect." She steps back, surveying her work. "There. Now you don't look lopsided."

"Thank you." I meet her eyes in the mirror. "Lily, I know today might be difficult—"

"Why would it be difficult?" She moves away, picking up a crystal flute and pouring herself champagne with the confidence of someone who's done it many times before. I guess I should stop her, tell her she's too young to drink. But I don't. I want her to have a good day today. I want her to feel like a part of it all, of us. "I'm happy for Dad. He deserves to move on."

The words are right, but something in her tone worries me. She sips the champagne, watching me over the rim of the glass.

"Mom always said Dad was intense when he wanted something." She traces the rim of the glass with one manicured finger. "Like a hunter. Single-minded. She thought it was romantic, how he pursued her after they met at that gallery opening."

I force a smile. I can't say he actually pursued me. He didn't have to. "He is passionate about the things he cares about."

"Things. People." Lily shrugs, setting down the glass. "He fixates. Mom said sometimes it was exhausting, being the center of someone's entire world." She tilts her head, studying me. "Do you feel that way yet? Like you can't breathe sometimes because he's just so... present?"

My mouth goes dry. I know I'm not Benjamin's entire world. Lily is. But he treats me well. "I love how attentive Benjamin is."

"Of course." Lily smiles, a perfect replica of polite interest. "I'm sure it's different with you. Mom was probably just being dramatic. She had episodes like that, especially toward the end."

Episodes? The word hangs between us, pregnant with implications I'm afraid to explore. Is she trying to put me off her father? She's never said anything so pointed to me before. Barely ever mentioned her mother.

"Your veil looks perfect now," Lily says, changing subjects with whiplash speed. "You're going to be a beautiful bride." She moves toward the door, pausing with her hand on the knob. "Oh, and Emma? Dad hates when women wear red lipstick. Says it looks cheap. Just FYI."

The door closes behind her before I can respond. I turn back to the mirror, studying the rich crimson on my lips that the makeup artist spent twenty minutes perfecting. Benjamin has never said anything about disliking red lipstick. He complimented this exact shade last month.

Just pre-wedding jitters, I tell myself, reaching for a tissue to blot my lips slightly. Just a teenage girl processing complex grief. Nothing more.

But as I stare at my reflection, at the slightly paler lips and the perfect veil Lily adjusted, an uneasy feeling settles in my stomach alongside the butterflies. For a moment, I see myself through Lily's eyes—an intruder in a story that was supposed to end differently.

I push the thought away. Today is my fairy-tale ending. I've waited five years to be noticed by Benjamin Stone. Nothing—not nerves, not the ghost of his first marriage, not even the daughter I still need to win over—will take this day from me.

. . .

The white runner stretches before me on the sand. The ocean crashes rhythmically to my right, providing percussion for the string quartet's rendition of Pachelbel. I clutch my father's arm, grateful for the support as my heels sink slightly with each step. All those faces turned toward me—the curious, the judgmental, the celebratory—blur into a haze of expectation. I focus instead on Benjamin, waiting at the end of this tenuous white path, his smile steady and sure.

"You good?" Dad whispers, patting my hand. His rough touch—that of a builder—anchors me to reality. It always has.

I nod, unable to speak past the knot in my throat. My bouquet—white roses and blue hydrangeas—trembles in my grip. The Florida sun beats down, surprisingly intense for October. Sweat prickles beneath my veil.

The white chairs arranged in neat rows on either side of the aisle hold Harbor Heights elite—Robert's business associates, Margaret's charity board friends, Benjamin's colleagues from the hospital. I recognize the managing partners from Stone Advertising in the third row, their curious eyes tracking my progress. They've watched me climb from junior copywriter to account executive over five years. Now they're watching me become a Stone.

I lift my chin, focus on Benjamin's face. His eyes never leave mine, steady and certain. Whatever people think doesn't matter. Benjamin chose me.

Me.

We reach the altar—a simple driftwood arch draped with white fabric and blue flowers. Dad kisses my cheek, places my hand in Benjamin's, and steps back. I watch him stand awkwardly in front of my mother, not knowing whether to sit down on the empty chair beside her. Divorced for years, they've barely seen one another. I smile and gesture for him to sit.

Benjamin's fingers close around mine, warm and delicate, trained from years of surgical work. Hands that save children. Hands that now hold my future. And I turn back toward him.

"You're breathtaking," he whispers.

The minister begins the ceremony. Words about love and commitment wash over me, familiar and strange all at once. I'm getting married. To Benjamin Stone. The man I watched from afar for years, inventing reasons to be in meetings where he might appear, volunteering for projects at his father's agency that might put me in his path.

I never planned for Alice to die. Never wished for it. But when tragedy cleared a path to Benjamin, I didn't hesitate to take it. Does that make me terrible? The thought flashes through my mind, unwelcome and disquieting. This isn't opportunism. This is love. This is destiny.

"The rings, please," the minister says.

Lily steps forward, her bridesmaid's dress rippling in the sea breeze. The blue fabric matches her eyes, which remain cool and assessing as she holds out the satin pillow. Benjamin reaches for my ring, and I notice a slight tremor in his hand. Stress? Emotion? His jaw tightens—the same tension I noticed earlier on Lily's face when she entered my dressing room.

Something passes between father and daughter as their eyes meet—a silent communication I can't decipher. Benjamin's fingers brush Lily's as he takes the ring, and she flinches almost imperceptibly. So slight I might have imagined it, except for the flush that rises on Benjamin's neck. Embarrassment? Nerves? I can't tell.

The moment stretches, elastic and uncertain, before Lily steps back into line with the other bridesmaids. Her face settles into polite blankness.

Benjamin takes my left hand. The platinum band slides cool and heavy onto my finger, his voice steady as he recites his vows. I respond with mine, surprised at the clarity of my own voice despite the confusion swirling inside me. The ring I place on his finger is new—he removed his previous wedding band when he proposed, and the tan line has long since faded.

"If anyone can show just cause why this couple cannot lawfully be joined together in matrimony, let them speak now or forever hold their peace."

My heart stutters. My eyes flick involuntarily to Lily, half expecting her to step forward with some revelation, some reason why I don't deserve her father. She remains still, but her gaze intensifies, pinning me like an insect to a board.

One second.

Two seconds.

Three.

The minister continues, and relief floods through me so powerfully I almost sway on my feet. Benjamin's grip tightens, steadying me. Always steadying me.

"By the power vested in me by the state of Florida, I now pronounce you husband and wife." The minister beams. "Dr. Stone, you may kiss your bride."

Benjamin's hands frame my face, gentle but possessive. His lips meet mine, and the kiss is perfect—not too brief, not inappropriately passionate. Just right for a man who does everything with precision. The guests applaud. Someone whistles—probably one of the surgical residents seated on Benjamin's side.

We turn to face our audience, hands clasped. Mr. and Mrs. Stone. No—Dr. and Mrs. Stone, according to the embossed napkins Margaret insisted on. I kept my name professionally, but I know how the Harbor Heights crowd will refer to me now. Mrs. Stone. Benjamin's wife. No longer Emma Caldwell, but an extension of the Stone legacy.

I search the crowd, finding my parents' tearful smiles, Robert's approving nod, Margaret's careful composure. The sun catches my new ring, sending prisms of light dancing across Benjamin's dark suit jacket. I did it. I actually did it. The thought blooms, warm and victorious in my chest. Five years of watching, waiting, hoping—and now he's mine.

My gaze drifts to Lily, standing slightly apart from the other bridesmaids. The careful blank expression has slipped, revealing something raw underneath. Not grief, as I might expect on her father's wedding day. Something darker. More calculated. Her eyes meet mine, and I feel a chill despite the warm sun.

The moment passes. Lily's face rearranges itself into a smile that doesn't seem genuine. Benjamin tugs my hand gently, and we step forward together to walk back down the aisle while our guests shower us with biodegradable confetti that catches in my veil and sticks to Benjamin's shoulders.

I am Mrs. Benjamin Stone now. I have everything I wanted. I know it might sound a little harsh, but the fact that I don't even have to deal with his ex-wife makes me happy. I know I could never compete with her, and I don't have to. Everything is perfect.

So why does Lily's expression follow me like a shadow, darkening the edges of my triumph as we walk toward our future together?

TWO

The revolving door spits me into the lobby of Stone Advertising with a whoosh of air-conditioned chill. Five years at the company, and I still feel like an imposter. Before Stone, I was pulling all-nighters at Wexler & Gray, surviving on vending machine coffee and determination, my desk lamp the only light on the entire floor at 3 a.m. I'd earned my MBA taking night classes while everyone else was building relationships at happy hours. Now I'm not just Emma Caldwell, aspiring to be creative director. I'm Mrs. Benjamin Stone. The doctor's wife. The boss's daughter-in-law. And I have more power than I could have ever imagined.

I smooth my skirt, checking my reflection in the polished brass elevator doors. The woman staring back looks the part—tailored blazer, subtle makeup, wedding ring catching the light. But her eyes give her away. Too wide. Too uncertain.

"There she is!" Marissa from accounts waves frantically from across the lobby. "Back from paradise!"

I paste on my presentation smile. "Good morning!"

She scurries over, coffee sloshing dangerously close to the

rim of her mug. "Tahiti looked amazing! Those Instagram posts? I died. Literally died."

"Thanks, it was beautiful." I don't mention that Benjamin spent half the honeymoon on conference calls with the hospital. That I lay alone on our private beach while he discussed a complicated pediatric case in the air-conditioned villa. That's not the narrative people want. I didn't mind that he was busy though. He's always busy saving the world one child at a time. It's part of what I love about him.

The elevator arrives with a dignified ding. Inside, Jason from the digital team gives me a congratulatory fist bump. "Stone's wife! How's married life treating you?"

"Wonderful." I fiddle with my wedding band. Three weeks, and it still feels foreign on my finger. A brand I didn't earn.

"Always knew the doc had good taste." Jason winks as the doors open on the third floor. "Half the office had bets on when he'd notice you."

My smile freezes. When he'd notice me. Like I was an object gathering dust on a shelf, waiting to be selected.

The creative department buzzes with Monday morning energy. I navigate between desks, accepting congratulations, deflecting questions about the ceremony ("Intimate," I say, not "Small"), about the honeymoon ("Relaxing," not "Lonely"), about married life ("Perfect," not "Terrifying").

My desk sits in the corner with a view of Tampa Bay—a position that signals my importance without the isolation of an office. Robert Stone believes in "visible leadership." Margaret prefers "keeping an eye on investments." I sink into my chair, exhaling for what feels like the first time since entering the building.

"Surviving the gauntlet?" Jen asks, rolling her chair closer. My assistant. My ally. The only person here who really sees me. She knows I don't enjoy this type of attention.

"Barely." I boot up my computer, the routine a comfort. "Did the Hartman pitch get moved up?"

"About a week. But we're in good shape." She taps my notebook. "Your pre-wedding notes were better than most people's final drafts."

I flip through the pages, finding my place. Work makes sense. Advertising follows rules I understand—identify the need, create the solution, package it beautifully. It's a territory I know. Unlike marriage to a man I've dated for less than a year. I wasn't sure what to do when he took those long work calls during dinners. Was a wife not a priority?

"Emma?" Jen's voice drops to a whisper. "You okay?"

"Fine. Just jet-lagged." I arrange my pens in a perfectly straight line. "Let's review the Hartman copy before—"

"Delivery for Mrs. Stone!"

I flinch at the name—still strange, still not mine—as the receptionist appears with a vase the size of a small child. White roses and orchids explode from crystal, drowning out everything else on my desk.

"Someone's husband remembers her first day back," the receptionist coos, setting down the monstrous arrangement. Heads turn throughout the department. Whispers ripple. I become acutely aware of the women watching—some with envy, others with calculation, all with judgment. I blush.

"He's spoiling you," Jen murmurs, plucking the card from its plastic fork.

I take it before she can read it. *Welcome back, beautiful. Counting the hours until tonight. All my love, B.*

The flowers overwhelm me with love for him—their sweetness, their ostentatious display, their public declaration of possession. His possession. I am his now. I can still hardly believe it. My fingers brush the velvet petals, and suddenly I'm back to our first dinner. The restaurant where the staff knew him by name. Wine I couldn't pronounce. His focus—a spotlight I couldn't escape, didn't want to escape.

The second date, where he brought me a single white orchid. "I noticed it in your office. Thought you might like one at home too." He'd been watching me. Learning me. The way I arrange research materials by color. My preference for the left side of the table at meetings. The way I twist my hair when I'm thinking.

Benjamin Stone was watching me. Me.

The third date, when he kissed me against my apartment door, his surgeon's hands precise in their exploration. "I've never felt this way," he whispered. "This is different." His certainty was contagious, because being wanted so completely was intoxicating.

The proposal came six weeks later. "We belong together. I've never been surer of anything." The urgency of it all—the rushed engagement, the quickly arranged ceremony before his hospital schedule filled up, the instant transition from single professional to doctor's wife.

"Earth to Emma." Jen waves a hand in front of my face. "Staff meeting in ten. Want me to move this botanical garden somewhere less distracting?"

I nod, unable to explain the sudden unease creeping up my spine. The flowers are beautiful. The note is loving. My husband wants me. So what if it all went a little fast? When you know, you know, right? That's what Benjamin said. What's wrong with that?

"Put them in the break room," I say. "Everyone should enjoy them."

As Jen carefully lifts the vase, I start organizing my desk for the day. Laptop centered. Notes to the left. Coffee to the right. Control in the small things.

My hand stops on an unmarked envelope nestled between

folders. Cream colored. Expensive. My name—*Emma Stone*—written in flowing script I don't recognize.

"Was this in the morning mail?" I ask, holding it up.

Jen shrugs, struggling with the massive arrangement. "Wasn't there when I sorted earlier."

I slide my finger under the flap, curiosity momentarily overriding the persistent anxiety that's followed me since the wedding. No return address. No postmark. Hand-delivered, then.

I open the envelope, and the beautiful handwriting inside is clear as I tug the fancy paper out. As I read the first words, I can barely breathe.

To Benjamin's new wife, with love from the wife he killed.

THREE

I slip into the Vista conference room, the smallest of Stone Advertising's glass boxes, and watch the color drain from my face in the mirror opposite me. The fishbowl effect makes me uneasy—anyone walking by can see me—but the frosted band across the middle provides just enough privacy. My fingers tremble as I pull out the paper again. I check my watch: seven minutes until the staff meeting.

It's heavy, expensive—the kind used for wedding invitations or funeral announcements. I unfold it carefully; breath caught in my throat as I read the words again.

"To Benjamin's new wife, with love from the wife he killed."

The room tilts. I grab the edge of the conference table, steadying myself. The words blur, then sharpen with terrible clarity. The letterhead: Alice Graham Stone. I think about the first time I heard about her car accident.

I check the door—still closed, no curious onlookers—and force myself to continue reading.

To Benjamin's new wife, with love from the wife he killed.

If you're reading this, two things are true: I am dead, and you've just married my husband. I don't know your name yet as I write this, but I know you exist. You're probably smart, ambitious, and kind. You're probably eager to impress the family too. That was me, years ago. I'm guessing that's you now.

I wonder if you're wearing my ring? No, he wouldn't reuse it. Ben is too careful for that. He probably took you to Cartier, made a show of letting you choose, but guided you toward what he wanted all along. Did you feel special? Chosen? I did too.

My stomach clenches. The room suddenly feels too small, too warm. I tug at my collar, loosen the top button of my blouse. How could she know these details? The boutique where he took me. I think about the way he steered me toward the emerald-cut diamond.

The letter continues, and in my mind, I hear a woman's voice—not mine, but what I imagine Alice sounded like. Refined. Confident. Dead.

I met Benjamin at the opening of a gallery. He was the handsome doctor everyone wanted to meet. When he focused on me, it felt like standing in a spotlight. Like I was the only person in the room. He called the next day. And the next. Sent flowers to my office—white roses and orchids, my favorite. How quickly he learned my preferences, my habits, my desires. Did he do that with you too? It feels magical, doesn't it? Like he can read your mind.

Our courtship was a whirlwind. Three months from first date to proposal. "When you know, you know," he told me. He was so certain, so confident. I felt chosen. Special. The luckiest woman alive. Ten months later, we got married.

The first year was perfection. The dream home in Harbor Heights. Vacations to exotic places. He would give me his complete attention, making me feel like the center of his universe. Did you get that too? The complete, undivided Benjamin Stone experience?

Then I got pregnant with Lily. That's when things changed.

My hands are ice cold now, despite the sweat beading along my hairline. I check my watch again. Four minutes until the meeting. I should stop reading. Should throw this away. Should pretend I never saw it. It must be some joke, a cruel one, but a joke.

I can't stop.

It was subtle at first. The cooling. The distraction. More hospital calls, more emergencies. I understood—he was saving children's lives. How could I compete? But it wasn't just time. It was the scrutiny. The questions. Where had I been? Who had I spoken to? Why was dinner late? Why was the house not perfect?

After Lily was born, I became irrelevant. A caretaker for his child. A manager of his home. The flowers stopped coming. The compliments dried up. The sex became mechanical when it happened at all.

I tried to leave once. Packed a bag while he was at work. His father called within the hour—how did he know?—said he knew of a gallery, someone within his social circles, they were offering me a promotion, a raise. One I couldn't refuse. "The Stones stick together," Robert told me. "And you're a Stone now."

I stayed. For Lily. For my career. For the life I thought I deserved.

A knock on the glass makes me jump. Jen points at her

watch, mouths "Meeting." I hold up one finger—just a minute—and turn back to the letter, heart hammering against my ribs.

> *I told Ben I was concerned about my car. I told Ben I was concerned about the brakes feeling soft. He said I was being paranoid. I was going to my sister's in Gainesville. It's a long drive, and I wanted to make sure my car was okay. It was serviced at Mack's Auto Shop.*
>
> *If you're reading this, I never made it to my sister's.*
>
> *Be careful, New Wife. The flowers will stop coming. The warmth will fade. And if you try to leave him, remember: I tried too.*

The letter ends there.

I'm going to be sick.

My heart pounds so hard I can feel it in my fingertips, in my temples, behind my eyes. The room spins slightly. I press my palms flat against the cool conference table, trying to ground myself.

This must be a joke. A cruel prank from someone at the office. Maybe Lily? The teenager hates me enough to forge a letter from her dead mother. She works at the agency from time to time, delivering mail. It could be her.

But how would she—or anyone—know those details? The specific way Benjamin courted me. The timeline that matched Alice's exactly—from first date to proposal.

The white roses and orchids.

The Cartier ring.

And the flowers this morning... aren't they already starting to fade? The honeymoon where Benjamin spent more time on his phone than with me.

The brakes. My stomach lurches as I remember Benjamin insisting on driving my car to the shop a few months ago. The same garage. "Just routine maintenance," he'd said. "Don't worry about it."

The door opens. Jen sticks her head in. "Emma? Robert's asking for you. Are you okay? You look like you've seen a ghost."

A ghost. I guess that's a way to put it.

The letter crinkles as I fold it with trembling fingers, sliding it back into the envelope.

"I'm fine," I lie. "Just reviewing some notes. I'll be right there."

She hesitates, concerned. "You sure? You're white as a sheet."

"Just hungry." I stand on wobbly legs. "Skipped breakfast."

As I follow Jen to the meeting, my mind races. The letter could be fake. Should be fake. Someone must have sent it pretending to be Alice. But if it isn't—if Alice really wrote it before she died—then what does this mean? What is she implying? That Ben knew about the brakes? That it was his fault?

Nonsense. He loved her. I know him.

The conference room door looms ahead. Behind it, Robert and Margaret wait.

I touch the envelope in my pocket. Whatever happens next, I can't let them see my fear. Can't let anyone know what I've just read.

After all, it must be a joke.

Right?

FOUR

I push open the front door of the Morrison Estate where I live with Ben and Lily. I've felt the overwhelming presence of the letter in my purse all day. The foyer of our home stretches before me, cavernous and cool. Late-afternoon light slants through the tall windows, catching dust motes that dance in golden shafts. I set my keys in the silver dish by the door—a wedding gift from Margaret.

I follow the blue glow of the television into the living room. Lily's there, curled into the corner of the white sectional. Her fingers tap rhythmically on her phone, thumb flying over the screen.

"Hey, Lily." I try to make my voice sound normal, but it's almost too bright; it sounds forced. "How was school?"

She doesn't look up. Doesn't acknowledge me at all. Just keeps scrolling, the light from her phone illuminating her pale face in the dimming room. I stand there, purse still clutched in my hand, waiting for a response that won't come. This silent treatment is familiar territory now. She's barely been speaking to me since we got home from the honeymoon. I'm not sure if she's just upset at the fact that she had to stay with her grandmother and grandfather in an even quieter home than this.

My mind flashes back to our first meeting, after Benjamin proposed. He'd arranged dinner at his—our—home, his eyes bright with anticipation as he introduced me to his daughter.

"Lily, this is Emma," he'd said, his hand warm at the small of my back. "The woman I told you about."

Lily had stood in this same living room, her posture rigid, her eyes flickering over me with clinical assessment. She'd been wearing all black then too, though today's ensemble is less deliberate in its mourning symbolism. She'd looked at me, then at her father's hand on my waist, then back to my face.

"Hi," she'd said, the single syllable dropping like a stone into still water. Her eyes never quite met mine, focusing instead on a point just past my shoulder. "I've seen you before. You work for Grandpa."

"I do. At the agency." I'd stepped forward, hand extended. She'd taken it briefly; her fingers cool and limp in mine. "I've seen you there too, delivering mail. It's nice to really meet you, Lily. Your dad talks about you all the time."

She'd withdrawn her hand. "I'm sure he does." Then she'd turned away, picked up a book from the coffee table. "I have homework."

Benjamin had filled the awkward silence with chatter about dinner plans, but the message was clear: I wasn't welcome. I was an intruder. A replacement.

"It's completely normal behavior for a teenage girl," my mom had said when I called her and told her about the meeting. "She'll come around eventually. Just give her time."

Now, almost a year later, I still stand in this living room feeling like a visitor who's overstayed her welcome. I set my purse on the kitchen counter in the room next door, careful to keep the letter hidden inside. I don't want to tell anyone about it.

"Did you eat anything after school?" I ask, opening the refrigerator, not expecting an answer.

Silence stretches between us, then: "Yogurt."

I close the refrigerator door slowly. "Dinner will be ready in about an hour."

She doesn't respond, but she doesn't need to. I pull out the cast-iron skillet from the cabinet beneath the counter.

Her hair is pulled back today, revealing the delicate line of her jaw. Benjamin's jaw. She has his eyes too, but where his are warm, hers are guarded, watchful.

I had thought that, with enough time and patience, she'd see I'm not trying to replace her mother. That I just want to belong here, with her and Benjamin. That we could be a family, not the fractured unit we are now. But this letter changes everything.

The accusations in the letter make my hands tremble. Benjamin, a killer? The man who spends twelve-hour days in pediatric surgery, saving children others have given up on? Absurd. But what makes my stomach truly clench is knowing someone slipped into my office—my private space—and left this poison for me to find. I force myself to breathe. Benjamin couldn't have done what this letter claims. He's a pediatric surgeon, for God's sake. He saves children. This has to be some twisted joke.

The garage door buzzer interrupts my thoughts. The familiar rhythm of it—three short bursts, then silence—signals Benjamin's arrival from the hospital. Lily looks up from her phone, her expression shifting subtly. Not quite a smile, but a softening around the eyes. She uncurls from the couch, setting down her phone for the first time since I arrived. I hear his key in the door, the thud of his briefcase on the tile.

"Hello? Anyone home?"

"In here," I call, wiping my hands on a dish towel.

He appears in the doorway, still in his white coat, wrinkled from a day of rushing between surgeries and consultations.

Dark circles shadow his eyes, but his face transforms when he sees me—the exhaustion melting away, replaced by something that looks like relief.

"There you are," he says, crossing the room in three long strides. His arms enfold me, and I let myself sink into his embrace, inhaling the hospital antiseptic mingled with his cologne. His hands press against my back, pulling me closer, his chin resting on top of my head.

How can these be the hands of a killer? How can this warmth conceal such coldness? No, it's nonsense. Nothing but a cruel joke. Alice's death was an accident.

"Rough day?" I ask against his chest.

"Better now." He pulls back, studies my face. "You look tired. Everything okay at the agency?"

Before I can answer, or consider sharing what happened today, Lily clears her throat from the doorway. She stands with her arms crossed, watching our reunion with unreadable eyes.

"Hey, kiddo." Benjamin's face lights up again, differently. The love there is uncomplicated, unconditional. He opens one arm, inviting her into our embrace.

She doesn't move. "I'm going to shower before dinner."

Benjamin's arm drops slowly back to his side. "Okay. Smells good in here. What are we having?"

"Mahi-mahi," I say, stepping out of his embrace. "Your favorite."

His smile is grateful, but his eyes follow Lily as she turns away, disappearing up the stairs without another word. The moment she's gone, his shoulders slump slightly.

"She talked to me," I offer. "Said she had yogurt after school."

Benjamin's eyebrows rise. "Full sentences? That's progress."

"One word. But still."

He kisses my forehead, and I close my eyes against the flood of conflicting emotions. The letter in my purse. The accusations. The love I feel for this man. The fear that's taking root alongside it. I won't let it. I refuse to. I love him. I saw how Alice's death crushed him.

"I'll go change," he says. "Then I'll help with dinner."

I watch him follow Lily's path up the stairs, his steps heavy with fatigue. The house falls silent again, but it's a different kind of silence now. More comfortable now Benjamin is home.

I turn back to the stove, focusing on the simple task of making dinner for my new family, trying not to think about the dead woman's words hidden in my purse. Trying not to wonder if I'm cooking for the man who killed her.

FIVE

"So I told Mrs. Halverston that her entire thesis was fundamentally flawed," Lily says, her voice animated as she recounts her debate class triumph to Benjamin. They sit across from each other at our glass-topped outdoor table, the sunset painting everything in coral and gold. Benjamin leans forward, completely absorbed in her story, nodding at exactly the right moments. The pool lights have clicked on automatically, casting blue ripples across their faces. I set down a platter of grilled mahi-mahi in the space between them. Neither looks up. I pour sparkling water into Lily's glass, careful not to interrupt.

"Dad, she actually cried," Lily continues, her eyes gleaming with the particular satisfaction of a seventeen-year-old who's bested an authority figure. As Benjamin and Lily laugh together, I wonder if I should mention that I spoke to a friend about the internship she really wants at my old agency in New York. Maybe that would finally give us something to talk about. Maybe that would finally get her to see me.

The fish sits untouched on the platter between them, the delicate aroma mingling with the salt tang of the ocean breeze. Lily's laughter tinkles as she looks out, but Benjamin's attentive gaze never wavers from her face, his features etched with parental pride.

"Mrs. Halverston won't forget that debate anytime soon," he chuckles, a slight furrow in his brow as he glances toward me, as if remembering my presence for a fleeting moment before refocusing on Lily. "Your argument must have been quite compelling."

"It was all about logical fallacies," Lily explains, her hands weaving through the air in animated gestures. "She was basing her entire premise on an *ad hominem* attack—"

"That's my girl," Benjamin interrupts, his voice resonating with paternal admiration. "You have your mother's gift for rhetoric."

The mention of Alice, even indirectly, tightens a knot in my stomach.

"How was work?" I ask, the question falling flat as I sit down in a chair, but I feel awkward, like I interrupted something. I serve Benjamin some of the fish and rice. Lily just pours some rice onto her plate, then looks at it with disgust.

Benjamin looks up, grateful for the attempt. "Good. Challenging case—infant with a congenital heart defect. But we've scheduled the surgery for next week. Parents are terrified, of course, but I think we can give them a good outcome."

"That's wonderful," I say. This is the Benjamin I fell in love with—compassionate, confident, committed to saving children's lives. Not the man Alice's letter described.

More silence. I take a sip of water, the cool liquid a brief relief against the tightness in my throat.

"Mom used to make mahi-mahi with cayenne pepper," Lily says suddenly, her voice slicing through the quiet. "Dad loved it." She doesn't look at me when she talks.

My fork pauses midway to my mouth. The bite of fish dangles there, suddenly unappetizing. My stomach tightens, a familiar knot forming beneath my ribs. I lower the fork slowly, careful to keep my expression neutral. This isn't the first time she's made these comparisons. It won't be the last. But each one lands with precision, finding the soft places in my armor.

Benjamin's knuckles whiten around his knife. "Emma's cooking is excellent," he says, his voice deliberately soft but threaded with tension. "Different, but excellent." He turns to me, his eyes apologetic. "How's the Hartman campaign coming along? Your presentation is coming up soon, right?"

The redirect is obvious, but I'm grateful for it. I force a smile, setting down my fork. "It's tomorrow. We're in good shape, though. The client wants something edgy but accessible—the marketing equivalent of wearing ripped designer jeans." My attempt to say something Lily would understand falls flat, but I continue anyway. "The creative team came up with a concept using augmented reality. Users can scan the product and see themselves in different scenarios with it."

I continue talking about work, pushing my food around on my plate. Benjamin nods at appropriate intervals, his surgeon's fingers tapping thoughtfully against his water glass. "Have you tried approaching Dad with the concept boards first instead of the budget?" he asks, always knowing exactly how to navigate his father's ego. It's ironic that he chose scalpels over spreadsheets, walking away from the family business that's consuming my life. "Maybe lead with the children's hospital angle—he's always had a soft spot for pediatrics."

I nod, thinking we're both working so hard to fill the space that Lily's comment carved open, like surgeons desperately packing gauze into a wound that won't stop bleeding.

I steal glances at her as I talk. Her eyes are narrowed slightly, fixed on her plate. Her jaw is clenched, a muscle jumping rhythmically near her temple. Is she angry? Or is there something else behind her eyes—a flicker of regret, perhaps?

Benjamin's gaze never lands anywhere for long. He looks at

me, then at Lily, then at the centerpiece—a crystal vase filled with white lilies. His fingers tap against the glass.

I've stopped talking, I realize. The silence has returned, heavier than before.

"We're using a similar approach for the children's hospital fundraiser," I say, grasping for the thread of conversation. "Your father thinks it will help donors visualize the impact of their contributions."

"Dad already convinced half of Tampa's millionaires to donate," Lily says, surprising me by joining the conversation. "Last year he showed them videos of his surgeries. Gross, but effective."

Benjamin's lips quirk up. "I believe the technical term is 'compelling medical footage,' not 'gross.'"

"Whatever. You made Mrs. Thornton cry with that before-and-after of the cleft palate repair."

"She wrote the biggest check of the night," Benjamin counters, a hint of pride in his voice. "But it wasn't just about the money. I'm very proud of how this repair turned out and can still remember the look on the kid's face when we removed the bandages. The way he looked at himself in the mirror that first time, even with the swelling. 'I'm fixed,' he told his mom. Like it was that easy. Like I was some kind of magician and not just a glorified plumber with a scalpel."

I watch this exchange with a strange feeling in my chest—part envy at their easy banter, part hope that I might someday be included in it. There's a rhythm to their conversation, a familiar dance of words that comes from years of knowing each other. I'm still learning the steps.

"I should let Emma handle the presentation next time," Benjamin says, turning to me. "She could probably double the donations without making anyone cry."

Lily makes a noncommittal sound, neither agreement nor dismissal. But she glances at me briefly, her expression less closed than usual. "You're good at that stuff. Making people want things."

The compliment—if it is one—catches me off guard. "Thank you," I say.

She shrugs again and returns to her food. The conversation dies once more, but something has shifted. The silence feels less brittle somehow.

I take another bite of fish, actually tasting it this time. It's good, though perhaps a bit heavy on the lemon. Maybe cayenne pepper would improve it. The thought doesn't sting as much as it should now. Instead, I file it away—a data point, a preference, something to remember for next time.

Because there will be a next time. And maybe, just maybe, we'll make it through a meal with more words than silence. Maybe Lily will look at me directly instead of past me. Maybe Benjamin will relax enough to set down his knife and fork at the same time.

Or maybe Alice's letter is true, and all of this—the house, the marriage, the tentative peace with Lily—is built on a foundation that will crumble. The thought makes my throat close up again.

I catch Lily watching me, her expression unreadable. But there's something different in her eyes—a curiosity that wasn't there before. "That internship thing you found," she says, not quite meeting my eyes, "do you really think I could get it?"

I sense a shift in Lily's demeanor, a subtle change in the air between us as she mentions the internship. It's a crack in her usual armor, a vulnerability she's allowing to show. Her question surprises me, the softness in her voice unfamiliar, almost fragile.

"You could definitely get it, Lily," I reply, cautious but genuine. I see a glimmer of uncertainty in her eyes, a flicker of doubt that she quickly tries to mask. Her guard is down for a moment, and it's a rare opportunity to connect, to bridge the gap she's been so intent on widening.

Lily's fingers toy with the edge of her napkin, a nervous habit I haven't seen before. The tension in the room shifts, the unspoken animosity between us momentarily dissipating. It's a fragile peace, but it's there, hovering between us like a delicate web.

"I'll help you with the application if you want."

"No, thanks. I can do it better myself," she says and leaves the table, forgetting to take out her plate, as I have told her to do a million times.

Benjamin catches my eye across the table and smiles slightly, as if to apologize. But oddly, I feel hopeful. She threw another dagger, but she also softened to me. Potentially because she now needs something from me, but still.

Our bedroom sits in the east wing, as far from Lily's room as the architecture allows. The distance was deliberate, Benjamin explained when I first moved in. "Teenagers need privacy," he said. "And so do we."

Tonight, I'm grateful for the separation. The thick walls and long hallway between us and Lily mean she won't spot me through the door as I stand in our bathroom, turning Alice's letter over and over in my mind. Who in their right mind would send a sick letter like this to me?

The marble counter is cold beneath my palms as I lean forward, studying my reflection. Same brown eyes, same wavy hair pulled back in a loose ponytail, same worry line between my brows that's deepened since this morning. Since the letter. I look unchanged, but I feel the shift inside me—a foundation cracking, certainties giving way to questions I never thought I'd ask.

Who would accuse Benjamin of hurting Alice? The accusation feels blasphemous even in the privacy of my thoughts. This man who saves children's lives. Who brought me chamomile tea with a splash of honey in bed this morning before leaving for surgery. Who looked at me across the dinner table tonight with such tender concern when Lily made her cutting remark. The same Benjamin who wept openly at Alice's memorial service, his voice breaking as he described the "tragic brake failure" that sent Alice's car over the guardrail that rainy night. The police report had been unambiguous—mechanical failure, the detective told everyone. A terrible accident that Ben couldn't have prevented, even though he'd just had the car serviced the week before. "Sometimes," Ben whispered to me months later when we first started dating, "I still wake up thinking I could have saved her if I'd just taken her car in sooner, or maybe to a different auto shop. How could they have missed this?"

That Benjamin—a murderer? Impossible.

Who would pretend to be Alice and make such an accusation? To mess with me. To destroy my happiness.

I brush my teeth methodically, buying time. The bathroom is a neutral zone, a place where I can think without Benjamin reading my expression. He's uncannily good at that—noticing the smallest flicker of emotion, the slightest shift in my voice. It's what makes him an excellent doctor. It's what makes him impossible to hide things from.

Water runs down the drain in a perfect spiral. I watch it disappear, wondering what else has been washed away in this house.

"Emma?" Benjamin's voice filters through the door. "Everything okay in there?"

I rinse my mouth, pat my face dry. "Fine. Just tired."

When I open the door, the bedroom comes into focus like a painting. He sits propped against the headboard, reading glasses perched on his nose, medical journal open on his lap. The bedside lamp casts a warm glow over the crisp white sheets, the plush carpet, the framed photos of Lily on the dresser. A perfect scene of marital normality.

He looks up, smiles. "Thought you might have fallen asleep standing up."

"Almost."

I cross to the bed, sliding under the covers on my side. My side. After just six months, we established these territories—his nightstand cluttered with medical journals and half-empty water glasses, mine with novels and hand cream. His closet filled with precisely arranged suits and hospital scrubs, mine with the colorful dresses and tailored blazers that Margaret subtly suggests aren't quite right for a doctor's wife.

Benjamin returns to his journal, but his free hand finds mine under the covers, fingers interlacing automatically. This unconscious affection—the casual touches, the instinctive reaching—this is what makes Alice's, or whoever wrote the letter, accusations so impossible to believe. How could these hands that hold mine so gently have done what she suggests?

I should show him the letter. Let him explain. Watch his face when he reads it. Ask him who he thinks may have written it.

Or I should burn it. Forget I ever saw it.

"What are you reading about?" I ask instead, delaying the decision.

"Experimental procedure for repairing hypoplastic left heart syndrome." He turns the page, thumb brushing over a diagram of a child's heart. "There's a team in Boston doing incredible work."

"Mmm." I let my head rest against his shoulder, breathing in the clean scent of his T-shirt. "Thinking of trying it?"

"If the right case comes along." He closes the journal, sets it aside. "What's on your mind? You've been quiet since dinner."

This is my opening. My chance to pull the letter from my

nightstand drawer where I hid it after changing clothes. To ask the questions burning inside me.

Instead, I say, "I was thinking about Lily. She seemed a little less hostile tonight."

"I noticed that too." He shifts to face me, eyes brightening. "The yogurt comment. And she actually spoke to you at dinner."

"To criticize my cooking."

"To engage," he corrects gently. "She also seems interested in that internship. It's progress. Slow, but real."

I nod, tracing patterns on the sheet between us. "I was also thinking about Alice."

His body tenses—so subtle I might have missed it if I weren't looking for it. His fingers still against mine, then deliberately relax. "What about her?"

"Just that..." I search for a safe direction, away from accusations of murder. "It must be hard for Lily, seeing me try to cook her mother's recipes. Maybe I should find my own dishes instead of recreating what she remembers."

Benjamin's expression softens. "That's thoughtful. But don't erase yourself either. You're not Alice, and you shouldn't try to be."

"I know. But I also don't want to replace her." I pause, watching his face carefully. "Have you talked about her recently? With Lily, I mean."

He withdraws his hand from mine, reaches for his water glass. "Not much. It's still painful for her." He takes a sip, sets the glass down with precision. "For both of us, in different ways."

The conversation is closing, the door to this topic swinging shut. I could force it open, produce the letter like evidence at a trial. Watch his surgeon's composure crack or hold.

But I don't.

What if it damages something precious and fragile between

us? What if he thinks I believe it? Trust, once broken, is like a shattered bone. It can heal, but it's never quite the same.

"I understand," I say and lean over to kiss his cheek. "I think I'll read for a bit."

He nods, relief evident in the loosening of his shoulders. "I'm going to brush my teeth."

I watch him cross the room, the controlled grace of his movements. The man I married. The man I love. The letter stays hidden in my nightstand drawer. My secret, for now.

SIX

The atrium in the lobby of Stone Advertising is all glass and steel, forming a perfect cage. Employees buzz around like worker bees. It's a huge company with hundreds of employees, and these days I only have time to get to know my immediate team. Now I'm personally attached to the owners, most people give me a wide berth in the elevator.

I clutch my laptop bag tighter, knuckles white against black leather. Sleep never really came last night—just fractured moments of consciousness between nightmares of brakes failing, of cars plunging over cliffs, of Benjamin standing on the edge, watching.

The elevator doors slide open. I step inside. A junior copywriter slips in before the doors close, his expression brightening when he recognizes me.

"Morning, Mrs. Stone! Great to have you back yesterday."

"It's still Caldwell," I correct automatically. "I kept my name."

His smile falters. "Right, sorry. Big presentation today, huh? Robert's been talking it up all week."

The presentation. The Hartman pitch. My career-making moment. "Yes. Big presentation."

We ride in silence to his floor, where he exits with a too-cheerful "Good luck!" The remaining floors pass in a blur of digital numbers. With each ascending floor, my stomach descends. By the time the doors open to the executive level, my insides have rearranged themselves entirely.

The creative department hums with energy. I weave between desks, mumbling good mornings to colleagues whose faces blur together. Their voices follow me, snippets of conversation floating like debris.

"—looks exhausted—"

"—honeymoon glow didn't last long—"

"—Stone men are intense, always have been—"

Jen intercepts me at my desk, coffee extended like a peace offering. "You look like you need this more than I do."

I accept the cup, the warmth seeping into my icy fingers. "Thanks. Rough night."

"Trouble in paradise already?" She grins, then stops when I don't return the smile. "Kidding. Obviously."

"Obviously." My voice sounds hollow even to me.

Jen's eyes narrow with concern. "The Hartman deck is ready for final review. Robert wants a run-through at eleven before the clients arrive at two."

"Great." I set down my bag, pull out my laptop. My fingers hover over the zipper of the inner pocket where Alice's letter now lives. I shouldn't read the letter again. Should focus on work. Should pretend everything is normal.

"You sure you're okay?" Jen leans closer, lowering her voice. "You can tell me if—"

"I'm fine." The words come out sharper than intended. "Just need to focus."

She retreats, hurt flickering across her face before her professional mask slides back into place. "I'll hold your calls."

Guilt twists in my stomach as she walks away, her coffee mug—the one with *World's Okayest Copywriter* that we bought together at that street fair in Tampa—dangling from her index finger. Jen's been my work confidante for years, through my promotion, through her disastrous Tinder phase, through the night she sobbed on my couch after her mother's diagnosis. Another casualty of Alice's letter—my ability to look my best friend in the eye without imagining her reaction if I told her my husband's dead wife is sending me mail. I haven't even had a chance to ask about Jason leaving her for his Peloton instructor. Two weeks ago, we would have dissected every cruel text message over pad thai at our corner table at Siam Palace.

I power up my laptop, open the Hartman presentation. The slides blur before my eyes, words and images swimming together in meaningless patterns.

My hand moves of its own accord, reaching into my bag, extracting the letter. The paper feels different than yesterday—less substantial, more real. I unfold it under my desk like a teenager with a note passed in class.

"If you're reading this, two things are true: I am dead, and you've just married my husband."

The words hit just as hard the second time. Third time? Tenth? I've lost count of how many times I've read it. Each repetition adds weight to her accusations, like layers of sediment turning to stone.

My fingers drum against the desk—rat-a-tat-tat—an unconscious telegraph of my anxiety. Across the department, heads turn at the sound. I force my hand flat against the surface. Breathe. Focus. The Hartman deck. Their slogan: "Reality, Enhanced." The irony isn't lost on me as I try to enhance my own reality, to make it something I can bear to inhabit.

I fold the letter back along its creases, but Alice's words remain suspended before my eyes.

"Emma?"

Vanessa, Robert's assistant, appears at my desk, clipboard in hand. "Mr. Stone wanted me to check if you need the conference room early for prep."

I start, nearly knocking over my coffee. "What? No. I'm—the regular time is fine."

She lingers, eyes taking in my disheveled appearance. "He also mentioned the Thornton Foundation materials need final approval by end of day."

"Right. Yes. On it."

Her eyebrows lift slightly. "He seemed to think you'd have questions."

"No questions." My smile feels like it might crack my face. "All good."

She retreats, and I know what her report to Robert will contain: Emma seems off. Not herself. Maybe the honeymoon's over already.

The thought of Robert discussing my marriage with Vanessa sends a chill through me. She's been his executive assistant for eight years—longer than most marriages last—and her loyalty to him has always felt like a wall between us. I've seen the way she watches me in meetings, her penciled eyebrows slightly raised, as if she's cataloging my every mistake for later discussion. Just a few weeks ago, I caught her lingering outside Robert's office after our budget presentation, her voice dropping to a whisper when I approached. If it wasn't for their thirty-year age gap, and her handsome realtor husband, I'd assume they were having an affair.

I check my watch. 9:47. Hours until the presentation, and I've accomplished nothing. I force myself to click through the Hartman slides, making random adjustments to margins and colors—busy work to appear productive while my mind races elsewhere. Two desks over, Marissa from accounts leans toward Lisa from digital, their voices dropping to a whisper as they glance my way.

My phone buzzes. Benjamin.

Hope your day's going well. Dinner with Mom and Dad tonight, don't forget. Love you.

Jen approaches again, tentative this time. "Creative team's ready whenever you want to rehearse the pitch."

"Thanks." I stand, gathering materials I haven't reviewed. Papers slip from my grasp, scattering across the floor. Jen drops to her knees, helping collect them.

"Seriously, Emma, what's going on? You've been off since yesterday."

I crouch beside her, reaching for the fallen documents. Our eyes meet, and for a second, I consider telling her everything. About Alice's letter. About the brakes. Lily's animosity since the wedding.

Instead, I say, "Just wedding hangover. Still adjusting to married life."

"I get it." She doesn't get it at all. "Big changes."

We stand, my presentation materials now a jumbled mess in my arms.

"I need to get some air," I say, dropping the papers on my desk. "Back in ten."

I don't wait for her response, just turn and walk—too fast to be casual, too slow to be running—toward the executive washroom. It's private. Secure. A place to breathe for five minutes without performing normalcy.

The letter burns in my pocket as I push through the door, Alice's voice echoing in my head: *Be careful, New Wife. The flowers will stop coming. The warmth will fade. And if you try to leave him, remember: I tried too.*

. . .

I don't remember the decision to leave the agency. One moment I'm in the executive washroom, splashing cold water on my face, and the next I'm in the parking garage, keys in hand. It's close enough to lunch—the perfect cover for disappearing. No one questions a midday absence. Even married to the boss's son, I'm entitled to sixty minutes of freedom. Today, I'll use them to uncover the truth.

My car chirps as I unlock it, the sound unnaturally cheerful in the concrete cavern. I slide behind the wheel, hands trembling as I insert the key. The engine purrs to life. Reliable. Safe. Benjamin had it serviced a few weeks ago. The thought hits me like a physical blow. Benjamin. My car. The brakes. I check them immediately, pressing the pedal to the floor. It responds with reassuring firmness. But would I know if something was wrong? Would Alice have known?

Before I know it, the exit ramp spirals upward. I don't even remember putting my foot on the gas. Sunlight blinds me as I emerge onto the street, the Florida heat an immediate assault. I navigate through downtown Tampa on autopilot, muscle memory guiding me toward Industrial Boulevard where Mack's Auto Shop squats between a discount furniture warehouse and a vape store.

The shop's sign flickers in the midday sun, neon tubing visible even in daylight. MACK'S AUTO. Where I know Alice's car was serviced before she died.

I park under a palm tree that offers more symbolic shade than actual relief from the heat. The asphalt shimmers, waves of heat distorting the air. My blouse sticks to my back as I cross the lot, heels entirely wrong for this environment. Everything about me is wrong for this—my clothes, my questions, my suspicions.

What am I even doing here?

The service bay doors stand open, offering glimpses of cars in various states of dismemberment. Rock music blares from unseen speakers, competing with the metallic symphony of wrenches and impact drivers. I step inside, the temperature dropping as I enter the shadowed interior. The smell hits me immediately—oil, rubber, metal, sweat. The perfume of mechanical surgery.

A man in blue coveralls notices me, straightens from under an elevated Honda. He wipes his hands on a rag that leaves more grease than it removes. "Help you, ma'am?"

"I hope so." My voice sounds foreign to my ears. Too high. Too tight. "I need to ask about a car you serviced. Not recently. Five years ago."

He squints, assessing my tailored dress and heels. "Records office is closed for lunch. Marge'll be back at one if you wanna come back."

"I can't wait that long." The desperation in my voice must register because his expression shifts.

"What's the name? I'll see what I remember, but no promises."

"Stone. Alice Stone."

Recognition flickers across his face. "Dr. Stone's first wife? The one who died in that accident up by Crystal River?"

My stomach clenches. "Yes. That's her."

He shakes his head, calls over his shoulder. "Hey, Anton! Lady here asking about the Stone woman's car. The one that went off the bridge."

A heavy-set man emerges from behind a tool cabinet, wiping his hands on a shop towel. His face is weathered, eyes sharp beneath bushy brows. "Why you asking about that?" His accent is Eastern European, words clipped and precise.

"I'm—" What am I? A suspicious second wife? An amateur detective? A potential next victim? "I'm trying to understand what happened. For the family."

The guy with the name Anton on his chest studies me, gaze traveling from my face to my left hand, where my wedding ring catches the fluorescent light. Understanding dawns in his eyes. "You're the new Mrs. Stone."

It's not a question. I don't deny it.

"We checked the entire car." He tosses the towel onto a workbench. "Nothing wrong with it."

"Nothing with the brakes?" I press.

"No problem with brakes." He shakes his head emphatically. "I remember because after accident, police ask same questions."

My heart pounds against my ribs. "But there was something wrong with her brakes. That's what caused the accident."

Anton shrugs. "Not our work. Maybe she take car somewhere else after."

"Or maybe someone tampered with them," I say, the words slipping out before I can stop them.

The shop falls silent. Even the rock music seems to fade. The first mechanic shifts uncomfortably. "Look, lady, we don't want any trouble. That was a tragedy, what happened to Mrs. Stone. But we only did what was on the work order. We checked the car like they asked. Checked the engine, and the brakes. Everything was fine. Nothing else."

Anton nods in agreement. "Dr. Stone bring car himself. Wait while we work. Take car after. That's all."

My breath catches. "Benjamin brought the car in? Not Alice?"

"Dr. Stone," Anton confirms. "He say wife too busy. He handle it."

The world tilts slightly. "When was this? Exactly?"

Anton confers briefly with the other mechanic in hushed tones. "Three days before accident. I remember because police very interested in this detail."

"Thank you." The words come out as a whisper. I turn, needing air, needing space to process this information.

"Mrs. Stone," Anton calls after me. "Police investigate very thorough. If something wrong, they find. It was an accident. No one could have prevented it. That's what they said. Now you let it go."

I walk away feeling confused. They checked the car. It was fine.

Three days later, Alice died when her car plunged off a bridge due to brake failure.

My hands tremble as I pull out my phone. Google search: "Alice Stone death Tampa accident." Dozens of results appear. News articles. Obituaries. Brief mentions in medical community newsletters praising Dr. Benjamin Stone's courage in returning to work "despite his tragic loss."

I click the *Tampa Bay Times* article, dated five years ago:

Local Surgeon's Wife Dies in Tragic Accident

Alice Stone, 39, wife of prominent pediatric surgeon Dr. Benjamin Stone, died yesterday when her car plunged off the Crystal River Bridge. Preliminary investigation suggests brake failure as the cause. Mrs. Stone was traveling to visit her sister in Gainesville when the accident occurred. There were no witnesses to the crash, but skid marks indicate she attempted to stop before hitting the guardrail. Dr. Stone, devastated by the loss, asks for privacy during this difficult time. The couple's teenage daughter was not in the vehicle...

Sweat beads on my forehead despite the car's air conditioning. My palms leave damp prints on the steering wheel as I scroll through article after article. Each confirms the same details: brake failure. No witnesses. A tragic accident that left a brilliant surgeon a widower and a young girl motherless. Exactly as Ben told me. Exactly as I remember from the office. Exactly as Alice predicted in her letter.

I keep circling back to the accident report. Benjamin had the car inspected beforehand—what more could he have done? Maybe I'm asking the wrong questions entirely. Not if Ben killed Alice, but who's trying to make me believe he did. Who benefits from planting these doubts? Who wants to drive a wedge between us?

The answer floats to the surface of my mind like a dark shape beneath ice. I try to push it down, but it rises anyway.

Lily.

SEVEN

I slam the car into park; the clock on my dashboard reads 2:37. I can't believe it. The presentation started thirty-seven minutes ago. Without me. I've never missed a client meeting in my years at Stone Advertising. Never been late. Never been anything less than perfectly prepared. Until today. I grab my bag and run toward the entrance door, heels catching on the pavement, nearly sending me sprawling. Physical injury would be a better excuse than the truth.

The lobby security guard gives me a quizzical look as I dash past, abandoning dignity for speed. "Hold the elevator!" I call to a man in a gray suit. He obliges, hand stopping the closing doors. I mumble thanks, then watch the numbers climb with excruciating slowness. A dozen scenarios play through my mind, each worse than the last. Robert's disappointment. The client's confusion. My team's embarrassment. My career imploding in real-time while I chased ghosts and suspicions.

The doors slide open on my floor, revealing a hushed executive floor. Eyes turn toward me—some curious, others gleeful at witnessing professional suicide. Jen intercepts me before I reach the main conference room, her expression a mix of concern and secondhand embarrassment.

"They finished a few minutes ago," she whispers, steering me away from the glass-walled room where staff are clearing coffee cups and presentation materials. "Robert did the pitch himself."

"Where is he now?" My voice sounds distant, hollow.

"His office. He asked to see you the minute you got back." She pauses, lowering her voice further. "Emma, what happened? I covered as long as I could, told them you had an emergency, but—"

"I'll explain later." I won't, but it's easier than the truth.

I move through the department on autopilot, aware of whispers following me like contrails. Marissa and Lisa fall silent as I pass, their expressions switching from gossip-hungry to professionally sympathetic so quickly it would be comical under other circumstances. The creative team averts their eyes, embarrassed for me or by me, I can't tell which.

Robert's corner office occupies the prime real estate of the floor—three glass walls offering panoramic views of Tampa Bay. His assistant's desk sits empty; she's probably taking a late lunch break, after witnessing Robert salvage the pitch I abandoned. I pause at the threshold, trying to steady my breathing, to prepare some explanation that won't sound insane or accusatory.

He sees me before I can knock, looking up from his computer with eyes so similar to Benjamin's, it makes my chest tighten. Same shape. Same intensity. My father-in-law has always loved me and been impressed with my work.

How do I explain this to him?

"Come in, Emma." His voice carries through the closed door.

I enter, closing the door behind me. The click of the latch sounds like a cell door locking.

Robert doesn't stand, doesn't offer me a seat. He simply

watches as I cross the expanse of plush carpet to stand before his massive desk—a supplicant awaiting judgment.

"I'm sorry," I begin, the words inadequate even as they leave my lips. "There was an emergency and I—"

"Stop." One word, quietly delivered, but it cuts through my explanation like a scalpel. "I'm not interested in excuses."

I fall silent, hands clasped before me to hide their trembling.

"Five years at this agency, Emma. Five years of exemplary work. Meticulous preparation. Perfect attendance." He taps his pen against the desk calendar, marking time with tiny percussive beats. "And then suddenly, weeks after marrying my son, you miss the most important presentation of the quarter. A presentation you've been preparing for months."

My face burns. Sweat trickles down my spine, soaking into the silk blouse that's already wilted from the afternoon heat and my frantic dash from parking garage to office.

"The Hartmans were disappointed. They specifically requested you, based on your previous campaigns. I had to explain that you were unavailable due to an unspecified emergency." His eyes narrow slightly. "An emergency so dire you couldn't even send a text message to alert us."

"I should have called. I know that was unacceptable and—"

"What was the emergency, Emma?"

If I lie, he'll know. If I tell the truth—that I was investigating his son's possible involvement in his first wife's death—I'll destroy everything. My marriage. My career. Possibly my safety.

"It was personal," I say finally. "A matter I needed to address immediately."

"Personal." He repeats the word like it's foreign to him. "More important than your professional responsibilities? Than your commitment to this agency? To the Stone family business?"

The Stone family business. Not just the agency, but the

entire enterprise of being a Stone. Of protecting the family name, its reputation.

"It won't happen again," I promise, voice steadier than I feel.

"No." Robert stands now, his full height imposing even across the desk. "It won't. Because if it does, Emma, marriage to my son won't protect your position here."

Something flickers across his face—before he continues, "Alice understood the expectations that come with being a Stone. The commitment to excellence. To family." He straightens his tie, a nervous gesture at odds with his controlled tone. "I had hoped you understood them too."

"I do." The lie tastes bitter. "Today was an aberration."

"See that it remains one." He sits back down, focus returning to his computer screen—dismissal without words. "The Hartmans have given us another chance. Presentation rescheduled for Monday. Don't disappoint them again."

"Thank you. I won't." I turn to leave, desperate to escape his scrutiny, to process what just happened.

"Emma." His voice stops me at the door. "Benjamin mentioned you seemed... distracted... last night. Said you were asking questions about Alice."

My hand freezes on the doorknob. "Just trying to understand Lily better. To help her adjust."

Robert studies me, his gaze eerily like his son's when Benjamin is assessing a difficult case. "Some subjects are better left alone. For everyone's sake." The warning in his tone is unmistakable. "Focus on your future with Benjamin, not his past with Alice."

I force a smile, grateful for the door under my hand—support when my knees want to buckle. "Of course. You're right."

He nods once, returning to his work. Conversation over. Threat delivered.

I escape into the hallway, legs trembling with the effort of appearing normal.

I walk back to my desk on unsteady legs, aware of eyes tracking my movement, of conversations pausing as I pass. My professional reputation lies in tatters—the account executive who abandoned her presentation, who disappointed the company's owner, who's already showing signs of instability barely a month into her marriage.

Whoever wrote that letter has got what they wanted. Upset my career, my relationship with my father-in-law, and my husband.

My computer screen shows seventeen new emails, three marked urgent. The Hartman deck sits open where I abandoned it hours ago.

I sink into my chair, fingers hovering over the keyboard.

I cannot let their letter derail everything I've worked for.

EIGHT

"You're quiet," Benjamin says, glancing sideways at me as we park between Robert's gleaming black Mercedes and Margaret's vintage Jaguar. "Still thinking about what happened with the Hartman pitch?"

I force a smile, though my lips feel numb. We're going to dinner at his parents', something that usually doesn't make me feel nervous, but after what happened today, it does. I'm usually Robert and Margaret's favorite, and sometimes I think they even prefer me over Benjamin. I was a bit of a class pet at work years before I got involved with Benjamin; I've always been someone they could trust. Depend on. But today is different. I messed up. I disappointed them, and here we are going to family dinner at their penthouse apartment.

"Just tired. It's been a long day."

"Dad will get over it." He reaches across the console, squeezes my knee. I didn't tell him why I was late. I just told him I went for lunch and lost track of time. That traffic slowed me down. "The Hartmans rescheduled. You'll wow them on Monday, and everything will be fine."

Everything will be fine. The platitude hangs between us,

absurd in its inadequacy. It feels like nothing will ever be fine again. It's like I can't snap out of this feeling of dread. Two days ago everything was perfect, but now it all seems to have been a lie. Was this what the sender of the letter wanted? To see me break apart? I think about Lily, and the insane thought in my head that she'd want to upset me. I've locked it away ever since I left the office, pushing the idea of her penning the letter as I'd redone my makeup. No. I need to ignore this. She would never pretend to be her own dead mother.

I stare up at the penthouse as the private elevator ascends to the seventeenth floor. The doors open to reveal twenty-foot floor-to-ceiling windows framing Tampa Bay. Outside, sailboats scatter like confetti across water that shifts from turquoise to cobalt. Inside, Italian marble gleams under recessed lighting, reflecting the sunset's amber glow across minimalist furniture that probably costs more than my parents' house. This isn't just luxury—it's the kind of calculated opulence that appears in architectural digests, not because it's unique, but because it embodies what new money looks like in Florida: expansive, exposed, yet somehow still impenetrable.

"We don't have to stay long," Benjamin offers, mistaking my hesitation for simple reluctance. "Early surgery tomorrow."

"It's fine," I lie, smoothing my navy-blue dress. I chose it carefully this morning—conservative but stylish—yet now I worry it's wrong. I never used to worry about what his parents thought of me.

Benjamin steps forward, calling out, "We're here!" with the easy confidence of someone returning to their childhood home.

The foyer opens before us like the mouth of some elegant beast. Marble floors gleam under the crystal chandelier. A sweeping staircase curves upward to the second floor. Fresh flowers—white roses and lilies, always white—spill from a massive silver urn. The air smells of beeswax and lemon oil and money.

And everywhere, watching from gilt frames, are the Stones. Generations of them stare down from the walls—Robert's father, the founding patriarch of Stone Advertising; Margaret's mother, a renowned philanthropist; Robert and Margaret on their wedding day; Benjamin in his graduation cap and gown.

And Alice.

Alice with her striking dark hair, her intelligent green eyes, her subtle smile that suggests she knows something you don't. She's wearing emerald green in the picture, the color enhancing her eyes, her pale skin luminous against the dark background.

I can't look away from her.

"Emma, darling." Margaret appears from the direction of the kitchen, her silver hair swept into an immaculate chignon, her beige silk dress exactly the neutral elegance I anticipated. She air-kisses my cheeks, her perfume—something French and understated—enveloping me briefly. "How lovely to see you."

"You too," I say.

"You look tired," she adds. "Working too hard?"

"Not hard enough, according to Dad," Benjamin interjects with a forced laugh, leaning in to kiss his mother's cheek.

"Robert mentioned the presentation." Margaret's eyes flicker over me. "Such a shame. The Hartmans are important clients. That's why we gave you that account."

"I'm aware," I say, my voice tight. She's disappointed. She had higher hopes for me. I know this. I love Benjamin's parents and can't stand to disappoint them. "It won't happen again."

"Of course not." She smiles. "We all have off days. Drink?" She turns, heading toward the sitting room without waiting for my response.

Robert emerges from his study, crossing the foyer with the purposeful stride of a man accustomed to commanding rooms. He clasps Benjamin's hand firmly, clapping him on the shoulder with his free hand. "Son. Good to see you."

His greeting to me is a curt nod, not the warm welcome I

usually get, his eyes already moving past me toward the elevator doors as they open again.

Lily enters like she's stepping onto a stage, her timing impeccable. She drove here by herself as she always does. In the BMW that her grandparents gave her. She's wearing a simple black dress that somehow looks both age-appropriate and sophisticated. Her dark hair falls in perfect waves around her face, and I realize with a jolt that she's styled it exactly like the Alice in the portrait—swept to one side, revealing the elegant line of her neck.

"Grandpa!" She crosses the foyer with swift grace, embracing Robert with genuine affection. "I bought the book you mentioned. It's fascinating already."

"That's my girl." Robert's face transforms, the stern lines softening into something approaching tenderness. "Always curious, just like your grandmother."

Margaret appears at his side, drawing Lily into a hug. "Darling, you look lovely. That dress is perfect on you."

"Thanks, Grandma." Lily preens slightly under the praise. "It was Mom's."

The ghost of Alice thickens in the air between us. I catch Benjamin's expression—a flash of surprise, then pain, then careful neutrality.

I smooth my dress again, an anxious gesture I can't seem to control. Behind me, reflected in the mirror, I see the family conversation flowing without me. Robert has his arm around Lily's shoulders. Margaret is saying something that makes Benjamin laugh. They form a perfect composition—grandfather, grandmother, father, daughter. No space for me in the frame.

Is this all part of Lily's plan? To make me miserable? To make me feel like an outsider? Maybe even to make me fear Benjamin? Enough for me to leave and get out of her life for good? Could she really be that cunning?

It's odd that I've received this letter and Lily's references to her mother have turned up a notch. Is she baiting me? I try to shake the idea away.

"Let me freshen your drink, Robert." I turn, attempting to insert myself back into the circle, holding out my hand for his empty glass.

"No need." Margaret intercepts smoothly. "Only I know exactly how he likes it. Why don't you tell us about that new restaurant you mentioned, Lily? The one near your school?"

Just like that, I'm redirected, sidelined. My attempt at small talk—at performing the role of helpful daughter-in-law—deflected. I retreat a step, then another, until my back touches the cool wall. From this vantage point, I can see Alice's portrait again. Her eyes seem to follow me, her slight smile knowing.

"Shall we move to the dining room?" Margaret's voice cuts through my thoughts. "Dinner is ready."

The family moves as one entity, flowing from foyer to dining room in synchronicity. I follow a step behind, separate, watching the back of my husband's head as he walks alongside his daughter. My heels click against the marble, too loud. The sound broadcasts my presence, my otherness. I am not silent and graceful like Margaret. Not poised and perfect like Lily. Not confident and commanding like Robert. I've never felt so detached from them.

The dining room stretches before us like a showroom from *Architectural Digest*. A Lindsey Adelman chandelier—bubbles of hand-blown glass suspended from brass branches—casts a warm glow onto the twelve-foot Molteni dining table, its matte black surface reflecting nothing. Ghost chairs, transparent and eerily empty, surround it. In the corner, a Noguchi floor lamp curves like a question mark beside a Barcelona chair no one ever sits in. Three identical Koons balloon dog sculptures—electric blue, canary yellow, and hot pink—stand sentinel on the Carrara marble sideboard. This space, like everything in the

Stone penthouse, is designed to broadcast success without appearing to try.

Robert takes his position at the head of the table without discussion. Margaret glides to the opposite end, her movements fluid and practiced. Benjamin pulls out a chair for me on one side, then sits beside me. Lily settles directly across, her posture perfect, her expression unreadable. For the first time, the seating arrangement doesn't feel accidental—it places me with my back to the doorway, unable to see who might enter, while positioning me directly in Robert and Margaret's lines of sight. An arrangement that feels like it's designed for observation. For interrogation. Or is this just my anxiety?

Maria materializes beside Robert, her black uniform blending with the shadows as she tilts the wine bottle over his glass. She circles the table, filling each crystal vessel without a word. When she reaches Lily, I notice the subtle change—a fractional softening around her eyes, the barest hint of recognition passing between them. Fifteen years she's been with the family, moving through these rooms like a silent witness to birthdays, arguments, celebrations. The same hands that now pour my wine once served Alice, who sat exactly where I sit now.

Did she notice anything strange before Alice died? Does she have suspicions of her own?

"The '82 Bordeaux," Robert announces, lifting his glass. "I've been saving it for a special occasion."

"What are we celebrating?" I ask, attempting to join the conversation.

Robert's smile doesn't come off as genuine. "Family," he says simply, and takes a sip. "Having you both back from honeymoon."

The first course arrives—some sort of seafood terrine garnished with microgreens. I lift my fork, conscious of how the silver feels unnaturally heavy in my hand. Every movement feels observed, evaluated. I'm back in the pitch meeting I never attended, being judged for a presentation I never gave.

"Emma," Robert begins, setting down his fork with surgical precision. "Benjamin tells me you're preparing to rescue the Hartman pitch on Monday."

Not asking if I'm prepared. Telling me I'd better be. I swallow a bite that suddenly tastes like nothing. "Yes. Everything's ready. The creative team has been working overtime to refine the concept."

"The concept wasn't the problem," Robert says, cutting a perfect portion of his terrine. "The problem was the absence of leadership. Your absence, specifically."

Benjamin shifts in his seat beside me. "Dad, I don't think dinner is the place—"

"When is the place, Ben?" Robert interrupts, his tone still conversational though his words are anything but. "Emma is family now. And in this family, we discuss business at dinner. We always have."

The "we" hangs in the air. A history I'm not part of. Traditions established long before I arrived. Rules I'm expected to know without being told.

"It was unacceptable," I admit, meeting Robert's gaze directly. "It won't happen again."

"You've been distracted lately," he continues as if I hadn't spoken. "Not just yesterday. The Calloway revision was three days late. The quarterly projections you submitted contained mathematical errors. And Jennifer tells me you've been taking extended lunches."

My cheeks burn. He's been tracking me. Having me watched. Of course he has—he's Robert Stone. Nothing happens in his company without his knowledge. Nothing happens in his family without his approval. And it was only one lunch.

"Emma's been adjusting to our new life together," Benjamin

offers, his hand finding mine under the table. A gesture meant to comfort, but his palm feels clammy against mine. "Marriage is a big change. Moving into the Morrison Estate. Becoming a stepmother. It's a lot at once."

His defense is weak, almost infantilizing. Poor Emma, overwhelmed by adult responsibilities. I want to pull my hand away but force myself to keep it still beneath his.

"Marriage is indeed an adjustment," Margaret agrees from her end of the table. "Though some adapt more naturally than others."

The server reappears, clearing the first course. The brief interruption does nothing to dispel the tension in the air. If anything, it heightens it—a pause in the interrogation that only signals more to come.

"Mom never allowed her personal life to affect her work," Lily says into the silence, her voice deceptively casual. "She was promoted six months after I was born. Mom always said proper planning was the key to balancing everything."

The invisible Alice takes her seat at the table. I can almost see her there, between Lily and Robert, nodding in agreement. The perfect wife. The perfect mother. The perfect employee. The impossible standard I will never reach.

"Your mother was exceptional," Robert agrees, his expression softening momentarily. "She understood what it meant to be a Stone."

My fork trembles against the fine china as the main course arrives—some kind of roast with perfectly turned vegetables arranged in a geometric pattern. The clink of metal against porcelain sounds thunderous to my ears. I set the fork down before anyone notices the tremor in my hand.

"We expected more from you, Emma," Robert continues, cutting his meat with precise, even strokes. "Especially given your... special connection to the family." The pause before "special" turns the word into something else entirely. A euphemism for nepotism. A reminder that I owe my position—perhaps even my continued employment—to my relationship with Benjamin.

"Emma's been with the agency for five years," Benjamin says, a hint of irritation finally entering his voice. "She earned her position long before we were involved."

But did I? The doubt creeps in, unwelcome but persistent. Would I be in my position at thirty-one without the Stone name attached to mine? Without Robert's influence? Without Benjamin's interest?

"Of course, she did," Margaret soothes, though her smile suggests otherwise. "Emma's always been talented. That's why we have such high expectations."

The word "we" again. The royal we. The family we. The we that excludes me even while discussing me.

I try to take a bite of food, but my throat constricts. The meat might as well be sawdust. I reach for my water glass, nearly knocking it over in my haste. Benjamin steadies it, his fingers brushing mine—a touch that once sent electricity through me but now just adds to my unease.

"I understand the expectations," I say, setting down my glass carefully. "And I appreciate the opportunity to prove myself." The corporate language feels safe, a shield against the personal attack disguised as professional concern.

"Opportunities must be seized, not squandered," Robert replies, his gaze piercing. "The Hartman account represents thirty percent of our projected growth for the next fiscal year. Failure is not an option."

Failure. The word echoes in my head. What happens to those who fail the Stones? What happened to Alice when she tried to leave? What will happen to me if I ask the wrong questions, discover the wrong secrets?

"The Hartmans will love the presentation," Benjamin assures his father. "Emma's concept for their campaign is revolutionary. Exactly what they're looking for."

"We'll see on Monday," Robert says, the matter closed for now.

The remainder of the main course passes in uncomfortable silence. I push food around my plate, creating patterns that look like I've eaten more than I have. My stomach is knotted too tightly for food. My mind races with implications, connections, fears. Robert knows something is wrong. He's noticed my distraction, my lunch trip—today's trip to Mack's Auto Shop. Does he know where I went? What I asked about? Has Benjamin told him about my questions regarding Alice?

The plates are cleared, and I stare at the empty space before me, wishing I could disappear as efficiently as the evidence of my barely touched dinner. But there's no escape. Dessert is coming. More conversation. More scrutiny. More time trapped in this beautiful prison.

The dessert arrives—a golden-yellow tart nestled on bone china plates with delicate blue borders. The scent of lemon and butter fills the air, bright and deceptively cheerful. Margaret watches my face as the server places a slice before me, her eyes never leaving mine as she announces, "Alice's lemon tart. A family favorite. I had Mrs. Winters make it especially for tonight."

Of course she did. Nothing in this house happens by accident. Not the seating arrangement. Not the interrogation disguised as dinner conversation. Certainly not this tart, which arrives like a final exhibit in the case against my belonging.

"It looks delicious," I manage, my voice sounding thin even to my own ears.

"Mom made this for every special occasion," Lily says, her fork poised above her slice. "Birthdays, anniversaries, Dad's promotions. She said the secret was in how she prepared the lemons."

I glance at Benjamin, searching his face for a reaction to this coordinated reminder of his dead wife. He's looking down at his plate, a small furrow between his brows the only indication that he recognizes the emotional minefield we're navigating.

"She would zest them by hand," Lily continues, warming to her subject, eyes bright with what looks like genuine enthusiasm. "Never with a machine. Said it released the oils better. And she'd roll each lemon on the counter before cutting it—something about getting more juice that way."

The tart sits untouched before me, a yellow accusation. I lift my fork, take the smallest bite possible. The flavor explodes on my tongue—bright, sweet, with an underlying bitterness that seems too perfect a metaphor for this entire evening.

"Delicious," I say automatically.

"Not quite like Alice's," Margaret muses, taking a deliberate bite of her own. "Mrs. Winters never gets the crust quite as flaky. Alice had the most remarkable touch with pastry."

"She did," Robert agrees, his tone softening for the first time all evening. "Remember that Christmas when she made twelve different desserts?"

"She stayed up three nights straight to finish them," Lily adds. "But she still made it to my winter concert the next morning. Front row. She never missed anything important."

The implication hangs in the air between us. Unlike you, who missed the Hartman presentation. Unlike you, who isn't really a Stone. Unlike you, who will never measure up to the ghost we keep enshrined in portraits and recipes and carefully curated memories.

The tart turns to paste in my mouth. I reach for my water glass, trying to wash down the flavors of inadequacy and suspicion. The cool liquid offers momentary relief before the knot in my throat reforms, tighter than before.

Seeing this, Margaret reaches for my hand and squeezes it. "I would love to get some of your favorite recipes so we can all enjoy them here. I'm sure you have some that are just as excellent. If you care to share them, that is. Some people are weird about that sort of thing."

"Of course," I say, feeling slightly better. "I would love to share them."

"Speaking of family occasions," Margaret continues, setting down her fork, "we really should discuss my birthday in December. I think Emma should be in charge of it this year."

I look at her, surprised. I know Alice used to handle everything, and never thought Margaret would think of letting me anywhere near it. Margaret sips her wine, her eyes never leaving my face. "I'm sure Benjamin can help you navigate it all. There are certain... politics... involved in who sits where. Alice understood that instinctively. I know you will too."

"Mom," Benjamin finally interjects, his tone carrying a note of warning. "Emma's got enough on her plate right now with the Hartman account."

"Of course," Margaret concedes. "I don't want to overwhelm you. There's plenty of time to learn our little family traditions."

"No, it's not too much. I would love to help," I say proudly.

Margaret smiles. "Then it's settled."

Robert sets down his napkin, a signal that dinner is concluding. "Well, Emma, we look forward to hearing about your triumphant return with the Hartmans on Monday. Benjamin, I expect you'll be at the hospital board meeting tomorrow?"

"Seven a.m.," Benjamin confirms. "We're discussing the new pediatric wing funding."

"Excellent. Lily, your grandmother and I would love to have you come over this weekend if you'd like."

Lily brightens visibly. "That would be great, Grandpa. I have that English paper to write, and Grandma promised to help me with it."

Benjamin's hand finds mine under the table, squeezing gently. The pressure is meant to reassure, but it feels like restraint. His thumb moves across my knuckles in a gesture that once made my heart race but now sends unease crawling up my arm.

"We should probably head out," he says, glancing at his watch. "Early meeting followed by surgery tomorrow."

The escape route appears, and I seize it with barely concealed desperation. "Yes, you need your rest."

The process of leaving the Stone penthouse involves as much ceremony as dinner itself. In the foyer, Lily embraces her grandmother with genuine warmth, then turns to Robert, rising on tiptoes to kiss his cheek. "Thanks for dinner, Grandpa. I'll bring those books back next time."

"Keep them as long as you need, sweetheart," he says, his voice gentler than I've heard it all evening. "Your mind is the most important thing you can develop."

Benjamin hugs his mother, shakes his father's hand. Their goodbyes are affectionate but restrained—the Stone men don't display emotion openly, even with each other.

For me, there is a warm hug and a cheek kiss from Margaret. "Do take care of yourself, Emma. You look exhausted."

From Robert, a curt nod and pointed reminder: "I'm counting on you, Emma. I still trust you and believe in you. Just need to make sure that we're giving the Hartmans our best."

The night air when we finally step outside feels like freedom. They still believe in me. I can still make things right. Benjamin guides me to the car with his hand at the small of my back.

As we drive home, I stare out the passenger window. Tampa's lights blur past, streaks of neon and streetlamps that mirror the chaos in my mind. Benjamin drives in silence for several minutes before reaching across the console to take my hand. "That wasn't so bad, was it?"

He's right. I nod and look at him with warmth in my eyes. I love him so much.

"Thanks for trying to help me out," I say.

"They love the way you handle Lily," he adds, squeezing my fingers. "Did you notice how she actually talked to you tonight? That's progress."

Progress. As if Lily's detailed description of her mother's lemon tart technique was an olive branch rather than a weapon.

"She misses Alice," I say, testing the waters, watching his profile in the dim light of the dashboard. "They all do."

His jaw tightens almost imperceptibly. "Of course they do. But that doesn't mean they can't care about you too. Mom and Dad care a lot about you," Benjamin says, turning onto our street, the Morrison Estate appearing.

I know he's right. They've always liked me a lot. I'm being silly. It's probably just that stupid letter. It's messing with my head. I need to stop letting it. I need to forget about it. I say nothing, watching our house grow larger as we approach. Knowing I need to get to the bottom of this letter if I have any chance of forgetting about what it said.

NINE

I walk the gauntlet of glass-walled conference rooms at work this morning, clutching my portfolio like armor. Each expansive space is named after a famous ad campaign. The Volkswagen "Think Small" room currently holds the digital team, their faces illuminated by the blue glow of screens. They glance up as I pass, conversations pausing just long enough to make it obvious I'm the topic. I keep my chin high, steps measured. The clack of my heels against the polished concrete floor announces my presence like Morse code: E-M-M-A-I-S-H-E-R-E. My mistake hasn't been forgotten.

I spent the weekend baking Lily's favorite double-chocolate brownies, the kitchen counters dusted with cocoa powder as I tried to decode the mystery of the letter. For a moment, I'd convinced myself it was her—seventeen and angry, penning letters in her dead mother's name. I'd decided to confront her softly. I'd even practiced my approach: casual voice, no accusations. "Sweetheart, if there's something you want to tell me..." But then I'd knocked on her bedroom door, music blaring behind it, and she'd opened it just enough to see the offering, and her eyes had narrowed before taking the plate without a word. And I'd lost my nerve. I'd found the brownies dumped in the trash, crumbled into yellow dust atop coffee grounds. I had no idea what to do next, so did nothing at all.

Now, the open-concept workspace sprawls before me—a sea of white desks punctuated by collaborative pods where creatives huddle over tablets. Digital screens line the walls, displaying our current campaigns in high-definition glory. The Sunset Shores Resort video loops silently—my campaign, my concept, my success.

"Morning, Emma," Jen says. "Nervous much?"

"Is it that obvious?" I adjust my portfolio.

"Your name's on the calendar for the big conference room." She shrugs. "Plus, you've got that look."

"What look?"

"You know what I mean."

I don't, but she walks away before I can ask what that's supposed to mean.

I weave through the workspace toward my desk in the strategy corner. Conversations dim as I approach, then resume slightly louder once I've passed, like waves parting around an unwelcome obstacle. My desk sits exactly where it did before I became Mrs. Benjamin Stone, but somehow it feels like I'm occupying someone else's space.

"Rough morning?" Ryan pauses at the edge of my desk. He's been my creative partner for three years, but lately, he's been careful around me—as if my marriage might have changed our working dynamic overnight.

I force a smile. "The pitch is ready, if that's what you're worried about."

"Wasn't worried." He rocks back on his heels. "Though Robert did call and ask me yesterday if we were on track."

My stomach tightens. "He asked you? Not me?"

Ryan shrugs, expression carefully neutral. "Probably just double-checking. You know how he is."

I do know how Robert is. Meticulous. Strategic. Nothing accidental about his movements, especially not conversations about million-dollar accounts. The fact that he bypassed me to check on our progress with Ryan isn't a coincidence. It's a message. Normally, he always comes straight to me.

"Well, we're on track," I say, more sharply than intended. "The deck is ready. The mock-ups are done. Unless there's something you haven't finished?"

"All good on my end." He backs away slightly. "Can you meet with Robert at eleven to run through everything one last time?"

I nod, already turning to my computer. The screen flickers to life, displaying my half-finished slide deck.

That's when I see it. A plain white envelope centered perfectly on my desk. No postmark. No return address. Just my name—*Emma*—written in elegant cursive across the front.

I freeze, coffee mug halfway to my lips. That handwriting. I've seen it before, on recipe cards in Benjamin's kitchen cabinets. On margin notes in books on his shelves. On a birthday card to Lily I found when cleaning out the guest room closet, signed: "All my love, Mom."

Alice's handwriting.

My pulse hammers in my throat. I glance around the office. Everyone seems absorbed in their own work, no one watching for my reaction. Who put this here? When? My desk is in clear view of at least fifteen people. Someone walked up and placed this envelope on my desk, and no one thought to mention it.

Or everyone saw and no one's saying anything.

My hands shake worse now, fine tremors that force me to set down my mug before I spill again. Sweat prickles along my hairline despite the aggressive air conditioning. I shouldn't open it. I should throw it away. I should call Benjamin.

I do none of those things.

Instead, I check once more that no one's watching, then

slide my finger under the sealed flap. The paper gives way with a whisper. Inside is a single sheet of cream-colored stationery, folded precisely in thirds. The same elegant handwriting fills the page, black ink against a pale background.

My heart thuds so loudly I'm certain the entire office can hear it. My mouth goes desert dry. This isn't possible. Alice Stone died five years ago. I never met her. I didn't know her.

But here is her handwriting, addressing me directly on the first line.

Dear new wife,

The words swim before my eyes. I fold the letter quickly, stuffing it back into the envelope as footsteps approach my desk. Jessica from HR appears, tablet in hand, talking about benefit forms I still need to update with my new marital status. I nod mechanically, sliding the envelope into my purse, fingers lingering on the paper as if it might bite. The weight of it seems to pull my entire bag down, creating a gravitational field of dread.

My wedding ring catches the light as I withdraw my hand from my purse. The diamonds Benjamin chose so carefully suddenly seem like tiny, glittering eyes, watching my every move as I try to focus on Jessica's words about insurance policies and emergency contacts.

All I can think is: Alice is speaking to me from beyond the grave. And I have no choice but to listen.

The women's restroom on the fifth floor is always empty this time of morning. I lock myself in the last stall, hands trembling as I pull the envelope from my purse. Ten minutes until my meeting with Robert and Ryan. Ten minutes to read a letter from a dead woman. I lean against the cool wall, my heart battering against my ribs like something wild trying to escape.

TO HIS NEW WIFE

The letter feels heavy in my hands, impossibly heavy for a single sheet of paper.

I unfold it carefully, smoothing the creases with shaking fingers. The handwriting flows across the page in elegant loops and swirls—confident, artistic strokes that match the recipes in Benjamin's kitchen drawers. The woman I never met but whose presence fills every corner of our home.

My stomach lurches.

I take a deep breath and read.

Dear new wife,

We haven't met, but I feel I know you already. You're sleeping in my bed now, using my bathroom mirror, perhaps even wearing my robe when the nights get cool. That's not an accusation—just a statement of fact. Life continues after death. Spaces get filled. I understand this better than most.

I'm writing to share a story that keeps replaying in my mind. Something about memory—how it preserves certain moments in perfect detail while others fade completely. This particular memory refuses to fade, and I think perhaps it's because it wasn't meant for me alone.

It was our second anniversary when Ben gave me the charm necklace. A beautiful thing—silver links holding six delicate charms, each with its own story. We were in our bedroom—I wonder if it's your bedroom now?—with morning light streaming through the windows. Ben had that look he gets when he's planned something perfectly. You've seen it, I'm sure. That slight smile that appears only at the corners of his mouth, the way his eyes follow your reaction to ensure you're appropriately appreciative.

He placed the necklace on my chest, while closing it behind my neck, the silver cool against my skin. "Each charm repre-

sents something about us," he said, his fingers brushing mine as he pointed to them one by one.

A paintbrush—*"For the night we met at your gallery and for your art."*

A miniature book—*"For reading Lily bedtime stories together."*

A sailboat—*"For our trip to the Keys."*

A house—*"For our home."*

A rose—*"For the flowers I bring you every Friday."*

And then the sixth charm—a small silver heart. A locket, he told me, though it was sealed shut when he presented it. "This one's special," he said, his voice dropping to that intimate tone he uses when he wants my complete attention. "It holds a secret. Something just for us."

I tried to open it, of course. The little heart felt warm compared to the other charms, as if it contained something alive. But Ben stopped me, his fingers closing around mine with that gentle-firm grip he uses in moments of control disguised as affection.

"Not yet," he said. "Some other time."

I wore the necklace every day, the charms jingling with every movement, the sealed heart resting against my chest. I couldn't stop thinking about what might be inside. A tiny photo? A lock of Lily's baby hair? Perhaps a miniature love note?

But at dinner one night—a reservation at Maison Bleu, the same hushed corner where we always sat—the locket wasn't there. I felt it halfway through the chilled oyster appetizer, my throat tightening as I touched the empty chain at my collarbone.

Ben's face paled. He rifled under the table, flagged down the waiter to scour the coat check, and even called our sitter to sweep through the nursery, the closet, the car. Each desperate search ended the same: nothing. "I'm so sorry," he whispered, voice folding in on itself as he reached for my hand. "I must have clipped it poorly. We'll find it—or I'll replace it."

I believed him. Why wouldn't I? His regret felt genuine. But three days later, while shuffling papers in his desk drawer, I discovered a small velvet pouch stashed behind his passport. Inside lay the locket—its silver heart glinting, untouched. Not lost... reclaimed.

My breath caught at a tiny hole drilled into the clasp, almost invisible. I pried it open and found a micro-SD card. My blood ran cold as I slid it into my laptop: bedroom shadows, my sleeping face, my hair splayed across the pillow. Then a sound made me raise my head, and there he was, looking at me, smiling.

He was recording my every move. A small hidden camera in my locket, making sure he knew everything I was doing. All the time.

I never told him I'd found it. Instead, I watched. I mapped every silent corner of his house—where the cameras peeked from the crown molding, where the microphones lay behind picture frames. I tracked his late-night drives, the calls he took in the dark of his car.

A month later, the necklace he'd given me—the one I wore every day—vanished. This time he said I'd left it at the gym. He'd get me a new one. He never did. Another loss. Another hollow apology. Another promise.

Perhaps you've felt it too—his attention that isn't love but something far colder, something that watches you sleep. Or maybe you're still in that first, dizzying stage, where his intrusion feels like devotion.

Either way, I wanted you to have this. Use it as you will.

With what's left of my bravery,

Alice

The signature crawls across the paper in a jagged flourish. My coffee churns sour in my stomach. The stall walls press in as I fold the letter with trembling fingers, the final words branded behind my eyes.

But as I fold the letter with fingers that feel disconnected from my body, I notice what I missed before—a postscript in smaller writing at the very bottom of the page.

P.S. Maybe you can find my necklace. I'm sure he still has it.

The letter slips from my fingers, floating to the bathroom floor. I stare at it, unable to move, unable to think clearly. The necklace. The locket. The hidden camera. None of this makes sense. Benjamin isn't secretive—he's protective. He isn't controlling—he's attentive. Isn't he?

My phone buzzes in my pocket—a reminder for my meeting. I grab the letter from the floor, folding it hastily and shoving it deep into my purse. The paper feels contaminated somehow, radioactive with doubt.

I flush the empty toilet to maintain the illusion of normalcy, then unlock the stall door on legs that feel like water. At the sink, I splash cold water on my face, watching my reflection in the mirror. The woman staring back looks frightened, her eyes too wide, her complexion too pale.

"Pull it together," I whisper to her. "This isn't real. This isn't possible."

But as I dry my hands, my wedding ring catches the fluorescent light, the diamonds suddenly looking less like stars and more like small eyes staring at me. Benjamin chose this ring carefully, spending weeks selecting the perfect stones, the perfect setting. He's particular about jewelry. Particular about everything.

Including me?

I straighten my blouse, check my lipstick, and walk out of

the bathroom on autopilot. The hallway stretches before me like something from a dream, elongating with each step. I don't know what I'm dealing with here. A warning from a dead woman, sent knowing her husband would find another victim? Or a letter from her daughter trying to ruin everything?

And at the end of the hallway, the conference room where Ryan and Robert wait to discuss our pitch, unaware that my entire world is shifting beneath my feet.

The letter in my purse seems to pulse with each step, a reminder that some questions, once asked, cannot be unasked. And some answers, once found, cannot be unknown. He's my husband, for crying out loud. I love him. I know him.

Don't I?

TEN

Robert sits across from me in the conference room, fingers drumming a slow, deliberate rhythm on the polished table. Ryan is next to me, totally silent as always; he normally just jumps in, never leads. I shuffle my presentation materials, trying to organize thoughts that refuse to align. The second letter burns in my mind—same elegant handwriting, same impossible sender. What does it all mean? I can't focus on campaign metrics when all I see are brake lines and repair shop receipts and Alice's name signed at the bottom of a page that shouldn't exist.

"These projection numbers seem optimistic," Robert says, tapping the spreadsheet I've laid before him. His voice sounds distant, underwater. "What market research supports this growth pattern?"

I stare at the numbers that meant something yesterday but are now just symbols floating on paper. Which page am I on? I flip through my notes, papers rustling too loudly in the silent room.

"The, um, the focus group results from last month showed strong positive response to the emotional testimonial approach." My voice sounds thin, uncertain. Not the voice of a future senior account executive. Not the voice Robert hired five years ago.

"Emma?"

I snap back to the present. Robert's eyes narrow, the wrinkles at their corners deepening with concern or annoyance. I can't tell which. Maybe both.

"Sorry, yes. The demographic breakdown is on page seven." I fumble with my tablet, advance through slides that suddenly make no sense. Charts with colored bars. I stop on what I hope is page seven, but the numbers swim before my eyes.

In the first letter, Alice—or Lily—detailed how Benjamin insisted on taking her car for servicing three days before the accident. Why didn't they find anything wrong with the brakes? She had told him she was worried about them. They didn't feel right. Too soft...

"These figures don't match what you sent over yesterday," Robert says, comparing his printout to my screen. His jaw tightens—the same tension I've seen in Benjamin's face when he's displeased but trying to control it. Like father, like son.

"I updated them this morning based on the latest..." I trail off, mind blank. Latest what? I wasn't updating figures this morning. I was locked in a bathroom stall.

Reading words coming from beyond the grave.

Robert watches me, waiting. The silence stretches between us, elastic and uncomfortable. I take a sip of water.

"Based on the latest social media analytics," I finish lamely, knowing it makes no sense. The ROI projections wouldn't change based on Instagram likes.

My hands tremble slightly as I advance to the next slide. The tremor isn't new—it started after the first letter. Small vibrations that make it hard to apply mascara or hold my coffee cup without spilling. Benjamin noticed it this morning, asked if I was getting sick. His cool palm against my forehead, checking for fever. Doctor's instinct. Husband's concern. Killer's touch?

No. Stop it. This is insane.

"Emma, let's talk about budget allocation." Robert's voice cuts through my spiral. "You've dedicated thirty percent to traditional media, but at the last meeting we agreed on a digital-forward approach."

Did we? I don't remember. The days have blurred. Sleep comes in fractured increments, broken by dreams of Alice watching me from dark corners of our bedroom. Her bedroom. Of Benjamin watching as the car drives off the bridge.

"I can adjust that," I mumble, flipping through papers. My mind keeps circling back to the second letter.

"Emma." Robert's voice sharpens. "Are you even prepared for this meeting?"

The question slices through my scattered thoughts. I look up to find his eyes locked on me, assessing, calculating. Not just my father-in-law now, but the CEO of Stone Advertising, evaluating a failing employee.

"Yes, of course. I just—" I reach for my water glass, needing something to do with my hands. My trembling fingers knock it sideways. Water cascades across the table, soaking my carefully prepared notes. Blue ink bleeds into expanding puddles.

"Shit!" I grab napkins from the coffee service, dabbing frantically at the spreading liquid. "I'm sorry, I'm so sorry."

Robert pushes his chair back to avoid the dripping edge. His sigh carries the weight of disappointment. I keep my head down, cheeks burning with humiliation as I mop up my mess. Just like I'm trying to mop up the mess of my thoughts, my suspicions, my fear.

Ben wouldn't kill anyone. He's a good man. I love him. He saves children's lives. His hands are steady, skilled, precise. Surgeon's hands. Hands that could, perhaps, disconnect brake lines with the same precision they use to repair tiny hearts.

No. This is crazy. I'm losing my mind.

"Let's reschedule," Robert says, setting down his Montblanc

pen. His eyes crinkle at the corners as he reaches for a handkerchief from his breast pocket—monogrammed RS in navy thread—and dabs at the water spreading across my presentation boards. "These things happen to the best of us. Remember when I spilled an entire pitcher of water on the Westfield execs?" He gathers his papers with one hand, still blotting with the other. "When you've had time to properly prepare, we'll try again. Tomorrow morning? I can block off the first two hours, give you my undivided attention."

"I am prepared," I insist, but the evidence against me spreads across the table in soggy clumps of paper. "I just—I didn't sleep well, and there's been some personal—"

"Whatever's happening in your personal life needs to stay there," Robert says, straightening his suit jacket with a tug. Ryan is sitting at the table still, looking embarrassed on my behalf. "We can revisit this when you're ready."

"Robert, please." I sound desperate now. Pathetic. "I can walk you through the core strategy now. The materials were just supporting documentation."

He pauses, considering. For a moment, I think he might give me another chance. Then his eyes flick to the ceiling, that subtle tell Margaret mentioned once—the way Robert looks up when he's made a decision he knows others won't like.

"We'll talk later," he says. "And Emma? I suggest you leave whatever's distracting you at home from now on. Please."

He walks out, Italian leather shoes silent on the carpet. Ryan follows him right after, leaving me alone. Through the glass walls, I watch Robert stride across the office floor, nodding to employees who straighten instinctively in his presence. No one looks at me in the conference room. No one wants to witness my humiliation.

I sink back into my chair, surrounded by wet paper and ruined plans. My career isn't the only thing unraveling. It's my mind. My marriage. My grip on what's real and what's imagined.

Ben wouldn't kill anyone. He's a good man. I love him.

My fingers leave damp prints on the glass table as I push myself up.

I walk through the conference room doorway, materials clutched to my chest. The carpet seems to tilt beneath my feet as I step into the open-plan office. Every head doesn't turn—that would be easier to dismiss as paranoia. Instead, it's the careful not-looking, the studied focus on screens that weren't so fascinating thirty seconds ago. The weight of peripheral attention presses against my skin as I make my way toward my desk.

My heels sink into the carpet. Left foot. Right foot. Keep moving. Don't run. The water stains on my presentation materials darken the papers, spreading like evidence of some crime. In a way, it is criminal—the death of my professional reputation, witnessed by everyone who matters in my career.

"—completely lost it in there—"

The whispered fragment reaches me as I pass the creative pod. Jen and Mark, heads bent close together, fall silent when they notice me approaching. Jen offers a tight smile. Mark suddenly finds his keyboard fascinating.

"Morning meeting go okay?" Jen asks, her tone carefully neutral. News travels fast here—of course they already know about my disaster with Robert. Ryan told them.

"Fine," I lie, the word brittle on my tongue. "Just some technical issues with the slides."

Mark nods too enthusiastically. "Happens to everyone."

Except it doesn't. Not to me. Not to Emma Caldwell, the account executive known for meticulous preparation and flawless presentations. Not to the woman who landed the Hartman account through sheer strategic brilliance two years ago—before I even knew Benjamin would notice me, despite what people might think now.

I continue past them, feeling their eyes on my back. More whispers follow, too low to catch, but the tone is unmistakable. The same tone used for office gossip about affairs and firings and spectacular professional flame-outs.

"—wonder if Robert will reassign the account—"

"—probably only kept it because she's married to—"

I pick up my pace, nearly stumbling in my haste to reach my desk. My sanctuary in this suddenly hostile landscape of whispers and stares. But even here, privacy is an illusion. The open-plan design Robert insisted on during the last renovation means everyone can see me unraveling.

I collapse into my chair, setting down my presentation boards—stained and torn at one corner—with trembling hands. My computer screen glows with thirty-seven unread emails. I've never failed this completely. Never lost control of a meeting. Never disappointed Robert so thoroughly that he questioned my very place here with that particular frown that makes the scar above his eyebrow turn white. I pull out my phone, my first instinct to call Benjamin. He would reassure me. Tell me that everyone makes mistakes. That my career isn't over because of one disastrous meeting. Just like last month when I'd forgotten to include the demographic research in the Westlake proposal and he'd driven forty minutes in rush-hour traffic to bring me the flash drive, kissing my forehead in front of the entire creative team and whispering, "You've got this, Em. They can't touch you."

My finger hovers over his name in my contacts. I stare at the screen until his name blurs, imagining his response if I called right now about the letters and who I thought was writing them. His voice would soften with concern, then harden when I mentioned his daughter might be involved. "Emma, she's just a kid," he'd say, that protective edge creeping in. The same tone he uses in hospital boardrooms when defending his patients. I set the phone down without calling.

Who can I trust if not my own husband? The thought sends a chill through me despite the office's aggressive air conditioning. I've never been the paranoid type. Never been the woman who jumps at shadows or sees conspiracies in coincidences. Yet here I am, doubting the man I married based on letters that shouldn't exist that might have been sent by his daughter.

My gaze drops to my hands, and I notice my nail polish—the pale pink I applied so carefully last night—is chipped on three fingers. Ragged edges where I've been picking at it unconsciously. Another sign of my unraveling. The Emma Caldwell everyone knows would never allow such imperfection. Would never leave the house with chipped nail polish or wrinkled clothes or presentations that fall apart under basic questioning.

I open my desk drawer, searching for the emergency nail polish I keep for touch-ups. Instead, my fingers brush against smooth paper. The envelope. The letter.

I pull back as if burned, but then find myself reaching for it again, drawn by some perverse need to confirm it's real. The envelope slides smoothly into my hand, my name written across the front in that elegant script that matches Alice's recipe cards.

Did I leave it here? I thought I'd put it in my purse. Have I completely lost track of what's real?

I slam the drawer shut, suddenly afraid someone might see.

I need to get out of here. Away from curious eyes and whispered judgments. Away from the evidence of my professional collapse.

I gather my purse and jacket, ignoring the mess of wet papers on my desk. They can wait until tomorrow—if I still have a job tomorrow. If Robert doesn't decide that nepotism has its limits.

Standing makes me realize how shaky I am, how little I've eaten today. Black spots dance at the edges of my vision again. I grip the edge of my desk until they clear, then force myself to walk normally toward the elevator. Don't run. Don't show weakness. Just another day at Stone Advertising, just heading out for a late lunch.

"Leaving early?" Ryan materializes beside the creative department's coffee station, concern etched across his features.

"Just for an hour or two." My voice sounds distant to my own ears. "Need to grab some materials from home for tomorrow's follow-up with Robert."

The lie comes easily. Too easily. I've never been a good liar before—Benjamin teases me about how my left eye twitches when I try to fib about surprise gifts or dinner reservations. But lately, lying feels like self-preservation. Necessary for survival.

Ryan studies my face. "You don't look great, Emma. Maybe take the rest of the day off and work from home tomorrow. I can take the meeting with Robert. Get some rest."

Is that concern or dismissal? I can't tell any more. Can't trust my own judgment about the simplest interactions.

"Maybe I will." I press the elevator call button, desperate for the doors to open. For escape.

More eyes follow me—or maybe they don't. Maybe I'm imagining the weight of attention, the silent assessments, the conclusions being drawn. The line between reality and paranoia blurs more each day.

The elevator arrives with a soft chime. I step inside, turning to face the office as the doors begin to close. A final glimpse of the world I've built over five years—the accounts I've landed, the campaigns I've created, the respect I've earned through talent and determination. All potentially unraveling because of letters that shouldn't exist and suspicions I can't shake.

As the doors slide shut, I catch one last fragment of conversation from passing colleagues:

"—wonder what's really going on with her and Dr. Stone—"

Then silence. Blessed, temporary silence as the elevator begins its descent. I lean against the wall. My reflection in the polished metal doors shows a stranger—hair escaping its careful styling, makeup smudged under one eye, complexion pale with stress.

"What is happening to me?" I whisper to this unfamiliar version of myself, the words barely audible even in the enclosed space.

The elevator doesn't answer. It continues its smooth downward journey, carrying me away from the wreckage of my professional identity and toward something potentially worse—a home filled with questions I'm afraid to ask and answers I'm afraid to hear. As the doors slide open to the marble lobby, I straighten my spine. It's time I find out if Lily did send those letters, and if anything inside them—anything at all—might be true.

ELEVEN

The buzzing won't stop. It burrows into my dream—something about running through the Stones' penthouse's endless corridors—and pulls me gasping into consciousness. I'd planned to talk to Lily when I got home, to confront her carefully and sensitively, rehearsing what to say during the entire drive. "It's okay if you miss your mother," "I know this must be hard," "I'm not going anywhere. Nothing you could say will scare me away from making you and your father my family." But the house stood empty. No designer purse abandoned by the door, no playlist streaming from her bedroom. I checked my phone for messages, then wandered from room to room calling her name, my voice echoing against the vaulted ceilings. I sat in the living room for hours watching the front door. But nothing. No Lily. Only Benjamin who called and said he was going to be late. Eventually, I got tired and went to bed.

My phone vibrates across the nightstand like it's possessed, screen lighting up the darkened room in rhythmic flashes. I reach for it, eyes still sticky with sleep. Notifications. Dozens of them. Texts, calls, app alerts—all pouring in at 7:07 a.m. Something's wrong.

Benjamin's side of the bed is empty, sheets cold. Tuesday. Early surgery day. He left before dawn, kissing my forehead while I pretended to sleep.

My phone buzzes again in my palm. Jen. Three texts in a row.

Have you seen this?

Call me ASAP

Are you OK???

Below her messages, more of the same from colleagues, friends, even my college roommate I haven't spoken to since the wedding. All with the same link. All with the same frantic tone.

My thumb hovers over the link—a TikTok video. My heart stutters as I click it, screen brightness stabbing my eyes in the dim bedroom. The app loads, and a young woman's face fills my screen. Dark eyes staring intently at the camera. Shoulder-length black hair. Professional lighting. This is no amateur production.

"I'm Mira Patel, and this is part one of 'The Doctor's Wives.'" Her voice is measured, authoritative. "Five years ago, Alice Stone died when her car plunged off the Crystal River Bridge. The official report cited brake failure. A tragic accident that left renowned pediatric surgeon Dr. Benjamin Stone a grieving widower and single father."

My stomach twists. The woman—Mira—holds up a photo of Benjamin in his white coat, smiling that perfect smile that first drew me to him.

"Five weeks ago, Dr. Stone remarried." A photo of us on our wedding day appears. Where did she get that? It wasn't in the papers. "Emma Caldwell, a rising star at his father's advertising agency. A perfect Hollywood ending."

Her expression shifts, hardens. "Except there's nothing perfect about Dr. Stone's story. I've spent months investigating Alice Stone's death, speaking with sources close to the family, and what I've uncovered is disturbing."

I sit up straight, fully awake now. The sheets pool around my waist as I grip the phone tighter.

"Multiple sources confirm Dr. Stone displayed controlling behavior throughout his marriage to Alice. He monitored her whereabouts, isolated her from friends, and undermined her confidence through constant criticism."

My free hand finds my throat, resting against my racing pulse.

"A former colleague of Alice's described an incident six months before her death: 'She came to work with sunglasses on. When she took them off in the bathroom, I saw the bruise around her eye. She claimed she walked into a closet door, but her hands were shaking when she said it.'"

"No," I whisper to the empty room. "That's not—he wouldn't—"

Mira's face is solemn now. "Three days before her death, Alice told a friend she was planning to leave Benjamin. The same day, Dr. Stone personally took her car to be serviced. Three days later, those brakes failed, and Alice Stone was dead."

The view counter at the bottom of the screen reads 2.7 million.

I scroll to the comments, fingers trembling.

This man operates on CHILDREN? Terrifying.

Someone check on the new wife!

@HarborHeightsMedical why is this man still employed???

Stone family money covering up murder. Classic.

Thousands of comments. Tens of thousands of shares. Hashtags forming:

#JusticeForAlice

#TheRealDrStone

#CheckTheBrakes

My thumb moves frantically, searching for Mira Patel's profile. More videos. A series, each with millions of views. Part two posted three hours ago. I click, heart pounding against my ribs like it's trying to escape.

"Welcome back to 'The Doctor's Wives.' Today we're looking deeper into the Stone family dynamics and how they may have enabled Dr. Benjamin Stone's behavior."

She talks about Robert and Margaret. About their influence in Tampa. About how the initial police investigation was led by a Detective Lucas Ramirez, who golfed regularly with Robert and is a close friend of Benjamin. About how Harbor Heights Medical Center, where Benjamin performs his miracle surgeries, receives substantial donations from Stone family foundations.

A text appears on my screen, interrupting the video. Benjamin.

In surgery until noon. Everything OK?

Everything is not okay. Nothing will ever be okay again.

I call him, anyway, knowing he won't answer. His voicemail greets me—that warm, reassuring voice promising to return my call as soon as possible. The same voice that whispered "I love you" last night when he climbed into bed around midnight with a deep, exhausted, yet satisfied sigh. The same voice that, according to Mira Patel and her mysterious sources, belittled and controlled Alice until she tried to leave him.

Back to TikTok. Part three, posted just forty minutes ago. This one features a blurred-out figure—feminine silhouette, voice disguised—claiming to be a patient's mother who witnessed Benjamin's rage when questioned about a procedure.

"He was like a different person. The charm vanished. His eyes went cold. I've never been so afraid of someone in a white coat."

I check the view counter again. 3.2 million now. Climbing as I watch. The internet is devouring my husband, pixel by pixel.

My mind races back to Alice's letter. "'When you know, you know,' he told me." He was so certain, so confident. The same words he used with me. The same lightning-fast courtship. The same white orchids.

But no. Benjamin saves children. Benjamin holds my hand under the table at uncomfortable family dinners. Benjamin can't be this monster. I know he isn't. He's my husband. My one and only.

Then I remember my trip to Mack's Auto Shop. Anton's words echo: "Dr. Stone bring car himself. Wait while we work. Take car after." The pieces Alice tried to show me are now being scattered across the internet for millions to see, assembled by a stranger with a camera and a story to tell.

Comments continue flooding in—death threats now. Calls for Benjamin to lose his medical license. People tagging the hospital, the medical board, the police department. Some express concern for me. More express suspicion. This is insane.

She works for his dad. Probably in on it.

New wife looking nervous yet?

Anyone checked HER brakes lately?

My stomach heaves. I barely make it to the bathroom before emptying its contents. Kneeling on the cold tile, I wipe my mouth with trembling fingers.

How much does this Mira Patel know? How did she find out? The same questions I've been asking for days are now being shouted by millions of strangers. The suspicions I've harbored in secret are now hashtags and memes and calls for justice. And somewhere in Tampa, Benjamin is standing over an operating table, gloved hands steady as he repairs a child's heart, completely unaware that his life—our life—is imploding in sixty-second viral video increments.

My phone buzzes again. Jen.

Robert's called an emergency meeting. 8 a.m. Everyone's saying it's about the videos.

Of course. The agency will go into crisis mode. The Stone family reputation must be protected at all costs. That's what the dinner the other night was really about, wasn't it? Not my missed presentation, but my loyalty. My willingness to stand by the family narrative, whatever it might be.

I push myself up, feeling the weight of the world pressing down on me. My legs are unsteady as I make my way to the sink, glancing at the mirror. I see a pale face, eyes wide with anxiety—the look of someone watching their life unravel. I splash cold water on my face, hoping to wash away the fatigue and dread that cling to me.

I dress quickly, choosing a navy blazer that I hope projects confidence, and head out to my car, when my phone vibrates insistently in my pocket.

It's Lily's school.

TWELVE

St. Catherine's Academy rises like a fortress from its grounds, all Gothic spires and ivy-covered brick. The security guard at the gate recognizes me—or my car, at least. The black BMW Benjamin insisted we buy for "family outings." He waves me through without checking my ID, his eyes sliding away from mine too quickly.

I park in the visitor's lot, between a Mercedes SUV and a Tesla. Elite vehicles for elite families who pay elite tuition for their children to receive elite education. Now those same families are probably texting each other about the surgeon's daughter, the murdered mother, the second wife who might be next—or even worse, in on it.

The principal's voice on the phone had been clipped, professional. "Mrs. Stone, we need you to pick up Lily immediately. There's been an... incident." Not Stone Caldwell. Not Caldwell. Mrs. Stone. Like Margaret. Like Alice. He explained they had called Benjamin but he didn't answer, which makes sense, since he's in surgery. I guess since I'm married to him now, I am considered next of kin.

The administration building stands separate from the classroom wings, a deliberate buffer between teenage drama and adult authority. My heels click against the polished marble floors, the sound echoing down the empty corridor. Classes in session. Lily should be in AP Biology, not waiting in the principal's office. The poor girl. She'll be in bits. And here I'd been suspecting her of sending these letters... whatever is happening can't have anything to do with her. She wouldn't do this to her father.

A secretary looks up as I enter the office suite. Her expression shifts microscopically—recognition, then something like pity mixed with distaste. "Mrs. Stone. Dr. Howard is expecting you." She gestures to a closed door across the reception area.

I cross the space, aware of eyes tracking my movement. Two administrative assistants pause their typing. A student aide delivering paperwork stops mid-stride. I am a curiosity now. A spectacle. The woman who married a monster—or perhaps a monster myself.

Dr. Howard rises as I enter her office, extending her hand. Her grip is firm, her smile professionally neutral. "Mrs. Stone. Thank you for coming so quickly."

Lily sits in one of two chairs facing the principal's desk. Her back is ramrod straight. She doesn't turn when I enter. Doesn't acknowledge my presence at all. Doesn't look upset.

"Please, sit down." Dr. Howard gestures to the empty chair beside Lily. I lower myself into it, resisting the urge to reach for my stepdaughter's hand. Her fingers are curled into tight fists on her lap, knuckles white with tension. I turn, expecting to see the remnants of tears on her face, but it's blank.

"I'm sure you're aware of the... situation... developing online," Dr. Howard begins, carefully selecting each word. "Unfortunately, it has made its way into our student body."

"The videos," I say flatly. "About Benjamin. About Lily's mother."

She nods, a small vertical line appearing between her

brows. "Yes. This morning when Lily arrived at the school, several students approached her with... inappropriate comments and questions."

"What kind of comments?" My voice is too high, too tight.

Dr. Howard glances at Lily, who continues staring straight ahead, silent and rigid. "I believe 'murderer's daughter' was used. And questions about whether she..." The principal hesitates, clearly uncomfortable. "Whether she feared for her own safety."

My stomach drops. "That's—they said that to her face?"

"Social media encourages a certain boldness," Dr. Howard says, the understatement almost laughable in its inadequacy. "When Lily reacted—"

"I punched Trevor Malcolm in his smug face," Lily interrupts, voice flat and cold. "After he asked if my dad killed my mom to be with you."

The words hit like physical blows. I struggle to breathe normally, to maintain composure. "Lily, I'm so sorry—"

"Don't." She cuts me off, still not looking at me. "Just don't."

Dr. Howard clears her throat. "Given the circumstances, I've decided not to pursue disciplinary action for the physical altercation. However, I do think it's best for Lily to go home for the remainder of the day. To give things time to... settle."

Time to settle. As if this viral storm will blow over in a few hours. As if Lily will ever be able to walk these halls without carrying the weight of those accusations.

"Of course," I agree. "Thank you for your understanding."

"St. Catherine's stands behind its students," Dr. Howard says, her practiced phrase ringing hollow in the tense office. "And we don't tolerate bullying of any kind."

Except they did tolerate it. Long enough for Lily to feel cornered. Long enough for her to lash out physically.

Gathering Lily's things takes ten excruciating minutes. We walk through empty corridors to her locker, the principal trailing at a discreet distance. Lily spins her combination, yanks books from shelves, stuffs them into her backpack. I stand uselessly beside her, aware of faces peering through classroom door windows, teachers pausing mid-sentence to watch our procession.

"Is there anything else you need?" I ask as she slams the locker shut.

"To disappear," she mutters, hoisting her backpack over one shoulder.

The walk to the parking lot feels endless. Students who should be in class find reasons to be in the hallway—water fountain trips, bathroom passes, convenient errands to the office. They stare openly, whispers following in our wake.

"That's her—"

"—saw the TikTok—"

"—wonder if she knew—"

The sunshine when we finally exit the building feels like a mockery. It should be raining. Storming. Something to match the darkness swirling around us. Instead, it's a perfect Florida day, bright and merciless.

A few parents are in the parking lot too—early pickups, forgotten lunches, scheduled appointments. Their conversations stop as we approach. A woman in tennis whites actually steps back, pulling her daughter closer as we pass, like murderous tendencies might be contagious.

I unlock the car with trembling fingers. Lily walks to her own car, yanks open the door, throws her backpack onto the floor, and slides in, immediately pulling out her phone. I walk to her car and poke my head inside.

"We'll figure this out, Lily," I finally say as she starts the engine. "Your dad would never hurt anyone. These videos—they're lies. Someone with an agenda trying to—"

"You don't know anything about my dad," she cuts in, voice low and dangerous. "Or my mom."

I sigh and look at her, painfully aware of watching eyes around us. "I know your father loves you more than anything. I know he's a brilliant surgeon who saves children's lives. I know—"

"You know what he wants you to know." She stares out the window, profile sharp against the bright day. "Just like my mom did."

Her words send ice through my veins. "What does that mean, Lily?"

She doesn't answer. Just taps furiously at her phone, the screen angled away from me. I catch glimpses—TikTok's distinctive interface, message notifications popping up, her thumb scrolling rapidly through comments.

"Who are you texting?" I ask, trying to keep my voice casual and failing miserably.

"None of your business."

I move closer, and glance over, catching sight of a notification banner before she can angle the phone away:

Mira Patel commented on your message.

My heart stutters. "Lily, do you know anything about these videos?"

Her eyes meet mine for the first time, cold and challenging. "What if I do?"

I stare at her in disbelief. "These videos are destroying your father's reputation. His career. Our lives."

"Maybe they're just exposing the truth." She turns back to her phone, fingers flying over the screen. "Maybe that's what my mom would want."

Lily remains engrossed in her phone, periodically angling it further from my view. I stand there, mind racing with implications.

"Do you mind?" she says, signaling that she wants to close

the door, and drive away. I pull back, and she slams the door. Then she rolls down the window and looks at me, her expression unreadable.

"You know what Trevor said after he asked if Dad killed Mom to be with you?" Her voice is eerily calm. "He said I should watch my back around both of you now. Because if Dad could do it once..."

She lets the sentence hang unfinished, then rolls the window back up before I can respond, taking off without looking back.

THIRTEEN

The house feels like it's holding its breath. Since returning from Lily's school, I've moved through the rooms in a daze, checking social media compulsively. Lily has locked herself in her room, refusing lunch, ignoring my knocks. I've called Ben seventeen times. Each time, straight to voicemail. Harbor Heights Medical Center won't put me through to him—"Dr. Stone is still in surgery," they repeat, voices professionally neutral. By six o'clock, two more videos have been posted. By seven, Ben's face is on the local news. By eight, headlights finally sweep across the driveway, and I stand in the foyer, heart hammering, waiting for my husband to walk through the door.

The lock turns. Benjamin enters, still wearing scrubs beneath his jacket, eyes shadowed with exhaustion. For a moment, he looks exactly like what he claims to be—a dedicated surgeon coming home after saving lives. Not a man whose past is unraveling on social media, whose reputation is being shredded in sixty-second videos.

"Sorry I'm so late," he says, setting down his bag. "Complex resection took longer than—" He stops, finally registering my expression. "Emma? What's wrong?"

My throat tightens. Does he really not know? Has he been so immersed in surgery that he's missed the digital wildfire consuming our lives?

"You haven't heard?" My voice sounds strange, distant. "You haven't seen the videos?"

"Videos?" His forehead creases with confusion. "What videos?"

I pull out my phone, hands trembling slightly. "The hospital didn't tell you? Your friends and family didn't message you?"

"I was in surgery all day. Back-to-back cases. I haven't even had time to look at my phone." He steps closer, concern etching deeper lines around his eyes. "Emma, you're scaring me. What's going on?"

The distance between us feels vast and unbridgeable. I hold up my phone. "This woman. A TikToker named Mira Patel. She's made a series of videos accusing you of killing Alice."

The color drains from his face. "What?"

"She says you were controlling. Abusive. That Alice was planning to leave you, and you tampered with her brakes." Each word feels like glass in my mouth. "Millions of people have seen them. It's all over social media. Local news even picked it up."

He takes the phone from my hand, staring at Mira's image with something between shock and recognition. "This can't be happening," he whispers.

"You know her?" The question comes out sharper than I intended.

"She interviewed me. About a year ago." He looks up, eyes wide. "A student journalist doing a piece on pediatric surgery. She seemed... intense. Asked a lot of personal questions about how I balanced work and being a single father. I thought it was odd, but harmless."

He taps the screen, and Mira's voice fills the space between us. "Multiple sources confirm Dr. Stone displayed controlling behavior throughout his marriage to Alice..."

Benjamin's expression crumples. Not anger. Not indignation. Pain. Raw and unfiltered. "This is insane," he says, voice breaking. "I loved Alice. I would never have hurt her."

He looks so genuinely wounded, so authentically devastated, that I know he could never have done this.

"There's more," I say, taking the phone back, scrolling to the latest video. "Six videos now. Each with more detailed accusations."

We move to the living room, sinking onto the sofa as I play video after video. Benjamin watches in horrified silence, occasionally shaking his head or whispering, "That's not true" or "It didn't happen like that."

The latest video features Mira standing outside Mack's Auto Shop. My stomach drops. The same place I visited, asking the same questions.

"Anton Kravitz confirmed to me that Dr. Stone personally brought Alice's car in three days before her death," Mira says on screen. "He waited while they changed the oil and did a thorough check-up, including the brakes, then drove it home himself. Three days later, the brakes failed catastrophically."

Benjamin's hands clench into fists. "Yes, I took her car in. She asked me to! She was busy with a presentation at the gallery. I was trying to help."

"Did you know she was concerned about the brakes?" I ask quietly.

His eyes snap to mine, suddenly sharp. "What?"

"Alice. Did she tell you she was worried about the brakes feeling soft?"

He stares at me, something shifting in his expression. "How would you know that?"

My heart pounds against my ribs. I've revealed too much. Shown my hand. "It's in the videos," I lie. "Mira mentions it."

He continues staring, eyes searching mine. I can't tell if he believes me. Can't tell if I believe him.

"Alice mentioned the brakes felt different," he finally says. "Not soft, exactly. Just different. I drove the car to the shop myself, it felt fine. I didn't think it was anything. I asked them to look at the brakes, and they said they were fine." He runs a hand through his hair, a gesture of frustration I've seen countless times. "Emma, you can't possibly think I had anything to do with Alice's death."

"Of course not," I say. "But these videos are convincing. People are believing them. Lily was sent home from school today because classmates were taunting her about having a murderer for a father."

"What?" He stands abruptly. "Why didn't you call me?"

"I did. Seventeen times. The school called you too, then called me when you didn't pick up."

"I need to see her." He turns toward the stairs, but I catch his arm.

"She's locked in her room. Hasn't spoken to me since we got home."

Something like suspicion flickers across his face. "What exactly did the kids say to her?"

I hesitate, not wanting to hurt him further. "That you killed Alice to be with me."

Pain contorts his features. He sinks back onto the sofa, head in his hands. "This is a nightmare," he whispers. "How could anyone think I'd hurt Alice? She was everything to me. To Lily."

A small sound draws my attention to the hallway. A floorboard creaking. The whisper of fabric against wood. Lily, standing in the shadows, listening. Our eyes meet briefly before she steps back, disappearing from view.

"I need to talk to her," Benjamin says, not noticing the exchange. "Make sure she knows none of this is true."

"Maybe give her space tonight," I suggest, thinking of the notification I glimpsed on Lily's phone. Thinking of how she angled the screen away from me. I need to know what she knows. What she thinks she knows. Before Benjamin has the chance to silence her. "It's been a traumatic day."

He nods reluctantly. "I'll check on her in the morning. And I need to call the hospital. And then my attorney. Figure out how to fight these accusations."

I watch him pull out his phone, shoulders hunched as he scrolls through missed calls and messages. The Benjamin before me looks genuinely devastated by these allegations. Authentically concerned for his daughter. Nothing like the calculating killer Mira Patel describes.

But Alice's letters warned me about exactly this—his ability to appear sincere, to make me doubt my own suspicions. And Lily seems to think he's capable of it too. Unless it's all just a game to her. To make me believe he is capable of it. So I will leave him, and she can be alone with him again.

I need to get to the bottom of these letters.

"I'm going to make tea," I say, standing. "Do you want some?"

He shakes his head, already dialing. "I need to call my dad. Then the hospital's PR team. Get ahead of this somehow." I leave him in the living room, his voice dropping to an urgent murmur as his father answers. The Stone family circling wagons. Protecting their own. Just as Alice said they would.

FOURTEEN

My phone rings. Ryan's name flashes on the screen.

"It's for the best," he says before I can even say hello. "I've been talking to HR."

I press my fingers against my temple, feeling a headache building. "They want me gone, don't they?"

"A sabbatical," Ryan corrects. "Paid leave until this blows over."

Relief washes over me, followed immediately by shame at feeling relieved. My phone buzzes against my ear—another notification. The seventh in the last hour. Another comment. Another accusation. Another stranger who thinks they know what happened.

"Emma? Are you still there?"

I want to tell him about the letters. Want someone to know I'm drowning. Instead, I say, "Yes. I'm here. It's fine. I'll take it."

What I don't tell Ryan is how I can't bear to face my colleagues' concerned looks, their whispered conversations that stop when I enter a room. They're worried about the videos, but they don't know about the letters. I haven't told anyone—not Jen, not even my mother. The weight of carrying this secret alone makes my shoulders ache. I really should talk to someone about it.

But I don't.

Instead, I find myself creeping into Lily's bedroom, my hands shaking as I ease open the desk drawer across from her unmade four-poster bed. The drawer resists, scraping against its track with a sound that seems to echo through the empty house. I pause, feeling Alice's presence in every corner of this meticulously decorated yet chaotically lived-in space. Her eyes follow me from the silver-framed photo on the nightstand as I sift through spiral notebooks and dog-eared textbooks scattered across the desk. I need proof that Lily is behind these letters. Ben had barely spoken to her at breakfast, just mumbled something about homework before rushing off to surgery. I'd been surprised when she didn't use the tension as an excuse to skip school, but now I'm grateful for the three-hour window before she returns. Still, every groan of the house makes my pulse spike.

And that's when I see it.

In the bottom drawer, I find stationery—cream colored, expensive, with a watermark I can't quite make out. The same paper as the letters.

I take a deep breath, trying to steady my shaking hands as I pick it up. The watermark remains elusive, a mysterious symbol barely visible in the soft light filtering through Lily's window.

It hits me like a physical blow—Lily has been orchestrating this torment all along. She is behind these letters. She must be. Why else would she have those same papers? Lily, with her quiet intensity and carefully constructed facade. Lily, who has been watching me, assessing me, planning her moves like a chess master.

My mind races, trying to connect the dots. Is she behind the videos too? I think of her words when she sped off outside the school. Is she trying to push me away from Benjamin, or save me?

I glance at Alice's photo, her serene smile juxtaposed against the turmoil brewing in Lily's room.

My phone vibrates again.

I look at it.

A text from Marissa in accounts:

Have you seen the latest? This is getting insane.

A TikTok link follows, the thumbnail showing Mira Patel's now-familiar face, her expression solemn as she stares directly into the camera.

My thumb hovers over the link. Don't click it. Don't feed the algorithm. Don't give her another view.

I click it.

"Welcome back to 'The Doctor's Wives,'" Mira begins, her voice carrying the gravity of someone who knows exactly how to hook an audience. "Today, we're looking deeper into the relationship dynamics between Dr. Benjamin Stone and his first wife, Alice. What appeared picture-perfect on the surface tells a different story when you know what to look for."

The screen splits to show photographs I've never seen before. Benjamin and Alice at some charity gala, his hand at the small of her back. Alice in a green dress at what looks like a hospital fundraiser, Benjamin standing close behind her. Their wedding photo—Alice in elegant white, Benjamin beaming beside her.

Mira's voice continues over the images. "Body language experts have identified several concerning patterns in these public appearances." A red circle appears around Benjamin's hand on Alice's back in the first photo. "Note the positioning—not supportive but controlling. His fingers are pressed firmly, directing her movements."

The circle moves to the second photo, highlighting Benjamin's posture behind Alice. "Classic dominance stance. He's not standing beside her as an equal, but hovering over her, monitoring." The circle shifts to Alice's face. "And here—the tight smile, the tension around her eyes. These are stress indicators, not genuine happiness."

My breathing quickens. This is ridiculous. Pseudoscientific nonsense. Anyone can circle random elements in photos and assign sinister meanings. Yet I can't look away as Mira methodically dismantles every image, pointing out supposed signs of control, domination, and fear.

"But perhaps most telling is the progression of photos over time." The screen fills with a timeline of images, Alice's face changing subtly across the years. "Notice how her smile becomes more fixed, her eyes less bright. Classic signs of a woman experiencing coercive control."

I take a sip of coffee to combat the dryness in my throat, my hand unsteady as I bring the cup to my lips. This can't be happening. These photos prove nothing. They're just snapshots, frozen moments being twisted to fit a narrative.

"Our source provided these images along with detailed accounts of Dr. Stone's controlling behaviors," Mira continues. She turns slightly, as if speaking to someone off-camera. "What else should we highlight here?"

A voice responds, just barely audible. A woman's voice, familiar in a way that makes my skin prickle. I increase the volume, pressing my phone closer to my ear.

"The hospital Christmas party photo," the off-camera voice suggests, clearing her throat before continuing. "Where he's gripping her arm."

That throat clearing. That specific cadence. I know that voice.

Rachel. My sister.

The sister I haven't spoken to in almost a year. The sister

who warned me about "controlling men" when Benjamin and I started dating. The sister who refused to attend our wedding, and whose last words to me were, "You never learn, Emma. You're walking into another trap."

My fingers fumble with the volume, turning it up to maximum as Mira follows Rachel's suggestion, highlighting a photo where Benjamin's hand circles Alice's upper arm.

"Perfect example," Mira says, circling Benjamin's hand. "The grip is tight enough to cause compression of the fabric. Notice Alice's expression—the smile doesn't reach her eyes."

I rewind the video, listening again to the off-camera voice. No mistake. It's Rachel. My own sister is feeding this TikToker information about my husband. Is she the "source" Mira keeps referencing?

I scan the frame desperately, looking for any visual confirmation. There—in the background. A mirror on the wall behind Mira catches a partial reflection. A woman with prematurely gray hair pulled back in a practical style. Rachel's distinctive profile as she leans forward, pointing at something out of frame.

I replay the video again, zeroing in on that mirror, freezing the frame where Rachel's reflection is clearest. She's wearing a blazer with something pinned to the lapel—the purple ribbon she always wears, a symbol of her work with domestic violence survivors. Her hair is grayer than I remember, her face thinner. But the set of her jaw, the way she holds her head—that's pure Rachel. Determined. Righteous. Convinced of her moral superiority.

My hands shake so badly I drop the phone. I snatch it up. Mira's face stares back at me, earnest and concerned as she wraps up her video.

"If you or someone you know is experiencing relationship patterns like these, please reach out for help. The signs are often subtle, but they matter. They mattered for Alice Stone. Don't let them be missed again."

The video ends, switching to a screen of suggested content—more accusations, more theories, more destruction packaged as justice.

Heat floods my face as I slam my palm against the desk. My sister. My own flesh and blood. The betrayal burns through me like acid, each heartbeat sending fresh waves of rage pulsing behind my eyes. I grip the edge of my desk so hard my knuckles turn bloodless, as if the wood might splinter beneath my fingers. The room sharpens around me, every detail in cruel focus. I want to scream. I want to break something. I want her to feel what I'm feeling right now.

Rachel. My sister is helping Mira Patel destroy my husband. My marriage. My life.

I know she didn't approve of me marrying him, but still?

I have to call Rachel. Confront her. Demand an explanation. Find out how deep this betrayal goes.

I need to understand why my own sister wants to destroy me.

FIFTEEN

Bayside Café squats between a discount furniture outlet and a pawn shop, its faded awning and foggy windows screaming "health code violation." Perfect. No one from Harbor Heights would be caught dead here, which means no one will witness this confrontation with my sister.

I arrive twenty minutes early, scanning the nearly empty parking lot for Rachel's car—a sensible Subaru she's driven for years. Not here yet. I secure a corner table, position myself with my back to the wall, facing the door. Old habits from childhood—always know where the exits are when Rachel's on the warpath. I check my phone: 12:47. Thirteen minutes until I face the sister I haven't spoken to in a year. The sister who's helping destroy my life.

The café's interior matches its exterior—worn vinyl booths in cracked mustard yellow, tables wobbling on uneven legs, fluorescent lights that make everyone look jaundiced. A bored server drops off a mug of coffee without asking if I want it. I wrap my hands around the thick ceramic, grateful for something to hold onto, something to ground me.

My phone lights up with a text from Benjamin:

Everything went fine with the Hospital's PR team. They have a plan. How's your day going?

How's my day going? I'm sitting in a greasy spoon waiting to confront my estranged sister about her vendetta against you. I haven't told him about my sabbatical and how I'm hiding from colleagues who whisper about my murderer husband.

Fine. Busy with Hartman prep.

I say, knowing I'll have to update him on my break from work when I see him later. I set the phone face down on the table, screen against the coffee-ringed wood. The ceramic mug beside it has gone cold, a film forming on the surface like skin.

The bell above the door jingles—that particular high-pitched chime that always makes me think of Christmas. My head snaps up.

Rachel.

My sister stands framed in the doorway, sunlight catching on her hair. She's been asking me incessantly to meet up for months, especially since the wedding she refused to attend, and I have been ignoring her. So it didn't surprise me that she was eager to return my phone call and moved whatever else she was supposed to do today to make room for me.

She pauses in the doorway, scanning the café until her eyes lock with mine. She looks both exactly the same and completely different. Her hair, always prematurely gray, is now entirely silver, cropped in a practical bob that frames her face. She wears no makeup, her skin pale against the navy blue of her blazer. The ribbon is still pinned to her lapel. She strides toward me with purpose. Her practical flats make no sound on the sticky linoleum. The messenger bag slung across her body is bulging.

"Emma." She stops at my table, making no move to sit. Her voice is exactly as I remember—low, firm, with that slight raspiness from years of speaking at rallies and support groups. While I was at college, I was in awe of my sister's strong values and her work with various charities in her spare time. But if she's attacking Benjamin, it doesn't feel as moral any more.

"Rachel." I gesture to the seat across from me. "Sit."

She slides into the booth, keeping her bag close to her body. We stare at each other across the chipped Formica, these familiar-stranger versions of ourselves. I search her face for the sister I once knew—the one who braided my hair for school, who taught me to ride a bike, who stood between me and our father's rage. All I see is the hard set of her jaw, the unwavering certainty in her eyes.

My wedding ring catches on a groove in the table as I spin it around my finger, and suddenly I'm seven again, curled into a ball inside the hallway linen closet, counting my breaths in the musty darkness. The click of the lock. The endless waiting. Rachel's voice, finally, whispering through the door: "It's me, Emmy. He's asleep now." Her small fingers sliding the bobby pin into the lock, her arms pulling me into the light, the smell of dust in her hair as she held me.

"You look thin," she says finally.

"You look old," I reply.

Her mouth twitches—not quite a smile. "Still direct, at least."

The server approaches and serves Rachel coffee. "I'm not staying long."

"No?" I lean forward. "I thought you'd want to explain why you're trying to destroy my life."

"I'm trying to save it." No hesitation. No doubt. Pure Rachel.

"By feeding lies to a TikToker? By helping her accuse my husband of murder?"

"Not lies, Emma. Facts." She unzips her bag, pulls out a

manila folder thick with documents. "Facts that you would see if you weren't so determined to repeat your patterns."

My coffee sloshes as I set the mug down too hard. "Don't psychoanalyze me. I didn't come here for therapy."

"Why did you come, then?" She places the folder between us but keeps her hand on it. "To convince me to stop? To beg for your husband's reputation?"

"I came to understand why my own sister would betray me like this." My voice cracks, a hairline fracture in my carefully constructed composure. "Without even talking to me first. Without giving me a chance to explain—"

"Explain what?" She cuts me off. "Explain how Benjamin Stone is different than David? How this controlling, manipulative man is somehow not like the last controlling, manipulative man you attached yourself to?"

David. My ex. The relationship Rachel warned me about, the one that ended with a restraining order and six months of therapy. The wound she knows exactly how to reopen.

"Ben isn't David." I wrap my arms around myself, suddenly cold despite the café's stuffy air. "He's a respected surgeon. He saves children's lives. He—"

"He isolated Alice from her friends." Rachel slides the folder toward me, flipping it open to reveal neatly organized documents. "He monitored her spending. He convinced her she was unstable, paranoid, unfit to make decisions."

All the things David did indeed do to me.

I remember Rachel's face in the rearview mirror as we sped away that night, her eyes darting to check if headlights appeared behind us. My hands had been shaking too badly to drive. "He'll find us," I kept saying, but Rachel just kept one hand steady on the wheel and the other on my knee. "Not this time," she'd promised, though we both jumped at every car door that slammed in the motel parking lot. Three days later, she helped me change my phone number, my email, my bank accounts—

methodically erasing the digital breadcrumbs that had let David track me down twice before.

She was a great help back then, but she believed Ben would be the same. She never even gave him a chance. She tried to stop me from marrying him. That's why we're estranged and why she didn't come to my wedding.

I stare at the papers before me—police reports, medical records, handwritten statements. My eyes catch phrases that stand out in stark black type: "suspicious bruising," "patient declined to explain injury," "expressed fear of returning home."

"Three separate ER visits in the last year of their marriage," Rachel continues, her voice taking on the clinical tone she uses in her support groups. "Always with a plausible explanation. Always at different hospitals. Classic pattern of an abuser who knows how to work the system."

"This doesn't prove anything." I push the folder away. "Accidents happen. People fall. Alice had a history of—"

"Of what, Emma? What did Benjamin tell you about her? That she was clumsy? Unstable? Prone to exaggeration?" Rachel leans forward, her gray eyes boring into mine over the rim of her chipped mug of black coffee. She's ordered the truck stop special—biscuits and sausage gravy, creamy grits, fried eggs and bacon—while my untouched avocado toast sits between us like a class divide. The waitress refills Rachel's cup for the third time, not bothering to ask if I want more of my water.

"Those are the stories abusers tell about their victims. I've heard them a thousand times."

"You don't know him." My hands clench into fists beneath the table, manicured nails digging into my palms. "You've never even met him."

"I've interviewed fifteen people who knew him and Alice. Her former housekeeper. Her colleagues. Her therapist." Rachel shovels a forkful of grits into her mouth, and my jaw hits the floor. How long has she been looking into him? She chews deliberately, mouth half open, reminding me of Sunday mornings in our childhood trailer when Dad was gone and we'd split a box of powdered donuts. Before she became the crusading journalist who couldn't stomach my "selling out" to Benjamin's world. The world of the rich.

"Her therapist spoke to you? That's a violation of—"

"Not about sessions. About what she observed at the couple's counseling Ben insisted on. How he dominated conversations, contradicted Alice, charmed the therapist into seeing his side." Rachel taps the folder. "It's all here. The pattern is textbook."

My chest tightens. "So you decided to be judge and jury? To help this—this internet vulture destroy his reputation based on circumstantial evidence?"

"Mira is giving voice to a woman who can no longer speak for herself." Rachel's expression hardens. "Someone needs to. The police didn't. The medical examiners didn't. His family certainly didn't."

"He loved Alice." The words feel hollow even as I say them. "He mourns her every day."

"He controls her narrative every day," Rachel corrects. "Just like he's controlling yours now."

Heat rushes to my face. "You don't know anything about my marriage."

"I know you quit the Johnson account because Benjamin thought it took too much of your time. I know you changed your hair because he preferred it longer. I know you've stopped wearing those silver earrings Mom gave you because he said they were 'tacky.'"

Each example lands like a slap. How does she know these details? Who has been watching me, reporting back?

"You're spying on me?" My voice rises, drawing glances from the few other patrons.

"I'm paying attention," Rachel counters, her voice

remaining frustratingly level. "Something you've never been good at when it comes to men."

I start to snap at her but catch myself when I notice the server lingering at the next table. I lower my voice instead. "Rachel, please. You've never given Ben a chance. I've found someone who makes me happy—who gave me the family I always wanted. Don't you see how this is tearing me apart? Try to understand what's at stake here. This family—they've become everything to me." I reach across the table, not quite touching her hand. "I've finally found where I belong."

Rachel's expression softens for just a moment before hardening again. "Is that really what you think this is about? That I'm trying to hurt you?"

"Then help me understand," I whisper, my voice cracking slightly. "Because right now it feels like you're determined to destroy the only real happiness I've ever known. Why?"

"Because I watched our mother die by inches in a marriage just like yours." Her voice drops to a harsh whisper. "Because I pulled you out of David's apartment when he put your head through a wall. Because Alice Stone reached out to me shortly before she died, and I didn't help her in time."

The café goes silent around us. Or maybe it's just the blood rushing in my ears, drowning out everything but Rachel's words.

"You're lying." My voice sounds distant, detached. I don't want to remember any of the things she's talking about. David is in my past. I'm a different person now. "Alice never knew you."

"She found me through my support group. Said she'd been following my work." Rachel's eyes never leave mine. "She was planning to leave him, Emma. She was terrified."

"No." I shake my head, rejecting the words, the implications. "I don't believe you."

"Look at the evidence." She pushes the folder toward me again. "Read Alice's own words. Then tell me I'm wrong."

I stare at the folder between us, this Pandora's box of accusations and evidence. Part of me wants to shove it off the table, to reject everything it contains. Another part, the part that's been awake at night since getting Alice's letters, wants to devour every page, every detail.

"You need to stop this," I say instead, my voice cracking. "Call off your TikTok attack dog. Take down the videos. Before they destroy everything."

"They're only destroying lies, Emma." Rachel zips her bag closed, preparing to leave. "The truth will survive just fine." She stands, drawing herself up to her full height. Heads turn toward our table, the other customers no longer pretending not to listen.

"Can we talk about this outside?" I say, gathering my purse, and the folder. "Please don't leave yet." Rachel nods once, already moving toward the door. Her back is straight, her stride purposeful. The posture of someone absolutely convinced of her righteousness. I need to convince her to stop this.

SIXTEEN

The folder burns in my hands as we stand in the parking lot, its contents—police reports, medical records, witness statements—weighing heavily. No prying eyes from the café windows now, just my sister and me and the accusations hanging between us like storm clouds.

"How long have you been doing this?" I ask, my voice steadier than I feel. "Investigating my husband. Building your case against him. Planning to destroy my life."

Rachel pushes her silver hair back from her face, the afternoon sun highlighting the lines around her eyes that weren't there a year ago. "Since I saw your engagement announcement in the *Tampa Tribune*."

"Wow. Just wow. And you couldn't have spoken to me about any of this?"

"I recognized the pattern." She leans against her car, arms crossed. "Successful doctor. Tragic widower. Quick remarriage to a woman who works for his family business. The same story I've heard from dozens of women in my support groups. And you've been bamboozled before."

"So you appointed yourself detective?" The folder crinkles

as my grip tightens. "Looking for evidence to confirm your bias?"

"I started asking questions." Her voice takes on the measured tone she uses when testifying in court—I've watched her do it twice, speaking for women who couldn't speak for themselves. "The domestic violence community is small, Emma. Alice's name had come up before. She came to me."

"As what? A victim? Based on what?"

"Based on the three separate ER visits with injuries inconsistent with her explanations. Based on her increasing isolation from friends. Based on her therapist's concerns that were never officially reported." Rachel pushes off from the car, taking a step toward me. "She gave me an SD card, told me it showed him recording her, keeping an eye on her every move, even when sleeping. He had put it in some necklace, she said. Without her knowing it. I watched it. It's bad. How do you know he's not doing the same to you?"

I touch my neck where my necklace used to be. I'm not buying all this Rachel is saying. I think she's making it all up. She wrote the letters and now she's trying to make me believe them by confirming the existence of those recordings. I don't believe anything she says.

"So you interviewed the housekeeper? Alice's friends? Without ever meeting Ben, without ever seeing them together, you decided he was guilty?"

"I talked to seventeen people who knew them as a couple." Rachel's eyes never leave mine, that same unflinching stare she's had since we were kids. "The housekeeper who saw Alice flinch when Ben raised his voice and drop a Waterford crystal vase that shattered across the marble floor. The colleague who noticed finger-shaped bruises on Alice's wrists during an art presentation at the Westwood Gallery, the same night Ben gave that speech about supporting women in the arts. The neighbor who heard arguments through open windows—always late at night, always ending with Alice apologizing while something crashed against the wall."

"And you couldn't pick up the phone before I married him?" My voice cracks. "Before the wedding?"

Rachel's face hardens. "I called you twenty-seven times in three months, Emma. Left voicemails. Sent texts. Emails with attachments. You blocked my number the week before your engagement party. I asked Mom to speak to you and she refused. I wanted to tell you what I knew but you wouldn't listen. He's bad news. He was abusive to his ex-wife. I have tried to tell you in so many ways and, in the end, I had to reveal him to the world. That's when Mira and I teamed up."

My throat tightens. "People argue. Marriages have rough patches. Doesn't mean he killed her."

"Her therapist was preparing to file a report with authorities when Alice died." Rachel's voice drops to a whisper. "She suspected ongoing emotional and physical abuse. Alice had bruises shaped like fingerprints on her upper arms—five perfect ovals of purple and yellow. A fractured wrist she claimed came from falling down stairs at their beach house in Naples. Three separate ER visits for 'household accidents' in six months—a kitchen knife slip, a tumble in the shower, a fall from a ladder while hanging Christmas lights." Rachel leans closer. "The day after Alice died, the therapist received a manila envelope Alice had mailed—containing a five-page letter detailing her fear that Ben would eventually kill her."

I swallow hard, my throat dry. Speaking of letters...

"Rachel, have you been sending me letters pretending to be Alice?"

"What are you talking about?"

"Don't play dumb. I have been receiving letters from someone pretending to be Alice, warning me about Benjamin. But I don't believe them. Any of them. Did you send them to scare me? To destroy my marriage, my life?"

Her eyes widen, genuine surprise flashing across her face. "What? No. God, no." But there's something in the way she looks down at her hands that makes me think she knows more than she's saying. I'm getting tired of people lying to me.

"If all you say is true," I say, fighting to keep my voice steady, "why didn't the therapist take it to the police? Why wasn't there an investigation?"

"There was. A cursory one." Rachel's mouth twists. "Led by Detective Lucas Ramirez, who closed the case in record time despite the therapist's statement."

I think of Robert at dinner, his cool assessment, his subtle threats. The way the Stone family closes ranks. Protects their own.

"You're making connections that don't exist," I say, but the conviction has leached from my voice. "Seeing conspiracy where there's only coincidence."

"Am I?" Rachel steps closer. "Then why did the mechanic who serviced Alice's car three days before her death suddenly receive an anonymous donation to expand his business? Why did the medical examiner who ruled her death accidental get a position on the Harbor Heights Medical Board six months later? Why has every person who questioned the official story been silenced, bought off, or intimidated? Even the guy that towed her car after it was pulled out of the water told me—off the record—that he received a donation right after."

"You sound insane." But my hands are shaking now, the folder threatening to spill its contents across the cracked asphalt.

"And you sound exactly like Mom did." Rachel's words land like a slap. "Defending Dad to the end. Finding excuses for the bruises, the controlling behavior, the isolation. Refusing to see what was right in front of you."

Anger flares, hot and sudden. "Don't you dare compare Ben

to Dad. Don't you dare use our childhood to justify this—this vendetta."

"It's not a vendetta, Emma. It's the truth."

"It's jealousy." The accusation bursts from me. "You've always resented my relationships, my ability to move on from what happened to us. You can't stand that I found happiness while you're still alone, still fighting the same battles, still seeing abuse everywhere you look."

Rachel flinches, the barb finding its mark. For a moment, her professional facade cracks, revealing the sister I grew up with—the one who took the brunt of Dad's anger to protect me, who worked three jobs to put herself through college.

"Is that what you think this is about?" she asks quietly. "That I'm so bitter about my own life that I'd destroy yours out of spite?"

"What else explains this crusade? This-this alliance with a TikToker who's turning my husband into a public villain without due process or evidence?"

"Due process failed Alice." Rachel's voice hardens again. "Just like it fails thousands of women every year. Sometimes public pressure is the only recourse."

"At the expense of an innocent man's reputation? His career? His daughter's well-being?"

"I told you. Alice contacted me three days before she died. That makes it personal to me."

The words hang in the space between us, stopping my next argument before it forms. Three days. The same timeline as the car service. The same as Anton confirmed.

"You're lying," I whisper, but there's no conviction in it. "I don't believe you."

"She found me through my support group website." Rachel's eyes hold mine, unflinching. "She said she was planning to leave him. That she had evidence but needed help getting away safely. We scheduled a meeting for the day after she died." Her voice catches, the only crack in her composure. "I was too late."

The folder nearly slips from my grasp. I clutch it tighter, knuckles white against the manila.

"I won't be too late for you," Rachel continues. "I won't watch another woman die because I didn't act soon enough. Especially not my sister."

"I'm not in danger." The protest sounds hollow even to my own ears.

"Check your brakes, Emma." Rachel opens her car door. "And read that folder. All of it. Then decide if I'm the enemy here. And take the letters seriously. Whoever they're from.

"Have you considered that Alice might not be as dead as everyone thinks? That she might be hiding because she's terrified of what he'd do if he found her? Think about it."

"Do you know she's still alive?" I say, but my voice must be less than a whisper as she's already sliding into the driver's seat, closing the door with a decisive click. Through the window, I see her hands grip the steering wheel—steady, resolute. The engine starts, and she backs out without another word, leaving me standing alone in the parking lot, the folder heavy in my hands.

I don't notice the car across the street at first, but when I do, it makes my pulse race. Inside sits someone, pointing a phone camera at my face through the open window. I recognize the car right away.

Is it Lily?

I fumble with my keys, hands suddenly clumsy with adrenaline, and when the door finally swings open, an envelope sits waiting on my seat, my name written in that now-familiar handwriting.

SEVENTEEN

My fingers hover over the envelope. Something about its plainness, its anonymity, sends a chill across my skin. I slip my finger under the flap, tear the envelope open with a sound that seems too loud in the quiet of my car. Inside, a single folded sheet of paper. No letterhead. No signature line visible. Just white paper with black type.

I unfold it slowly, hands suddenly unsteady.

The first line hits like a physical blow:

By now you know he's dangerous. I hoped my first letter would be enough to warn you, but if you're still there. Still with him. Still in danger. Perhaps this will convince you.

It was our anniversary. Five years married. I wore the green dress he liked, made his favorite dinner, even bought those ridiculously expensive scotch-filled chocolates he loves. Everything perfect. Then I mentioned my brother had invited us to visit him in Seattle. Just mentioned it—not even asked if we could go.

His face changed instantly. Like a mask dropping. One moment, my charming, smiling husband. The next, something cold and hard and frightening. He asked why I'd been talking to my brother without telling him. Said I was being secretive. Manipulative. Planning things behind his back.

I tried to explain it was just a casual conversation, nothing planned, but he wouldn't listen. His voice got louder. Mine got smaller. He followed me into the kitchen, standing too close as I cleaned up dinner dishes. Kept asking questions with no right answers. Why was I so desperate to get away from him? Was I meeting someone in Seattle? Did I think he was stupid?

When I turned away, his hand shot out, gripped my upper arm so hard I gasped. He spun me around to face him, fingers digging into my flesh. "Don't walk away when I'm talking to you," he said, his voice so quiet now, which was somehow worse than the yelling.

I started crying. Couldn't help it. The pain, the fear, the confusion—all of it bubbling up and spilling over. He watched me cry with this strange detachment, like he was observing an experiment. Still gripping my arm. Still leaving the bruises I'd have to hide at work the next day.

"I'm sorry," I said, though I didn't know what for. It's what he wanted to hear. The magic words that sometimes ended these episodes. Not this time.

"Sorry isn't good enough," he said, his voice cold and menacing. "You need to learn."

Learn what? I never knew. Just that I was always failing some test I didn't know I was taking. That night, he did something terrible. He locked me in the basement, the door slamming shut with a chilling finality, leaving me alone. Before he left, he placed a mirror in front of me, leaning on the wall. "Look at yourself," he instructed, his voice dripping with a sinister edge. "See what you've done." Then he left. My heart raced as I heard the unmistakable sound of a chain, heavy and metallic, being dragged across the floor above. Panic clawed at my throat as I realized he was sealing the door.

He left for work the next morning like nothing happened. Let me out of the basement. Kissed my forehead. Said he loved me. Left a coffee on the kitchen counter. The bruises on my arm formed a perfect handprint, five fingers of deepening purple. I wore long sleeves for days, hiding not only the marks but the fear that had taken root deep within me. This wasn't the first time. It wasn't the last. But it was when I knew I needed to start documenting everything. Start planning my escape.

By the way, did they ever find my phone when I died?

The final question pulls me from the horror of Alice's account like a slap. Her phone. I never thought about her phone. Was it recovered from the crash? Was it searched? What might it contain?

I fold the letter with numb fingers, tuck it back into my pocket. My heart pounds against my ribs like it's trying to escape. Rachel's words ring in my ears; are these letters really being sent from Alice beyond the grave? Or stranger still... did she really die? Or did she just escape?

I open a new tab in my phone browser. Type: "How to locate a missing cell phone from years ago."

The search results populate my screen. I begin to read.

The IT department sits on the third floor of Stone Advertising, fluorescent lights buzzing like trapped insects above rows of server racks. I take the back entrance and then the stairs to avoid running into any of my colleagues. I open the heavy door slowly, then venture deeper into territory where questions might be raised. Marcus Chen's workspace is tucked into the back corner—a glass-walled cube filled with monitors, hard drives, and tangled cables that remind me of exposed nerves. Perfect. Isolated. Private. I take a deep breath, rehearsing my story one more time before I knock on his door,

Alice's phone number burning a hole in my pocket alongside her new letter.

Marcus glances up from his array of screens, surprise flickering across his face. Account executives don't venture down here unless something's catastrophically wrong with their presentation decks.

"Emma? Everything okay with the Hartman files?" He pushes his glasses up his nose, already reaching for his keyboard.

"The files are fine." I slip inside, closing the door behind me, glad he hasn't heard about my time off quite yet. The space smells of electronics and stale coffee. "I need something else. Something... unofficial."

His eyebrows lift, interest piqued. Marcus has worked here longer than I have. And he's the head of IT. He knows the Stone family dynamics. He knew Alice.

"Unofficial as in off the books? Or unofficial as in potentially against company policy?" His voice remains neutral, but his eyes sharpen behind rectangular frames.

"Both, maybe." I settle into the spare chair beside his desk. "I need to locate a phone. Not hack it—just find its last location. From about five years ago."

His fingers stop their perpetual tapping. "That's... specific. And difficult." He studies my face. "And definitely not related to the Hartman presentation."

"It's personal." I lean forward, dropping my voice though we're alone. "I have a friend whose sister died suddenly. The family never found her phone. There might be photos, messages —things that would help them find closure."

The lie tastes metallic on my tongue. Marcus tilts his head, considering. I've never asked him for anything like this before. Never given him reason to doubt my integrity. He will have seen the news, heard the accusations against Benjamin. He's a friend of mine, and he owes me a favor.

"Five years is a long time for digital breadcrumbs," he says finally. "What's the number?"

I pull out the slip of paper where I've written Alice's cell number, copied from Ben's contacts, where he still has it saved. I don't say whose number it is. Don't need to. Marcus's eyes flicker with recognition as he takes it, but he doesn't comment.

"I'd need the account details. Carrier. Password."

"I don't have those." My heart sinks. "Just the number."

He drums his fingers on the desk, thinking. "There are ways. Not exactly above-board ways, but..." He glances at his door, then back to me. "This is important to your friend?"

I nod, trying to look appropriately solemn rather than desperate. "Very."

"Okay." He pulls out his own personal laptop, turns to his keyboard, fingers flying. "Give me a few minutes."

The "few minutes" stretch into fifteen, then twenty. Marcus works in silence, occasionally muttering to himself as he navigates through screens I can't begin to understand. I watch his reflection in the darkened monitor to my left—his focused expression, the occasional frown, the small nod of satisfaction when something works.

His office feels like a cave, insulated from the corporate world above us. Framed comic book art hangs on the walls between whiteboards covered in diagrams and code snippets. A collection of action figures guards his desk—superheroes frozen in mid-battle against invisible enemies. In any other circumstance, I'd find it charming.

"Huh." The sound pulls my attention back to Marcus. "That's interesting."

"What?" I lean forward, trying to decode the gibberish on his screen.

"This phone." He taps the monitor. "It didn't stop pinging when your friend's sister died. It kept going for almost a week after."

My pulse quickens. "What does that mean?"

"Could mean a few things. Battery lasted a while. Someone else had the phone. Or..." He glances at me. "The phone wasn't with her when she died."

Alice's phone wasn't in the car when it plunged off that bridge? Wasn't with her body? Was somewhere else entirely. My mind races with implications.

"Can you tell where it was? That last week?"

Marcus types again, bringing up a map with a glowing dot. "Last ping came from a cell tower near this location in Palm Harbor. Around the industrial district." He zooms in, the map resolving to show streets, buildings. "Looks like it's a storage facility. Park-Safe Storage on Industrial Boulevard."

A storage facility. Not the bridge where Alice supposedly died. Not the Stone mansion. Not any location that makes sense if Alice's death was truly an accident.

"What about account activity? Any calls or texts after... after the date of death?"

Marcus shakes his head. "That I can't access without carrier authorization. Just the location data from tower pings."

"Can you find out if she rented a unit at that storage facility?"

He studies me for a long moment, clearly weighing professional ethics against curiosity. Curiosity wins. He turns back to his keyboard.

"Their security's basic. Small operation." More typing. Several windows open and close rapidly. "Got it. Customer database. What name am I looking for?"

"Try..." I hesitate. "Try variations of Alice. Alice Stone. Alice Graham."

Marcus's fingers freeze over the keyboard. His face drains of color so quickly I think he might faint. "Alice?" he whispers, eyes darting to the door as if expecting someone to burst in. "Why would you—" He stops himself, swallows hard. His Adam's apple bobs twice before he continues typing.

Marcus scrolls through records. "Nothing under Stone. But there's an A. Graham who rented unit 237 five years ago. Paid for in advance. Cash."

"Cash?" That seems deliberate. Untraceable.

"Yeah. Unusual these days, but their system allows it with a cash deposit." He clicks through more screens. "Unit's still technically rented. They don't clear them out unless they need the space, especially if they're paid up."

"Is there... is there an access code? For the facility?" I shouldn't ask. Should stop here. But I can't.

Marcus hesitates, then sighs. "Facility uses a keypad entry. Code changes monthly." More typing. "Current code is 5291." He scribbles it on a Post-it, then pauses before handing it to me. "Emma, whatever your friend is looking for... I hope it brings them peace. But maybe some things are better left alone."

I take the Post-it, slide it into my pocket alongside Alice's letter. "I'll tell them you said that."

"This stays between us, right?" His eyes hold mine, suddenly serious. The fluorescent light catches on the small scar on his knuckles—the one he got when he punched through the server room wall after finding out his fiancée was sleeping with the CFO. I'd covered for him, told everyone he'd had an allergic reaction to medication and hallucinated. I even convinced Robert to let him keep his job. That was back when I was still Robert's favorite and he'd listen to anything I'd say.

Marcus fidgets with his security badge, twisting it between his fingers until the lanyard cuts into his skin. "Robert would have my job if he knew I accessed these systems for personal reasons. After everything you did for me..."

"Of course." I stand, straightening my skirt. "As far as anyone knows, I was never here."

At the door, I pause. "Thank you, Marcus. Really."

He nods once, already turning back to his legitimate work. I descend the stairs back to the main floor, mind racing. A storage unit in Palm Harbor. Paid for in cash under Alice's maiden name.

Her phone's last location.

What did she hide there? What was so important she needed to conceal it from Benjamin? From everyone?

And what will I find if I go looking?

EIGHTEEN

Darkness falls early in November, even in Florida. I wait until seven, when the last pink streaks fade from the sky, before driving to Palm Harbor. The storage facility sits between a defunct bowling alley and an auto parts store, its chain-link fence topped with rusting barbed wire.

I park two blocks away in the overlit lot of a fast-food franchise, tucking the BMW between a dented Dodge and a minivan with reindeer antlers. It's the kind of place that expects late-night pit stops from surgeons on call and Uber drivers striking gold at the drive-thru, not advertising execs with designer handbags and hearts pounding. I kill the engine, clutch the folder on the passenger seat, and sit a moment, waiting for my pulse to drop below 180. It doesn't.

The phone buzzes before I can psyche myself up. Benjamin. I hesitate, knowing if I answer, I'll need to conjure a version of myself who hasn't been circling this block for twenty minutes, a version who isn't about to break into a dead woman's storage room. I answer anyway.

"Hey. Everything okay?" I keep my tone light, tapping the car door with chewed nails.

He's whispering, like he's afraid someone's listening. "It's bad. Dad's convinced this is some kind of coordinated takedown. He wants to bring in the crisis PR team and—Jesus, Emma, my phone's been non-stop since before sunrise. We had two more reporters at the door." A ragged sigh. "Where are you? When are you coming home? I could use a glass of wine and some friendly eyes."

"I'll be home in a bit. Just running some errands. I went and had coffee with my mom." The lie stings on my lips as I say it. I hate lying to him. He's my husband, the love of my life. We should share everything with one another. Do life together. For better or for worse. I start to wonder if I'm just messing everything up for myself. For us?

"I'm still at my dad's but hope to get out of here soon. I miss you. It's been hell with the phone constantly ringing."

I make soft, supportive noises, ask if he's eaten, if he needs me to bring anything. He says no, just keep your head down, don't talk to press waiting outside. His voice is the thinnest I've ever heard it, a cracked eggshell of composure. I want to tell him I'm afraid too—afraid for us, for our future, for the story that keeps evolving with every post and ping. Instead, I say, "We'll get through it," because what else do you say to someone whose past won't stay buried?

The walk feels endless. I take the folder and tuck it under my arm, power walk across the vacant lot, and step onto the sidewalk. My heels click too loud, ricocheting off asphalt and stucco. I try switching to the grass, moving along the periphery of streetlight halos, but the dew instantly seeps into my shoes, cold and intrusive. I debate taking them off, but I'd rather risk a rolled ankle than a broken toe. The whole time, my heart batter-rams my chest. What am I doing?

I replay the past hour, searching for different outcomes. What if I'd gone straight home and crawled into bed beside Ben, sank into his warmth, and let him shield me from the noise? What if I'd called the police, admitted everything, let them sift through the letters and worked this all out for me? But the truth is, I know exactly why I'm here—why I have to be here. I think what Alice is saying is true. Part of me believes she's alive. Warning me. Rachel's voice is still fresh in my head, prickling the back of my neck.

"You trust too easily, Em. You always have. First Dad, then David, and now this—this Stepford surgeon with a dead wife and a daughter who hates you."

I wanted to scream at her, but the words stuck, because wasn't that always my flaw? Loving too hard, letting people in until they took what they wanted and left me with nothing but the ache. That's what Rachel never understood: sometimes the ache is better than the emptiness.

I pass two more houses, both with porch lights blazing and Ring cameras blinking blue. I keep my head down, shielding my face with the folder, wishing I'd thought to wear a hat or something less... memorable. This is breaking and entering. This is illegal.

This is necessary.

There's a moment, wedged between the nothingness of the empty street and the sharp, chemical tang of the letter in my bag, where I think about Dad. About the way he'd come home smelling of whiskey and salt air, slamming doors and demanding silence, as if the smallest sound could set him off. About the nights I'd press an ear to the wall, measuring the threat level on each syllable. For years, I promised myself I'd never marry a man like that. Never let anyone weaponize my love or make me feel small. Which is why, for all her warnings, I can't let Rachel's theory hold any water. I know men like my father. Ben is not that man.

The facility entrance features a keypad mounted on a metal post, illuminated by a single flickering bulb that attracts moths and casts jittering shadows. I glance over my shoulder—the street behind me empty, the bowling alley's neon sign dark, the auto parts store closed for the day. No witnesses. No cameras pointed this direction from what I can tell. My fingers tremble as I punch in the code Marcus gave me: 5-2-9-1.

A mechanical click. The gate slides open with a rusty groan. I slip inside before it fully retracts, eager to escape potential observation from the street. The gate closes automatically behind me with the same protesting sound.

Inside, the facility stretches before me in identical rows of metal doors. Fluorescent lights from the ceiling cast everything in a sickly pallor. The air smells of dust and damp. Unit numbers are stenciled in black paint above each roll-up door: 199, 201, 203.

I follow the ascending numbers, moving as quietly as possible. My shadow stretches and contracts as I pass under each light fixture. The concrete walkways amplify every sound—the soft pad of my steps, my shallow breathing, the rustle of my clothing. I'm the only person here.

Door 237 appears around a corner. A standard unit with a padlock securing the roll-up door. Nothing special to distinguish it from the dozens I've passed. Nothing to indicate it might contain secrets that could destroy my marriage, expose a murder, or perhaps even save my life.

I stare at the padlock. Sturdy but basic—a Master Lock 175, the same brand my father used on the closet door during his "teaching moments." The brass gleams under the hallway's fluorescent light, taunting me. I've watched enough crime shows to know the theory of lock-picking but possess none of the tools or skills required. What I do have is a platinum American Express Centurion card with Benjamin's name embossed next to mine in raised italic lettering. The irony isn't lost on me as I slide the black metal edge into the gap between the door and frame, feeling for the latch mechanism, my hands remembering the countless times I'd done this as a teenager, after being locked away for some minor infraction.

Minutes pass. Sweat beads on my forehead despite the cool evening air. The card bends alarmingly but doesn't snap. Just when I'm about to give up, something clicks. The door gives slightly. I've disengaged the latch.

I hesitate, hand on the handle. This is my last chance to turn back. To pretend I never found this place. To return to my life with Benjamin, to uncertainty, to potential danger.

I pull up.

The door rises with a metallic shriek that makes me wince. I freeze, listening for any response—footsteps, voices, alarms. Nothing. Just the distant hum of traffic.

The unit's interior is small, maybe five by ten feet, and nearly empty. Just a single cardboard box placed precisely in the center of the concrete floor. Dust motes dance in the beam of light that spills from the hallway. I step inside, pulling the chain for the overhead bulb. A naked lightbulb flickers to life.

The box is labeled in neat handwriting: "A. Graham." Alice's handwriting—I recognize it from the letters. My knees weaken. This is real. This is happening. This is evidence.

I kneel beside the box, hesitating before lifting the lid. Whatever Alice hid here, she meant it to be found—perhaps by the police, perhaps by a friend, perhaps by the next woman to marry Benjamin Stone.

The lid comes off easily, releasing a puff of dust that makes me cough. Inside: a cracked iPhone in a brown Louis Vuitton case. A manila envelope. A collection of photographs held together with a rubber band.

I reach for the photos first. The rubber band snaps as I remove it, too brittle from time and temperature fluctuations. The top image shows Benjamin and Alice on a beach, smiling at the camera, arms around each other. They look happy. Normal. In love. The next photo shows them at what appears to be a hospital charity gala—Alice in emerald green, Benjamin handsome in a tuxedo. More photos follow—holidays, vacations, ordinary moments made significant through preservation.

I search their faces for signs of what Rachel and Mira described—control, fear, abuse. Find nothing but ordinary smiles and ordinary poses. Was everything hidden beneath the surface? Or am I looking at genuine happiness before something changed?

The iPhone comes next. The screen is shattered, a spiderweb of cracks emanating from the bottom right corner. I press the power button, unsurprised when nothing happens. Dead after five years without charging. Whatever secrets it holds remain locked inside for now.

The envelope contains legal documents—life insurance policies, a copy of Alice's will, financial records. I skim them quickly, noting that everything was left to Lily, with Benjamin as trustee until her twenty-first birthday.

There's also a necklace. With charms. The one Alice talked about in her letters, which contained a small camera. I take a deep breath as I look at it in the light. The heart charm is still missing. I think of Rachel, who said she had the SD card. I guess it wasn't all made up. The necklace does exist, but did it really contain a camera? Would Ben do that?

I'm still not convinced.

Fear prickles at the base of my neck—fear of being discovered, fear of what I'll learn, fear of how it will change everything.

As I take a deep breath to steady myself, something else catches my eye in the box. I reach for it, my curiosity piqued. It's a thin metal object—a shim. I pick it up, turning it over in my fingers, holding it up to the dim light from the solitary bulb above. Its surface glints dully, and I wonder what purpose it served in this tangled web of secrets. After a moment, I place it back inside the box, my mind racing with possibilities and questions.

I make a decision. The phone goes into my purse. Everything else goes back in the box, arranged exactly as I found it. I'm hoping I can somehow open the phone and reveal the last days of her life. Maybe Marcus could do it. Maybe the police.

I replace the lid, turn off the light, slip out of the unit. The door rolls down with a softer sound than when I opened it, or perhaps my fear of discovery has sharpened my hearing. I reset the latch as best I can. From a casual glance, it should look undisturbed.

The walk back through the storage facility feels twice as long.

A car is parked across the street, headlights off, engine silent. I wouldn't have noticed it except for the brief flash of light inside—like a phone screen illuminating a face for just a second. The light vanishes immediately, but not before I glimpse a familiar profile.

Lily.

NINETEEN

Lily's car sits in the driveway of our home. My hands grip the steering wheel as I pull in beside it, my knuckles white, my pulse hammering in my ears. She made it home before me. I cut the engine but don't move, staring at the house that suddenly feels more trap than home.

Rachel's folder sits on the passenger seat. Alice's phone is burning a hole in my pocket.

The house is quiet when I enter, too quiet. No music from Lily's room, no TV from the den. Just the soft hum of the air conditioning and the tick-tick-tick of the grandfather clock in the foyer, counting down to something I can't name. Benjamin must still be with his father.

"Lily?" My voice echoes against marble and hardwood. No answer.

I move through the house, checking the kitchen, the living room, the sunroom at the back. Empty. Empty. Empty. Then a flash of movement catches my eye through the French doors—a figure moving along the side path to the backyard. Lily, her dark hair pulled back in a ponytail, her phone clutched in her hand like a weapon.

I yank open the door, step out onto the patio. "Lily!" She freezes, then turns slowly. "I saw you." The words come out in a rush, my anger propelling them forward.

She tilts her head, one eyebrow lifting in a perfect arch of disdain. "I have no idea what you're talking about."

"Don't lie to me." I step closer, the stone patio hot beneath my feet. "Why are you following me?"

"You're imagining things." Her arms cross over her chest, a barrier between us. "Maybe you should talk to someone about these paranoid delusions."

The words hit like a slap. Paranoid. Delusional. The same words Rachel said Benjamin used to describe Alice. "It was you, Lily. I know it was you."

"Whatever." She turns away, dismissive, but I grab her arm.

"No. Not whatever. You followed me. You photographed me talking to my sister. Why?"

She yanks her arm free, her cool facade cracking. "Don't touch me."

"Then stop lying to me."

"Like you're not lying to everyone?" Her voice rises, sharp and sudden. "Pretending to care about me? About Dad? Playing the perfect stepmom while you sneak around with people trying to destroy him?"

I close my eyes. It takes all my strength not to run away, to just stand there, breathing in the stale scent of rain-soaked mulch. "Lily," I say, keeping my voice steady, "you recently said something about your father not being who I think he is. What did you mean by that? Did you... Did you ever see anything happen between your parents that worried you?"

Lily's laugh this time is quieter, but no less bitter. "You want the truth?"

She steps closer, invading my space, and for a terrifying moment I think she's going to hit me. Instead, she just leans in, her breath cold and sharp against my cheek. "You know nothing about my mother," she whispers. "You never will." She pulls back, glancing toward the door leading inside.

I stand my ground, heart pounding. "Then tell me," I challenge, voice barely above a whisper. "Tell me what I don't know."

A terrible thought suddenly crystallizes: what if Lily isn't just grieving? What if Alice isn't actually dead? The letters, Lily's behavior, the way she seems to appear wherever I go—they could be working together, orchestrating this whole thing. Why else would this child be stalking my every move?

Lily's eyes narrow, a flash of something—pain? Anger?—darkening her features. "You think you can just waltz in here and replace her? You think he'll love you like he loved her?" Her voice is a low hiss, venomous. "We were perfect. Then you came along, with your sad eyes and your cheap perfume—"

"Lily, it's complicated—"

"It's not complicated at all." She steps closer, her face flushed with anger. "My mom died in an accident. Her brakes failed. End of story. And now you're helping spread lies about my dad."

"I'm not spreading anything. I'm trying to understand what's happening. You're the one who was talking to the TikToker."

"To tell her to stop spreading those lies."

"I don't believe you. You said that maybe it was the truth."

"Believe what you want. Maybe I was just messing with you, trying to get you to tell me how you really feel."

"I don't understand, Lily. What do you want? Why are you doing this?"

"You want to understand?" Her laugh is brittle, cutting. "Understand this: you'll never be half the woman my mother was. You're just trying to replace her, but you can't. No one can."

The words shouldn't hurt—I've heard versions of them

since the day I married Benjamin—but they do. They always do.

"I've never tried to replace your mother," I say, my voice steadier than I feel. "I just want us to be a family."

She cuts me off, words ratcheting up in volume. "You don't get to say that. You don't get to act like you're the victim here."

"I'm not." I can see the hurt in her, and beneath it, the terror of being left behind. It should make me feel maternal, but all I feel is exposed.

I risk another step closer, lowering my voice. "Lily. Please. I'm not trying to replace anyone. Especially not your mother. I know what it's like to lose someone and feel empty. But this isn't about me, or even Ben. It's about what you need. And I think you need to know the truth."

She scoffs, uncurling from her defensive stance just enough to glare at me. "The truth? What is that even? That you married him for the house and the money?"

"That's not—" I say, but then stop myself. "Do you," I start, desperate, "even believe what's being said in those videos online? I know you see them. I know you read the comments." My hands are shaking. I put them behind my back so she doesn't notice. "People are saying terrible things about your family. About your dad. I just want to understand what really happened. I want you to trust me." I almost add: help me. But I don't.

Lily doesn't move for a long time. She just stares. Maybe through me, maybe into the past.

Then, with a clipped finality, she says, "You don't know the first thing about trust."

"Lily, if you know something about your mother's death—something that wasn't in the reports—"

"I don't." Her voice is flat again, controlled. "You're twisting my words."

"I'm not twisting anything. You just said—"

The sound of the garage door opening cuts through our argument. Benjamin's car, pulling in. Lily and I both freeze, our heads turning toward the house like synchronized dancers.

"We're not done with this conversation," I say quickly, urgently.

"Yes, we are." Lily's expression shifts, a subtle rearrangement of features that transforms her from wounded to resolute. "We're absolutely done."

She brushes past me, her shoulders squared, her step purposeful. I follow, my mind racing with questions. What secrets is Lily keeping? What else does she know about her mother's death that she's not telling?

The answer feels close, tantalizingly so, but Benjamin's arrival has slammed a door between me and the truth. For now.

The kitchen door swings open as Benjamin steps into the house. His face brightens when he sees us, then immediately clouds with concern. He's always been good at reading rooms, at sensing emotional undercurrents.

"What's going on?" he asks, eyes moving from Lily's flushed face to my rigid posture. The question hangs between us, deceptively simple. Before I can answer, Lily's entire demeanor transforms. Her shoulders slump, her chin trembles, and tears—tears that weren't there seconds ago—well in her eyes. The steel in her spine melts away, replaced by a vulnerability that makes her look younger, smaller.

"Dad," she says, her voice catching on the word. She takes a half step toward him, her hands twisting together in front of her. "I was just getting some air and—" Her voice breaks. A perfect, practiced break.

"What's wrong, sweetheart?" Benjamin sets his briefcase on the counter, moves toward his daughter with the instinctive response of a parent to a child in distress.

"She's been interrogating me." Lily's voice trembles now, a masterful performance. "She thinks I'm behind those horrible videos. She accused me of following her, spying on her."

Benjamin's gaze snaps to me, suddenly sharp, suddenly cold. "Emma? What's going on? Why are you attacking Lily?"

"I'm not attacking her," I say, struggling to keep my voice level. "I saw her there, Ben. She was parked across from the café where I was meeting Rachel, taking pictures of us."

"Rachel?" His forehead creases. "Your sister Rachel? The one you haven't spoken to since before the wedding?"

I take a breath, realizing too late that in telling Benjamin about Rachel, Benjamin might not believe me when I tell him my suspicions about Lily. What I really need is five minutes alone with my husband to tell him what I think Lily has been doing.

"Yes. I reached out to her about the videos. I realized she's been working with Mira Patel, the woman making them."

Benjamin stares at me, his expression shifting from confusion to something harder. It's only then that I notice how tired he looks, the dark circles under his eyes and stubble on his jaw. "You're meeting with people actively trying to destroy our family? And you're accusing Lily of what, exactly? Documenting your betrayal?"

"It's not betrayal to try to understand what's happening, or trying to get them to end this," I say, heat rising in my cheeks.

"Stop." His voice cuts through mine, sharp as a scalpel. "Emma, that's enough."

"But she just told me—"

"I said that's enough." He steps between us, physically positioning his body to shield Lily from me. His back is straight, his shoulders squared—the posture he adopts in the hospital when delivering difficult news, when establishing authority.

"I'm not making this up," I say, fighting to keep my voice steady. "She was taking pictures of me meeting Rachel."

"She's twisting my words because she's trying to make you look guilty."

I stare at her over Benjamin's shoulder, watching her burrow closer to her father's side, her fingers clutching at his white coat. The same fingers that held a phone camera trained on me hours earlier. The same lips that just spat accusations at me are now trembling with fabricated fear.

"Ben, please," I try again. "Just listen—"

"No, Emma." His voice is softer now but no less firm. "I think you need to take some time to cool off. These videos are clearly affecting you more than you're admitting."

"They're affecting all of us," I counter. "That's why we need to talk about what's happening, what Lily knows—"

"Leave Lily out of this." His arm curls around his daughter's shoulders, pulling her closer. "She's a child who's being traumatized by these accusations against me. By videos tearing apart our family. And now by her stepmother interrogating her in our own home."

"I wasn't interrogating her. I was asking about something she said. Something important about—"

"Emma." My name in his mouth is a warning. "Enough."

The finality in his tone silences me. I stand there, suddenly aware of how the two of them form a unit—father and daughter, bound by blood and grief and secrets I'm not allowed to question. I am the outsider. The intruder. The threat. He's never spoken to me like this. I take a step back.

"I need to change," Benjamin says after a moment, his voice gentler but distant. "Lily, why don't you go start your homework? I'll check on you in a bit."

She nods, pressing her face briefly against his chest in a gesture of childlike trust. "Okay, Dad." Her voice is small, fragile. Nothing like the razor-edged fury she directed at me minutes earlier.

"And Emma, maybe it's best if you stay home from the

hospital fundraiser on Sunday. It's too important for me to be concerned about you. I can't mess this up."

They turn together, moving toward the stairs and leaving me standing alone in the kitchen. As they reach the doorway, Lily glances back over her shoulder. For just a fraction of a second, her mask slips. The vulnerability vanishes, replaced by something triumphant, something knowing. Her eyes meet mine, and I think I can see a ghost of a smile touch her lips—not the trembling, tearful one she showed her father, but something sharp and satisfied.

Then they're gone, their footsteps receding up the stairs, leaving me with the hollow echo of what just happened. Lily knows how to play Benjamin perfectly. Knows exactly which strings to pull to make him dance to her tune. Knows how to transform herself from aggressor to victim in the blink of an eye.

And I am left wondering which version of my stepdaughter is real—the vulnerable child seeking her father's protection, or the calculating young woman who just outmaneuvered me easily. The girl who might know what really happened to her mother.

I sink onto a kitchen stool.

Now I know for certain that she's trying to break up my marriage.

And I won't let her.

TWENTY

The master bedroom's ceiling soars fourteen feet above me, crown molding tracing elaborate patterns that draw the eye upward, away from whatever happens below. Benjamin was called to the hospital for an emergency surgery this morning, and I've been at home for hours, alone, worrying. I've paced the Persian rug so many times that my path is visible in the crushed fibers. Seven steps from window to bed. Nine from bed to bathroom door. A beautiful cage with antique fixtures and designer wallpaper. Every detail of the Morrison Estate whispers of old money, of secrets kept, of appearances maintained at all costs.

I brushed everything under the carpet last night, apologized to Benjamin and promised to make things right with Lily. We had a normal evening after that, and he told me his father's plans to get the videos forcibly removed from social media. Their lawyers were already working on it. I reassured him everything will be fine. That I'd spend today making things right with Lily. Now I just need to figure out my next move.

A shadow passes by the partially open door—Lily's distinctive silhouette, pausing for just a moment before continuing down the hallway. Is she checking on me?

Ben doesn't come home till after dinner. The distant sound of tires on gravel stops my pacing. Benjamin's car in the driveway, returning from the hospital. I glance at my reflection in the antique mirror above the dresser. Pale face. Tense jaw. Eyes too wide, too wild. I force my features into neutrality, smooth my hair, adjust my blouse. By the time the front door opens, I've composed myself into the wife he expects to find.

I listen to the familiar rhythms of his arrival. Keys on the entryway table. Briefcase set down by the stairs. Shoes off, placed precisely side by side. The refrigerator opening and closing—his usual post-work beer. Then silence where there should be footsteps ascending the stairs to our bedroom. I wait for him there. He always comes upstairs to shower and change after surgery.

Ten minutes pass. Twenty. My phone remains silent—no text explaining a delayed arrival upstairs. I strain to hear movement below, catching only occasional sounds. A drawer closing. What might be a muffled voice. The subtle creak of a chair.

After thirty minutes, concern overcomes caution. I move down the hallway, past Lily's closed door where music plays just loud enough to mask conversation, down the curved staircase with its gleaming banister. The main floor lights are dimmed, shadows pooling in corners and doorways. I follow the faint sounds to Benjamin's study at the back of the house.

The door stands slightly ajar, a thin slice of darkness within darkness. No lights on. No movement visible. But I hear it now —a soft, rhythmic sound. Breathing? No, something more broken than that. I push the door open wider, eyes adjusting to the gloom. Benjamin sits at his desk, back to the door, shoulders hunched and shaking with silent sobs. His white coat is crumpled on the floor beside him, a crease-free surgeon suddenly undone, unmade. This vulnerable tableau contradicts everything Alice's letters have suggested, everything Rachel's evidence implies. This is not a calculating abuser, a man who controls with cold precision. This is a broken man, crying alone rather than letting anyone see his pain.

"Ben?" My voice comes out barely above a whisper.

He startles, shoulders stiffening, but doesn't turn. "I need a minute, Emma. I'll be out soon."

I don't leave. Instead, I step into the room, cross the distance between us, place my hand gently on his shoulder. His body is rigid beneath my touch, vibrating with the effort of containing his emotion.

"What happened?" I ask, my earlier suspicions dissolving in the face of his raw grief.

"I lost her." His voice cracks. "Paige Matthews. Eight years old."

He looks up at me finally, eyes red-rimmed and swollen. "Her heart just... it wouldn't restart. I tried everything."

My throat tightens. While Lily's been trying to break us apart, he's been going through hell, and now he is carrying this unbearable weight all alone. Doesn't she realize how much her father needs me?

"I'm so sorry, Ben." I kneel beside his chair, taking his hands in mine. They're cold, these miracle hands that couldn't perform today. "It's not your fault."

"Her parents trusted me." A tear tracks down his cheek, and he makes no move to wipe it away. "They looked at me like I was some kind of god. Like I could guarantee their daughter would come home." His fingers tighten around mine. "How do you tell parents their child is never coming home?"

In this moment, I see only the Benjamin I fell in love with. The dedicated healer whose hands I've warmed between mine at 3 a.m. after six-hour surgeries. The man who carries the weight of children's lives on his shoulders, whom I've held while he silently wept after losing a six-year-old patient last spring. The husband whose scrubs I've washed blood from, whose favorite meal I've learned to cook perfectly for those nights when he can barely stand after saving someone else's child. Not the monster from Rachel's folder or Alice's letters.

"You did everything you could," I say, reaching up to brush the tear from his face. "You always do."

He leans into my touch, eyes closing briefly. "I couldn't face coming upstairs. Couldn't bear to see you look at me and know I'd failed."

"You haven't failed." I rise, pulling him to his feet, into my arms. "One loss doesn't mean you're failing. Think of how many you have saved."

His body shudders against mine as he allows himself to be held, to be comforted. We remain like that for a few long minutes. When he finally pulls back, his face is composed again, the moment of vulnerability carefully tucked away.

"Thank you," he whispers, pressing his forehead to mine. "For not seeing me as weak."

"Never," I promise.

His kiss tastes of salt and gratitude. As we make our way upstairs, his arm around my waist, his body leaning slightly into mine, I feel the pieces of us clicking back into place.

We shower together. Benjamin's hands on my skin are gentle, reverent. Each touch an affirmation, each kiss a promise. I recommit to trusting him, to believing in us, as our bodies move together. And I make a silent promise to myself to do whatever it takes to protect this man.

TWENTY-ONE

I adjust the strap of my midnight blue gown—too tight across my shoulders, too loose around my waist. All this stress has already caused me to lose a bit of weight. Benjamin's hand rests at the small of my back as we enter Harbor Heights Country Club, five perfect fingers applying just enough pressure to guide me forward, to remind me of his presence. To anyone watching, we're the perfect couple—brilliant surgeon and his devoted wife, dressed in designer finery, smiling for the cameras that document the hospital's annual fundraiser. His touch is different than last night in the shower, but I try not to let it bother me. Benjamin has assured me everyone has forgotten about the accusations against him. Injunctions have been filed. The journalists have gone. Ben changed his mind and said he wanted me there after all. Now it's our turn to pretend it never happened.

"There's Dr. Landry," Benjamin murmurs, his breath warm against my ear. "New head of pediatric oncology. Potential donor for the wing." His smile never falters as he speaks through barely moving lips, teeth gleaming in the chandelier light. "I need to speak with him. Why don't you grab a drink at the bar? Those two ladies over there"—he nods toward a pair of silver-haired women—"they're on the hospital board. Might be good for you to introduce yourself."

Not a question. A statement dressed as one. He's already pulling away, his hand sliding from my back, severing our connection before I can respond. I watch him glide across the marble floor, his movements fluid and purposeful. He claps Dr. Landry on the shoulder, throws back his head in laughter at whatever the man says. Benjamin Stone, lifesaver, charmer, pillar of the community.

The love of my life.

The ballroom stretches before me, a gleaming monument to old Florida money. Potted palms create strategic privacy nooks between white-clothed tables adorned with roses and orchids. Ice sculptures of the hospital logo sweat slowly on buffet tables, where wait staff in crisp black and white arrange delicate canapés in perfect rows. The wealthy patrons of Harbor Heights circulate in designer gowns and bespoke suits, diamonds catching light, voices pitched to that particular register that signals money.

I reach the bar and ask for more champagne. My fingers trace the delicate beadwork at my waist—a gown Benjamin selected months ago. "The color brings out your eyes," he said earlier, helping me zip it, his fingers lingering at my neck.

I sip champagne that tastes of nothing and watch Benjamin work the room. He moves from group to group with practiced ease, a hand on an elbow here, a confidential lean-in there. Everyone responds to his presence—backs straightening, smiles widening, eyes lighting with the special glow reserved for those who believe themselves in the presence of greatness.

"Has he remarried already? The man doesn't waste time."

The voice catches my attention—elderly, female, pitched low but carrying in that way particular to women who've spent decades delivering devastating remarks at garden parties. I turn slightly, spotting the two women that Benjamin mentioned were on the hospital board, seated at a corner table partially concealed by a large floral arrangement. Both wear the uniform of Harbor Heights' oldest residents—pastel St. John knits, pearls, perfectly coiffed silver hair. I recognize them vaguely from previous events, longtime pillars of Tampa society.

"Though I suppose you'd be desperate for a bit of romance after Alice." The taller woman nods in my direction without looking at me directly. "I heard she was quite cold."

"What do you mean?" The other lady asks.

My breath catches. I step closer to the enormous arrangement of white roses and hydrangeas, positioning myself just out of their line of sight.

"She was always turning her nose up at poor Benjamin. She came from money, you see, much more money than he has. Old Boston family." The woman shakes her head, ice tinkling in her whiskey glass. "I always thought she faked her death to run off to the Bahamas."

The shorter woman leans forward, pearls swinging, and the two laugh. "I don't think she'd be happy to see Benjamin moving on so fast. I think their parents just wanted to see them married. She always thought she was better than him." She lets the sentence hang, arched eyebrows completing the thought.

My champagne flute freezes halfway to my lips. The women have moved on to discussing someone's daughter's divorce. I stare across the ballroom at Benjamin, now deep in conversation with the hospital board president. His hand gestures precisely as he speaks, surgeon's fingers sketching his vision in the air. He and Lily have always spoken so highly of Alice.

What if Alice isn't even dead? Is she alive somewhere living off that money? While writing letters to me? Is she still trying to play with Benjamin even now?

The thought strikes without warning, electric and terrifying. What if the crash was staged? What if the body was misidentified? What if Alice is doing all of this to break me and Benjamin up?

No. That's impossible. There was a funeral. A body.

I push away from the table, needing air, space to think. The champagne I've consumed on an empty stomach swirls unpleasantly. Faces blur as I move through the crowd, nodding mechanically at greetings, maintaining Stone family perfection while my mind races in frantic circles.

Rachel's folder. Would it contain financial information? Bank records? Could it lead a trail to where Alice is?

Across the room, Benjamin looks up, his eyes finding mine with unerring precision. His smile doesn't falter, but something in his gaze sharpens, assessing my location, my posture, my isolation. He excuses himself from his group, beginning to move in my direction through the crowd.

I straighten my spine, force my breathing to steady. My face arranges itself into the pleasant mask I've perfected as Mrs. Benjamin Stone. Inside, my heart hammers against my ribs, my thoughts spinning with new suspicions, new fears. Money, control, death—the pieces rearranging themselves into an even darker picture than I'd imagined. Benjamin has never mentioned any of this to me.

Stop it. This is insane.

Benjamin approaches, his smile warm. "There you are," he says, taking my elbow. "Come meet the new hospital board members. They're dying to talk to you."

I allow myself to be guided across the ballroom, feeling the pressure of his fingers through the thin fabric of my gown. The elderly women watch us pass, their eyes sharp with decades of observing the rise and fall of Harbor Heights' families. They see more than most, these guardians of social history.

I wonder what else they know about Alice Stone.

* * *

Once Benjamin is busy with mingling again, I retreat to the silent auction display, seeking refuge among the carefully arranged items on white-clothed tables. Crystal paperweights, weekend getaways to private islands, a tennis lesson with a former Wimbledon champion—all donated by Harbor Heights' elite, price tags starting where most people's monthly salaries end. My fingers hover over the bid sheet for a Hermès scarf, not because I want it, but because focusing on something—anything—might steady the tremor in my hands after what I've just overheard about Alice. I don't notice Margaret's approach until her rich perfume envelops me like an expensive fog, her presence materializing at my shoulder.

"Emma, darling." Her voice carries that particular musical quality reserved for public performances. "That scarf would be lovely with your coloring."

She reaches past me, her diamond tennis bracelet catching the light as she picks up the pen to sign her own name on the bid sheet, adding a figure that makes my eyes widen slightly. A power move disguised as generosity.

"Margaret." I turn, summoning a smile that feels like stretching plastic wrap across my face. "The gala seems to be a success."

"Appearances can be deceiving." Her own smile remains fixed, a perfect arrangement of lips and teeth. Today she wears dove-gray silk that whispers money with every movement, pearls gleaming at her throat and ears. Her hair catches the light in a way that suggests weekly appointments with Tampa's most exclusive colorist.

She guides me further along the auction tables, her hand resting lightly on my forearm. To anyone watching, we're mother-in-law and daughter-in-law admiring the generosity of

Harbor Heights' finest. Only I feel the slight pressure of her fingers, the subtle steering that brooks no resistance.

"This TikTok scandal is beyond damaging to our family name," she says, her voice dropping to a register only I can hear. The pleasant smile never wavers. "I'm worried. Benjamin is suffering. Three families have requested different surgeons this week alone. Robert is fielding calls from concerned clients questioning whether they want to remain with an agency associated with such... unpleasantness." We pause before a display featuring a week at someone's villa in Tuscany. The starting bid would cover my rent for six months back when I had my own apartment, my own life, my own reality. Margaret's smile tightens imperceptibly. Her manicured nails press into my arm, five perfect points of pain through the silk of my gown. "Benjamin mentioned that your sister is feeding information to this TikTok person."

My breath catches. "I haven't spoken to Rachel in—"

"We know you met with her." Margaret's interruption is smooth, practiced. "And I'm worried about you."

Across the ballroom, Benjamin holds court among a circle of adoring hospital donors. His head is thrown back in laughter at something an elderly woman in diamonds has said. His hand rests lightly on her shoulder—the perfect gentleman, attentive and charming.

"You need to get this under control," Margaret continues, her voice like silk over steel. "The videos. Your sister. Your own... erratic behavior."

I turn slightly, meeting her gaze directly. "My behavior?"

"Benjamin tells us you've been unstable. Imagining people following you. Attacking our granddaughter." Her eyes, so like Benjamin's in shape if not in warmth, study my face with clinical detachment. The gold pendant at her throat catches the light as she leans forward. "It's concerning, Emma. To all of us who care about you."

I twist my wedding ring, feeling the diamond dig into my neighboring finger. The accusation hangs between us. I need to know more. "Margaret, before all this happened... did Alice ever confide in you? About Benjamin? About their marriage?"

Margaret's perfectly lined lips tighten. "Alice was... cold. Even before the accident, there was something distant about her. Benjamin would bring her flowers, and she'd put them in water without a word. No smile, no thank you." She sighs.

"Do you think—" I hesitate, then plunge ahead. "Is it possible she's still alive?"

Margaret's laugh is like breaking glass. "Good heavens, no. But wouldn't that be just like Alice? To orchestrate something so cruel? To make us all suffer just to prove a point?" She reaches across and pats my hand. "The crash was devastating, dear. No one walked away from that."

"I guess it is kind of a crazy thought," I say.

Margaret's smile widens, revealing professionally whitened teeth. "Now, let's rejoin the party. Benjamin must be looking for you." She gestures across the room, where indeed, Benjamin is scanning the crowd, his expression pleasant but his eyes sharp and searching.

* * *

Margaret glides away, leaving me standing alone by a framed painting of Harbor Heights in its early days. I need air. Space. A moment to myself. But no sooner has Margaret disappeared into the crowd than Lily materializes at my side.

"You look like you could use this." Lily offers a flute of champagne, her smile sweet and seemingly innocent. The crystal catches the light as she extends it toward me, the bubbles rising in perfect formation. Her dress—designer, certainly expensive—transforms her from sullen teenager to sophisticated young woman. The couture bodice hugs her slender frame, the color bringing out blue undertones in her dark hair, which has been swept into an elegant updo that adds years to her appearance.

I accept the champagne, noting the perfectly applied makeup that makes her look startlingly like her mother. No seventeen-year-old achieves that level of cosmetic perfection without help. A makeup artist, perhaps? Margaret's hand, I suspect.

"I saw you talking with Grandma." Lily's voice carries just the right note of casual interest. "She worries about you, you know. We all do."

Before I can respond, she leans closer, her perfume—subtle, expensive, definitely not a teenager's choice—enveloping me as she whispers, "You pronounced Dr. Whitaker's name wrong earlier. Dad noticed."

My stomach drops. Dr. Whitaker—the new neurosurgeon Benjamin introduced me to during our initial circuit of the room. I'd called him Whittaker, an easy mistake.

"I'm sure he understood," I say, trying to maintain composure. "Simple mistake."

"Dad says details matter." Lily straightens a nonexistent wrinkle in her dress. "Especially with important people like Dr. Whitaker. His department could direct a lot of funding to the pediatric wing."

Her words land like a judgment, another small stone added to the barrier she's constructing between us. Before I can defend myself, Lily's face transforms—her gaze shifts past me, her shoulders pull back, and her lips curve into a genuine smile I've never seen directed at me. I turn to see Benjamin walking toward us, flanked by two colleagues in suits who must be hospital board members.

"What do you think of this piece?" Lily asks, smoothly changing subjects as she gestures toward a modern painting on display among the auction items. "Emma was just saying she finds it fascinating."

I wasn't. I hadn't even noticed the artwork until this moment—an abstract canvas of harsh red lines intersecting with black circles that means nothing to me. But now Benjamin stands beside us, his cologne mingling with Lily's perfume, creating a sensory barrier between me and the rest of the room.

"Was she?" Benjamin's hand settles at the small of my back. "Tell us what you find so compelling about it, Emma."

The trap springs shut. I stare at the canvas, mind racing. Art has never been my area of expertise. This was Alice's domain. Benjamin knows this—has gently teased me about my preference for advertising copy over gallery openings. Now I'm expected to expound on a painting I've barely glanced at, with both of them watching for any misstep.

"I-I appreciate the contrast," I begin, voice less steady than I'd like. "The way the red lines cut across the black circles. It's... dynamic."

"Dynamic," Lily repeats, the word stretched slightly, questioning. "And the artist's commentary on post-industrial alienation? Do you find that compelling as well?"

There is no such commentary. I'm certain of it. She's testing me, setting me up to fail in this small, public way.

"I hadn't considered that aspect," I admit, heat rising to my cheeks.

Lily's eyes gleam with subtle triumph. "Professor Harrington at school says modern art is all about social context. Don't you think that's true, Dad?"

"Absolutely." Benjamin smiles down at his daughter with genuine warmth. "Lily has quite an eye for art. Gets it from her mother."

The reference to Alice lands exactly as intended. I take a sip of champagne to hide my expression, the liquid tasteless on my tongue.

"Perhaps we should stick to what we know," Benjamin suggests, his smile never faltering. "Emma's talents lie elsewhere. Creative direction for advertising campaigns, not art criticism."

The gentle diminishment sounds like praise to anyone overhearing our conversation. To me, it's another cut. Lily nods in perfect agreement, her expression a masterpiece of daughterly admiration directed at her father and carefully masked disdain for me.

I glance around the ballroom, suddenly hyperaware of my complete isolation. The elderly women who gossiped about Alice now chat with Robert near the bar. Margaret works the room, stopping to speak with key important Harbor Heights socialites who then glance in our direction. The wait staff circulate invisibly, eyes downcast but ears open. Even the other guests—hospital board members, wealthy donors, Tampa society fixtures—seem part of an elaborate surveillance network, watching the drama of the Stone family unfold while pretending not to notice.

I'm trapped in Lily's sophisticated campaign to undermine me at every turn. All while questions about Alice's death multiply with each passing hour.

I don't know what to do.

The orchestra strikes up a waltz, the opening notes of Strauss floating across the ballroom. Couples begin moving toward the dance floor, a choreographed migration of wealth and privilege.

"Shall we?" Benjamin's hand presses more firmly against my back. His public face shows nothing but adoration for his wife. Only I feel the tension in his fingers, the subtle guidance that allows no resistance.

"Of course," I respond, the perfect doctor's wife accepting her husband's invitation to dance.

As Benjamin leads me toward the dance floor, I glance back

at Lily. She stands alone now, a younger reflection of Alice's portrait, watching us with a slight smile playing at the corners of her mouth. Our eyes meet across the thinning crowd, and in that moment, I see something unexpected in her gaze—not triumph, not hatred, but something more complex.

Then Benjamin's hand tightens at my waist, turning me to face him as the waltz begins, and Lily disappears from view. The music swells around us as we begin to move in perfect time, the Harbor Heights' elite smiling approvingly at the handsome doctor and his lovely wife.

TWENTY-TWO

I slip into Stone Advertising through the service entrance, avoiding the main lobby where questions might follow me. My heels make no sound on the industrial carpet of the back hallways as I make my way to the IT floor, heart hammering against my ribs like it's trying to escape. Marcus will be there. Marcus who owes me a favor. Marcus who can access records no one else can.

I find him hunched over his computer, the blue light reflecting off his glasses like miniature moons. He doesn't look up when I enter, fingers never pausing their relentless dance across his keyboard.

"You shouldn't be here," he says, still not looking at me. "Pretty sure Robert's in a closed-door with Legal right now."

"I'm not here for Robert." I close his office door softly. The click of the latch sounds final, like a commitment I can't take back. "I need your help."

Now he looks up, his fingers stilling mid-keystroke. "Again? I think we're even after I helped you last time." His eyes narrow behind his glasses.

"This is important." I move closer to his desk, lowering my voice though we're alone. "It's personal. And confidential."

Marcus leans back, chair squeaking in protest. "That's what you said last time. Those are the words people say right before asking me to do something that could get me fired."

He's right, of course. What I'm about to ask crosses every professional boundary. But I'm beyond caring about boundaries now. The letters have shattered all normal considerations.

"I need to look at financial records for Alice."

Marcus's expression shifts from irritation to disbelief.

"Your husband's dead wife? Are you serious?" He shakes his head. "Even if I could access them—which I'm not saying I can—why would you want to? We just found her phone and now you want me to do that? Isn't there enough heat on your family?"

My hands tremble slightly. "I've been receiving letters. Letters that suggest her death wasn't an accident or maybe even that she isn't dead."

"Letters from whom?" His voice sharpens with interest despite his obvious reluctance.

"They're signed by Alice."

The silence stretches between us, thick with implication. Marcus stares at me, assessing whether I've lost my mind. I don't blame him. I've asked myself the same question repeatedly.

"That's not possible." His voice drops to a whisper. "She died."

"I know what the official story is." I lean closer, keeping my voice low. "But what if it's not true? What if she's alive somewhere? I need to know if there were unusual financial movements before or even after her death."

Marcus rubs his temple, a gesture I recognize from our late nights preparing pitch decks. It means he's weighing options, calculating risks.

"We're even," he says finally. "After last time, we're even. This"—he gestures vaguely—"this is something else entirely."

"I wouldn't ask if it wasn't important." My voice catches, betraying how desperate I've become. "Please, Marcus."

He holds my gaze for a long moment, then sighs—the sound of professional ethics surrendering to human curiosity. "Five minutes. That's all you get. And if anyone asks, you threatened to expose my online poker habit."

"You have an online poker habit?"

"I do now." He turns back to his computer, fingers flying across the keyboard. "What exactly are we looking for?"

"Anything unusual in the months before her death. Large transfers, new accounts, unexplained expenses."

Marcus nods, typing rapidly. Security warnings flash across his screen, followed by dialogue boxes requesting passwords and authentication codes. He navigates through them expertly, his face bathed in the blue glow of secret access.

"Alice's financial records were part of the estate settlement," he mutters, more to himself than to me. "Sealed but still in the system because of the trust for the daughter—Lily, right?"

I nod, watching numbers and codes populate his screen.

"Here we go." His voice changes, interest overriding caution. "Standard checking and savings at First Tampa. Investment portfolio with Morgan Stanley. Retirement accounts." He scrolls through screens of information, pausing occasionally to drill deeper. "Nothing unusual on the surface. Regular income from the gallery. Joint accounts with Dr. Stone. Expected stuff."

My heart sinks. I'm chasing ghosts after all. Imagining conspiracies where there are none. Maybe I am losing my mind.

"Wait." Marcus's fingers pause. "This is interesting. Six months before her death, she opened an account in the Bahamas. Transferred substantial sums—like, six figures substantial—out of their joint investment account."

My breath catches. "Could it be legitimate? Art purchases for the gallery, maybe?"

"Gallery finances were separate. This came from personal funds." He clicks through several more screens. "And it gets better. The Bahamas account made regular transfers to a custodial account in Lily's name. An account Benjamin Stone doesn't appear to have signature authority on."

Alice was moving money—hiding it from Benjamin, ensuring Lily had access to funds he couldn't control. Why? Was she planning to leave him? According to the letters, she was. Was she also planning to take Lily away?

Or was she preparing for something worse?

"Can you tell if the accounts are still active?" My voice is distant, detached from the storm brewing inside me.

Marcus clicks through several more screens. "The Bahamas account has been dormant since her death. No withdrawals, no deposits. The custodial account for Lily shows regular small withdrawals—typical teenage spending patterns. Nothing that would raise flags."

"So not evidence of Alice being alive."

"Not financially, no." He glances up at me. "Though it does suggest she was preparing for something before her death. People don't usually move money to offshore accounts unless they're hiding it."

Another piece of the puzzle that doesn't quite fit. Alice moving money secretly. Lily's hostility toward me, trying to sabotage me. The letters that shouldn't exist.

"One more thing," I say, an idea forming. "Can you check the login history for my computer? See if anyone accessed my workstation on the morning before my presentation?"

Marcus frowns. "That's a different system. Security logs, not financial."

"But you can check it?"

He sighs again but turns to a different screen. More typing, more password prompts. "You suspect someone sabotaged your presentation? I heard it tanked."

"Just covering all possibilities."

The security logs appear, lines of code and timestamps that mean nothing to me but clearly speak volumes to Marcus. His eyebrows rise as he scrolls through the data.

"Well, well," he murmurs. "Someone logged into your station at 7:15 the night before using admin credentials. Made changes to files in your presentation folder." He looks up, face serious now. "The credentials belong to Lily Stone."

The air leaves my lungs in a rush. Lily. Of course. The perfect sabotage—destroying my professional credibility in front of her grandfather. Making me look unstable, incompetent. All while remaining the innocent teenager at home.

"She accessed my presentation files?" My voice sounds hollow even to my own ears. "Changed them before my meeting with Robert?"

Marcus nods. "Looks that way. Rearranged slides, altered some figures. Nothing that would be immediately obvious until you were in the middle of presenting." He closes the window quickly. "That's serious, Emma. Family or not."

My mind races between confrontation and calculation. I could tell Robert, show him the evidence that his precious granddaughter deliberately sabotaged a major client presentation. I could confront Lily directly, watch her teenage composure crack under the weight of exposure.

Or I could say nothing. Gather more evidence. Understand why a seventeen-year-old girl is so determined to destroy me—and what connection that might have to her mother's mysterious finances and possible faked death.

"Emma?" Marcus's voice breaks through my thoughts. "What are you going to do with this?"

I straighten, decision made—or at least, the next step clarified.

"Nothing. Yet." I meet his concerned gaze. "This conversation never happened. You never showed me these records."

He nods, relief evident in the softening of his shoulders. "Good call. Some secrets are better left buried."

But that's where he's wrong. These particular secrets have already clawed their way to the surface. The only question now is whether they'll drag me down when I try to expose them to the light.

I turn the key in the lock of my front door, the weight of Marcus's revelations pressing down on my shoulders like a physical burden. The house greets me with its usual perfect silence—the kind of quiet that costs money, insulated from the outside world by thick walls and expensive windows. I drop my keys in the dish by the door, the clink echoing through the foyer. Nothing looks different, yet everything has changed. Lily sabotaged my work. Alice moved money before she died. She's sending me letters.

The central air hums softly, maintaining a perfect seventy-two degrees despite the Florida heat pressing against the windows. I slip off my heels, feet sinking into the plush carpet as I move deeper into the house. A different sound breaks the stillness—the low, melodic humming coming from the kitchen. Benjamin. The tune is vaguely familiar, something classical he often plays during complex surgeries.

I pause at the kitchen threshold, watching him unobserved. He stands with his back to me, one hand holding a glass of red wine, the other leafing through what looks like medical journals. His surgeon's shoulders, broad and straight beneath his blue button-down, show no sign of the tension that's been my constant companion for days. He looks exactly like what he's supposed to be—a dedicated doctor unwinding after saving lives.

He turns, wine glass in hand, and his eyes—those warm brown eyes that I've trusted completely—immediately scan me from head to toe. A clinical assessment, it almost feels like the same one he gives patients.

"Rough day?" he asks, his voice gentle.

"Just busy." I move to the refrigerator, needing to do something with my hands, something normal. Inside, everything is organized with surgical exactitude—vegetables in their designated containers, proteins on the bottom shelf, condiments arranged by frequency of use. Benjamin's influence on our shared spaces. "How was surgery?"

"Successful. Repaired a ventricular septal defect in a four-month-old. The parents were beside themselves with gratitude." He takes a sip of wine, watching me over the rim of the glass. "You didn't answer my text about dinner."

Did he text? I can't remember. The phone in my pocket might as well be from another life—the life where Emma Caldwell was just worried about client presentations.

"Sorry. It's been hectic." I pull out a bottle of sparkling water, avoiding his direct gaze. "I'm not very hungry anyway."

"You need to eat." His tone shifts slightly, edging toward the authoritative voice he uses when patients don't follow instructions. "And you look like you haven't slept in days."

I haven't. Not properly. Not since the first letter arrived. Not since I started seeing Alice's handwriting everywhere, hearing her voice in my dreams, imagining her watching me from dark corners of rooms she once inhabited.

"I'm fine." I twist the cap off the water bottle, the crack of the seal unnaturally loud in the kitchen's perfect acoustics. "Just stress."

He sets down his wine glass and moves toward me, closing the distance I've been carefully maintaining, afraid he might know what's going on, what I have discovered about his precious daughter. His hands settle on my shoulders, warm and steady.

"But I'm worried about you, Emma. This isn't just work stress."

His closeness makes it hard to think clearly. The familiar scent of his aftershave—sandalwood and something clean, clinical—fills my senses. I still haven't told him I'm on a sabbatical. I'm surprised his parents haven't said anything. I fear he can read it on my face. I should pull away. Should maintain distance. But some treacherous part of me still craves his comfort.

"I haven't been sleeping well," I admit, offering a partial truth. "Dreams."

"Nightmares?" His thumbs press gently against the tight muscles at the base of my neck, a doctor's touch identifying physical symptoms.

"Just... vivid dreams. Hard to shake in the morning."

Benjamin studies my face, his gaze moving from my eyes to the dark circles beneath them, to my lips that feel perpetually dry from stress. "I might have something that could help."

He releases me and moves to the kitchen island where his medical bag sits—the leather satchel that travels with him between hospital and home, containing the tools of his profession and the authority that comes with them. He unzips a side pocket and produces a small orange prescription bottle, setting it on the marble countertop between us.

"These might help," he says, sliding the bottle toward me. "Low-dose zolpidem. Just enough to help you fall asleep without the grogginess in the morning."

I stare at the bottle, the white pills visible through the transparent plastic. My name isn't on the label. No patient name at all.

"Where did these come from?" My voice sounds strange, too high.

"Sample packs from the pharmaceutical rep." He shrugs, casual. "Many of my colleagues use them for sleep issues. Perfectly safe."

My fingers close around the bottle, lifting it to examine the contents more closely. The pills look innocent enough—small white tablets, unmarked.

"I'm not sure about taking sleeping pills." I turn the bottle over in my hands, buying time. "I've never needed them before."

"You've never looked this exhausted before." Benjamin's eyes never leave my face, tracking my reaction with the same attention he gives to surgical monitors. "Just for a night or two, until you get back on track."

The bottle feels heavy in my palm, weighted with implications. If I refuse, will he be suspicious? If I accept but don't take them, will he somehow know? The paranoia spirals through my thoughts, distorting normal marital concern into something sinister.

"Thank you," I say finally, closing my fingers around the bottle. "I'll think about it."

"Don't think too much." He smiles, the expression not quite reaching his eyes. "That's part of the problem. Your mind won't shut down."

If only he knew what thoughts were keeping me awake— letters from his dead wife, offshore accounts, sabotaged presentations, and the growing suspicion that his daughter is out to get me.

"I should get changed," I say, needing escape from his too-perceptive gaze. "Maybe lie down for a bit."

Benjamin nods, returning to his wine and journals. The

perfect picture of a concerned husband. Despite everything, my heart still aches with tenderness watching him. The gentle way he holds his glass, the furrow in his brow as he reads—these are the details that made me fall in love with him. These are the reasons I am still in love with him. These are the reasons why I refuse to let Lily come between us.

TWENTY-THREE

The envelope arrives just as I'm fastening my earrings—plain silver studs, not the ones my mother gave me. The sound of the mail carrier's small van startles me, hands already shaky from lack of sleep. I didn't take the pills.

I peer through the bedroom window to catch his retreating van, then hurry downstairs to retrieve the single cream-colored envelope propped into the mailbox. I stare at it, heart racing immediately. No return address. Just my name in handwriting I recognize instantly.

How did she know I'd hear the van? That Benjamin wouldn't find it?

I race back upstairs, clutching the envelope like it might dissolve in my hands.

Back in our bathroom, I tear it open with trembling fingers. The date at the top—three days before her death. My pulse pounds in my ears as I unfold it completely.

"If you're reading this—" The first line stops me cold.

"Emma? Are you ready?" Ben's voice floats up from downstairs, startling me so badly I nearly drop the letter. "We need to leave in five minutes if we're going to make it to my parents' on time."

"Almost!" I call back, voice cracking on the single word. I scan the first paragraph quickly, catching fragments: "—not what you think—" and "—proof is with Rachel—" and "—recording everything—"

Rachel. My sister. Once again the connection snaps into place. Rachel could have found the letters, then addressed them to me. Because she knew I wouldn't listen if she talked to me. She could even have written them.

"Emma?" Ben's voice again, closer now. Footsteps on the stairs.

I fold the letter with frantic haste, stuffing it deep into my purse with the others that I keep on me all the time. My hands shake so violently I drop my lipstick twice before managing to apply it, the red slightly overshooting my lip line. In the mirror, a stranger stares back—hollow-eyed, pale as milk, dark circles like bruises beneath eyes that dart constantly toward the door.

The bathroom door opens. Ben appears behind me, in the reflection, impeccable in his charcoal suit, a small frown creasing his forehead.

"Everything okay?" he asks, eyes scanning the bathroom counter, taking in the scattered makeup, the open drawers. "You look flustered."

"Fine," I say, forcing a smile that feels like it might crack my face. "Just running late. You know how I hate being late to your mother's."

His eyes narrow slightly, not buying the explanation but not pushing further. "You look tired," he observes, his doctor's gaze clinical, assessing. "Are you taking those vitamins I gave you?"

"Yes," I lie, meeting his eyes in the mirror. "Every morning."

His hand settles on my shoulder, warm and heavy. "Good. I worry about you."

* * *

In the car, Ben drives with one hand on the wheel, the other occasionally reaching across to touch my knee. He seems nervous. Uncomfortable. Such a mild word for accusations of murder. For millions of strangers picking apart his first marriage, his character, his possible guilt.

"Have there been more videos?" I ask, hoping he'll confide in me, and I can reassure him, though I know the answer to my question.

"Two more yesterday." His knuckles whiten on the steering wheel. "More 'expert analysis' of body language in photos. More anonymous sources claiming I was controlling. But the story hasn't been picked up by any other media." He glances at me, expression suddenly vulnerable.

Ben pulls up to the entrance of his parents' building and kills the engine. The sudden silence amplifies my shallow breathing and the rapid drumming in my chest. Another Stone family dinner—another performance without a script. This is the first time I've seen Ben's father since I took leave from work. I squeeze Ben's hand before he can ask if I'm ready.

"Hey," I say, summoning brightness into my voice. "I haven't heard from Rachel since our meeting. Maybe this TikTok nightmare is finally burning itself out?"

His fingers tense slightly against mine. "You think?"

"Absolutely. These internet scandals never last." I touch his cheek, ignoring the letter scorching through my purse like a live coal. "We'll get through this. Together."

He studies my face, his hand warm against mine. "My mother's probably wondering where we are."

I nod, already calculating how to navigate the evening. I need to get through this dinner, show them I'm fine, stable. The sooner I figure out what Alice—or Lily—is doing, the sooner I can reclaim my office on the executive floor and the career I've worked years to build.

His eyes linger on my face for a moment too long, searching for something. Doubt? Fear? Knowledge? Then he smiles, squeezes my hand, and releases it to exit the car. I remain frozen for three heartbeats, watching him round the hood to open my door. The perfect gentleman. The perfect husband.

Ben opens my door, extends his hand. I take it, stepping into the rainy night, the Stones' luxurious building looming before us.

The elevator opens to the penthouse, revealing Margaret standing there with a warm smile that reaches her eyes, her silver hair glowing softly under the chandelier light. "Benjamin, sweetheart," she says, embracing her son with genuine affection before turning that same maternal warmth toward me. "Emma, dear. Come in, come in." Her voice carries none of the judgment I've been dreading all day. I clutch my purse against my side, my stomach knotting at the thought of facing my father-in-law.

Robert materializes from his study, tumbler of amber liquid in hand. He doesn't bother with kisses, just nods at Ben and gives me a small smile. "Traffic?" he asks, though the question sounds more like an accusation.

"My fault," I say before Ben can answer. "Lost track of time while getting ready."

We move into the formal dining room, where crystal and silver gleam under the Lindsey Adelman chandelier. Against one wall, a floating credenza displays carefully curated objects: a small bronze sculpture, three art books stacked at a precise angle. Through floor-to-ceiling windows, Tampa's skyline glitters against the darkening sky.

The table could seat twenty, but the five place settings cluster at one end. Lily already sits in her usual spot, phone in hand, scrolling. She looks up, her smile warm for her father, cooling several degrees for me.

"You're late," she observes unnecessarily, slipping her phone into her pocket. "Grandma had to keep dinner warming."

"Traffic," Ben says, contradicting my explanation without a second thought. He kisses the top of Lily's head, a gesture that transforms her expression into something younger, more vulnerable. In these moments, I glimpse the child beneath the calculating teenager. The daughter who lost her mother at a tender age. I know she's angry that her mother has been replaced, but why would she want her father unhappy? In her attempt to push me away, she's hurting him.

Margaret is without help today, as Mrs. Winters is visiting her grandchildren in Pennsylvania. She serves us the first course—some delicate soup that smells of leeks and cream. Silence falls as spoons clink against bone china. The weight of Alice's letter presses against my side, where my purse hangs from the chair. I imagine I can feel heat radiating from it, as if the explosive revelations inside might spontaneously combust.

"I was speaking with Carl Hartman this morning," Robert says, breaking the silence as he sets down his spoon. "He's worried about you returning to work."

My spoon freezes halfway to my mouth. Here we go.

"Returning to work?" Ben says.

"I-I've been taking some time off since the failed presentation. I meant to tell you but..."

Ben tilts his head and looks at me. "You didn't feel like you could share that with me? With your husband?"

"I guess I was embarrassed."

"You have no reason to be. It wasn't a mishap," Ben says. "Emma's been under a lot of pressure lately. The social media situation has been difficult for all of us."

The social media situation. Such a clinical term for the

destruction of his reputation. For accusations of murder spreading across the internet like wildfire. But I'm grateful for his understanding and forgiveness. I can't believe he's not even angry at me for lying to him. He really is the perfect husband.

"Yes, well." Robert's mouth tightens.

"I'll rework the entire presentation together with Ryan, when I get back," I say, fighting to keep my voice steady. Fighting the urge to tell them there was an actual explanation for this mishap. Her name is Lily. Yet I don't say anything. This is not the time or the place. "The concept will be stronger, the messaging clearer."

"I certainly hope so." Robert's gaze is unforgiving. "I expected more from you, Emma. The company has a reputation to maintain."

"Dad," Ben says, a warning note in his voice. "Emma knows what's at stake."

I do know. My career. My marriage. All in the hands of a teenager who is trying to take me down at all costs. If only I had some evidence to prove she's behind it all, besides the logins that Marcus showed me. That could easily be explained away, I fear. I need evidence that she wrote the letters, that she tampered with my presentation, and possibly even that she's behind the TikTok videos. Maybe she thought I would be blamed for them, and Ben would throw me out of his house? That's why she did it?

Margaret silently clears the soup bowls, returning with plates of perfectly seared steak, asparagus, and roasted potatoes. The meal she always serves when discussing serious family matters.

"The asparagus looks beautiful," I offer, desperate to change the subject.

My fingers twitch with the urge to touch my purse, to feel the reassuring edge of Alice's letter. What secrets does it contain? I force myself to spear an asparagus instead, tasting nothing as I chew.

"The TikTok woman posted again today," Robert says, directing his words to Ben but watching me from the corner of his eye. Does he believe I'm behind it? "Something about inconsistencies in the police report. Your mother's had to field calls from three different charity boards asking if she wants to 'step back' from her duties."

Ben's jaw tightens. "My lawyer is exploring a defamation suit. These accusations are baseless."

"It's okay, Robert," Margaret adds, in an effort to reassure her husband.

"Baseless or not, they're damaging," Robert counters.

My gaze shifts to Lily, who watches this exchange with calculating eyes.

"I saw Mrs. Abernathy at school today," she says, changing the subject. "She asked about you, Dad. Said she's praying for our family during this 'difficult time.'" Her voice takes on a mocking tone for the last two words. "As if we need prayers. As if Dad did anything wrong."

"People love drama," Margaret says, patting her granddaughter's hand. "They'll move on to the next scandal soon enough."

My purse seems to pulse against my hip, the letter inside demanding attention. I need to read it.

"Emma, you've hardly touched your food," Margaret says, leaning forward with furrowed brows. Her hand hovers near mine on the table. "I'm worried about you. You look pale—have you been sleeping at all?"

"Not very well, no. Ben gave me something to help me. I'm just nervous about this whole thing, the lies, the videos," I say, forcing myself to take another bite of food I can't taste.

"You should be," Lily mutters, just loud enough for me to hear.

Ben's hand covers mine briefly on the table.

"Don't worry," he says, his gaze locked on mine with that practiced steadiness. "Everything will work out."

"Excuse me," I say, placing my napkin beside my half-eaten steak. "I need to use the powder room." Four pairs of Stone eyes track my movement as I stand and grab my purse from where it hangs on the chair. Does Lily know what's inside it? Did she want me to be spooked by her latest letter and bring it along to dinner? Am I simply playing into her hand? But I need to read it.

The powder room is a monument to tasteful wealth—marble sink, antique mirror, hand towels monogrammed with an elaborate "S." I lock the door with trembling fingers, then press my ear against it, listening for footsteps. Nothing. Just the distant murmur of dining room conversation.

I place my purse on the marble counter and extract Alice's letter, handling it like an unexploded bomb. The paper crinkles as I unfold it fully for the first time, spreading it beneath the soft lighting. Alice's handwriting flows across the page—hurried but precise, pressing hard enough to leave indentations I can feel with my fingertips.

The day starts perfectly. Sunlight streams through white orchids on the windowsill as Ben brings me coffee in bed. His smile seems genuine, his touch gentle. I almost believe this version of him—the loving husband, the attentive father, the brilliant doctor everyone admires. We spend the morning laughing, planning our future. A trip to Greece next summer. Lily's college options. The renovation to the east wing of the Morrison Estate.

But by afternoon, something shifts. A phone call I'm not meant to overhear. Ben in his study, voice low and urgent. "She's becoming a problem," he says. "No, not Lily. Alice." When I enter, he ends the call abruptly. Smiles too widely.

Asks about dinner plans as if I hadn't heard my name spoken like a diagnosis.

When I ask about the call, his face changes. Just for a second, but long enough to see the mask slip. His voice turns cold when I ask about it. His fingers dig into my wrist when I press for answers. A bruise forms on my wrist where he gripped me too hard. Later, he brings me jewelry to apologize.

I've been recording everything. Every conversation. Every "episode" Ben claims I've had but can't remember. Every pill he's given me that doesn't match my prescription. I know he's trying to get rid of me. I have become a "problem." I think he is planning on killing me. I'm scared. If you're reading this, you should be scared too.

A soft knock at the door jolts me back to the present.

"Emma?" Margaret's voice, clipped with impatience. "Are you okay? You've been in there an awful long time. Dessert is being served."

"Just a moment!" I fold the letter quickly, stuffing it back into my purse. I redo the red on my lips.

"Coming," I call, checking my reflection one last time. My eyes are too wide, my complexion waxy. I pinch my cheeks, force my features into a neutral expression, and open the door.

Margaret stands in the hallway, her hair gleaming under the sconces. Her gaze flicks to my purse, then back to my face.

"Everything all right? You were gone quite a while."

"Fine," I lie. "Just needed a moment."

Her smile is strange, awkward almost. "Of course. We've all been there, needing a moment."

We return to the dining room, where lemon tart—Alice's recipe, no doubt—awaits on delicate dessert plates. Ben and Robert are deep in conversation, their voices hushed but intense. They fall silent as I take my seat.

"We were just discussing this TikTok situation," Robert

says, his tone conversational but his eyes sharp. "The damage to the family reputation is becoming untenable."

"These accusations are absurd," Margaret adds, serving the tart with mechanical exactness. "As if Benjamin would harm a fly, let alone Alice. The woman had mental health issues. Everyone knew it."

Mental health issues?

"I had a call from the hospital board today," Ben says, not meeting my eyes. "They're suggesting a temporary leave of absence until this blows over."

"Unacceptable," Robert snaps. "The Stones don't retreat. We fight."

Fight what? The truth? The evidence Alice left behind? The proof I'm getting closer to finding?

Lily watches me over the rim of her water glass. "It's affecting me at school too," she says, her voice pitched to sound vulnerable though her gaze remains hard. "I know you all think it will blow over, but if I have to hear one more person accuse Dad of killing Mom, I'll explode." Her bottom lip trembles—a perfect performance. "I told them it's all lies. That my dad loved my mom. That he'd never hurt her."

Ben reaches across the table, squeezes his daughter's hand. "Of course I wouldn't, sweetheart. This will all blow over. The truth always comes out.

"We should go," he says, checking his watch. "Emma needs rest."

As we gather our things, Lily approaches me while Ben speaks with his father. She stands too close, her voice a whisper meant for my ears only.

"You don't belong here," she says, her eyes cold despite her smile. But before I can respond, the elevator announces a visitor with a soft chime.

Detective Ramirez emerges from the shadows, his badge catching the harsh fluorescent light. I recognize the small scar above his left eyebrow—a reminder of the fishing trip last summer when Ben's cast went terribly wrong. Lucas, who'd laughed it off over tequila shots on our back patio just weeks ago. Lucas, who taught me how to make authentic ceviche while our husbands argued about baseball. Now he stands before us transformed, shoulders squared beneath his department-issued jacket, eyes deliberately avoiding mine.

"Lucas," Ben says, surprise threading through his voice. "Wasn't expecting you tonight."

"I'm here officially," Ramirez replies, his familiar face suddenly foreign to me. "We need to speak privately. Both of you."

"My father's study should work," Ben says with forced casualness.

His fingers press into my elbow as he steers me down the hallway. Behind us, his parents and Lily settle themselves back at the dinner table, their faces composed into masks of polite worry.

TWENTY-FOUR

My heart slams against my ribs as we enter his father's study following Detective Ramirez. The detective who investigated Alice's death. Ben's friend. The man who declared her death an accident despite the suspicious circumstances. I expect to see the two friends embrace one another, but Ben seems tense already. No clap on the back, no handshake.

Ben has positioned himself by the fireplace, one arm braced against the mantel in a pose that would look casual if not for the white-knuckled grip of his fingers on the polished wood. Ramirez stands in the center of the room, his stocky frame somehow filling more space than it should.

"Emma," he says, nodding to me. His face gives nothing away, the professional mask firmly in place. "Sorry to interrupt your evening."

"It's fine," I manage, sinking onto the sofa. "Is everything all right?"

He doesn't answer immediately. Instead, he places a bulging file folder on the glass table with a soft thud. The folder is worn at the edges, as if it's been handled repeatedly, opened and closed countless times. A yellow sticky note peeks from between pages. My stomach clenches.

"I wanted to speak with you both in person," Ramirez says, lowering himself into the armchair opposite me. His polished shoes whisper against the marble tile as he crosses his legs. "There's been a development in Alice's case."

Ben's head snaps up. "Has this got something to do with the ridiculous accusations of these keyboard warriors?"

Ramirez nods slowly, his dark eyes moving between us. "New evidence has come to light that requires us to reopen the investigation."

The room seems to tilt beneath me.

"What evidence?" Ben asks, his voice tight. He crosses to sit beside me on the sofa, close enough that our shoulders almost touch.

Ramirez flips open the file, slow and deliberate, as if he's bracing for the detonation he's about to set off. "Over the past three months, we've received multiple reports that suggest Alice Stone's car accident—driving over the bridge into the water—may not have been an accident after all."

He lets the sentence hang for effect, watching Ben like a hawk, scoping for twitches.

I forget how to breathe. The room blurs at the edges; the art behind the detective's head seems to recede, leaving only the manila folder, the words echoing, and the sudden vacuum in my chest.

"What are you talking about?" Ben's words come out hoarse, shredded. "That's not right. This comes from that TikTok lunatic, doesn't it?"

Ramirez closes the file with a click. "It's not just the videos, Ben. We've been fielding anonymous tips, a few from inside the hospital, and we have reason to believe that someone may have tampered with Alice's brakes."

"You do know it's Emma's sister who is behind those videos,

right?" Ben says. "She's out to get me, because she's jealous of her sister's marriage. She never liked me and even tried to get Emma to not marry me."

"Be that as it may, you need to know that we have reopened the investigation. I'm here as your friend, Ben."

Silence. Ben is shaking his head, but not in a "no"—more like he's trying to knock the words loose from his skull before they settle. I glance at the folder, half expecting it to pulse like a telltale heart.

"I want to talk to Joseph," Ben blurts, then immediately flushes, eyes darting to me, seeking something—reassurance, forgiveness, a map out of this hell. I can't believe this is happening. It's a nightmare. Does Lily know what she's done? To her own father? "We're not answering questions without representation."

"I'm not accusing you of anything," Ramirez says, and his tone almost convinces me. "I'm just trying to build a timeline. Something doesn't add up. Your wife's car was serviced three days before the accident. The mechanic left a statement saying the brake lines were in perfect condition. But post-crash, examining the circumstances, it has become clear that the brakes failed."

Ben slumps back into his chair, all the fight gone. Sweat beads at his temples. "You think I sabotaged my wife's car?"

"Ben, I don't think that. You know this. But right now we're examining all possibilities. I have to. I was hoping you two could help me out."

"Okay," Ben says. "Of course, we will. But with what?"

I can barely breathe. Should I tell them about the letters? Would it help Ben if I did? But their content doesn't exactly paint him as the perfect husband. On the contrary. They might think they're actually from Alice, written before her death; they might end up being evidence against him.

"We'll need to interview everyone," Ramirez continues,

making more notes. "Family members, colleagues, friends. And we'll need access to your phone records, security systems, email accounts. Again."

Ben sinks back onto the sofa, suddenly looking exhausted. "Of course," he says, the fight gone from his voice. "Whatever you need. I want this resolved as much as you do."

Ramirez's gaze shifts to me, studying my face. What does he see there? Shock? Fear? Guilt? I try to arrange my features into an appropriate expression of concern, but my thoughts are spinning too fast to control my face.

"Emma," he says, his voice gentler now. "You look pale. Are you all right?"

"It's just a lot to take in," I manage. "I never knew Alice, but this is... unsettling."

Ramirez nods, but his eyes linger on me for a moment too long. Does he suspect me of something? Does he know about my visits to Mack's Auto Shop, my meetings with Rachel, my suspicions about Lily? Does he already know about the letters?

I watch him sigh, rubbing the back of his neck. "Look, I hate this as much as you do. Twenty years on the force and interviewing friends never gets easier." He glances at his watch—the one his husband, Miguel, gave him for their anniversary. I remember when they got married, how we all celebrated at that little Cuban place by the water. Now the air between us crackles with tension that makes my stomach knot. Ben's jaw tightens in that way that means he's building walls. I want to reach for his hand, bridge this sudden gulf between old friends, but my fingers remain frozen.

"Let's get through these questions so we can all go home," Ramirez continues. "You're still coming to Rosie's quinceañera Saturday, right?"

His phone buzzes. He glances at it, then silences it with an apologetic smile that doesn't reach his eyes. I find myself praying this will end, that we can somehow rewind to before all this started.

"One more thing before we start." He flips a page in his notepad, taking his time. "Alice withdrew a substantial amount from the family trust the morning she died. Transferred to an offshore account." His eyes meet Ben's. "Any thoughts on that?"

We exchange a glance. I think of what Marcus told me but can't reveal what I know. That the account was in Lily's name.

Ben shakes his head. "No idea."

"Okay," the detective says. "Let's get this over with. You can leave now, Ben. I'll start with Emma."

Before he leaves, Ben stands there, frozen, unwilling to meet my eyes. I realize, abruptly, that we're both terrified—but not of the same thing. I know in my heart that Lily did this. And this time she has taken it too far.

TWENTY-FIVE

Ramirez sinks into the leather armchair opposite me, deliberately placing a small digital recorder on the glass table between us. The device's red light blinks accusingly. He explained that he'd need to reinterview everyone connected to Alice at the time of her death and review every piece of evidence he had five years ago. But while he's here, he said it makes sense to interview me. For the first time. Ben and I merely nodded our heads in agreement. I've never been interviewed by a police officer before, but the quicker this is over with, the quicker I can confront Lily. End this silly game once and for all.

"For the record, state your name and relationship to Alice Stone," Ramirez says, his tone shifting from the almost friendly one he used with Ben earlier to something more formal, more detached.

"Emma Stone Caldwell. I'm..." I hesitate, the words sticking in my throat. "I'm married to her widower."

Ramirez nods, making a note in his small pad. "And when did you first meet Dr. Stone?"

"Five years ago. At Stone Advertising. I was presenting a

campaign for his father, Robert Stone, and Ben happened to be there."

"So this was before Alice's death?"

Death. The word hangs in the air between us. Death. Possible murder. Not an accident. Is this really true? If so, then it's a nightmare.

"Yes. He didn't notice me then, not till years later."

"And when did your relationship begin?"

"We started dating about a year ago," I say. "We married in October."

Ramirez's pen scratches across his notepad. "Did you know Alice before her accident?"

"No. I never met her. Only heard about her." I grip my hands together in my lap to stop them from trembling.

"Mrs. Stone, were you aware of the TikTok videos accusing your husband of involvement in Alice's death?"

"Yes." My voice comes out smaller than I intend.

"And what was your reaction to those accusations?"

I feel trapped, cornered. I keep thinking of the letters. Should I mention them? "I was... concerned. Shocked. It's a terrible thing to accuse someone of."

"But did you believe them?" Ramirez presses.

"I know my husband," I say, the non-answer hanging between us.

Ramirez watches me for a long moment, then shifts his focus. "Emma, are you aware that you were mentioned in one of the videos online? Made by the woman behind the account, Mira Patel. It was based on a text she received."

My heart stutters. "No. I mean, I'm sure they have mentioned me. What did it say?"

"The exact text read: 'Ask Emma about the phone.'"

The floor seems to drop from beneath me. Someone knows I found her phone. Knows I've been keeping it, carrying it, hiding it from Ben. I have tried to charge it and turn it on, but with no success.

My mind races, searching for a plausible explanation that isn't the truth. Before I can speak, Ramirez leans forward.

"I'd like to know what that's all about," he says, his eyes never leaving my face. "Her phone was never found."

The accusation in his tone catches me off guard. I'd walked in expecting routine questions, not this ambush. My throat tightens as I glance at the empty chair beside me where Ben should be. I hadn't thought I'd need him here. I was wrong.

"I don't know anything about a phone," I lie, the words tasting like acid. "I never met Alice. I never received anything from her."

Ramirez's expression doesn't change, but something in his eyes hardens. "Interesting. That's not the only thing, though." He pulls a photograph from his file and slides it across the table. It's me. Entering Mack's Auto Shop. The day I spoke to Anton about Alice's car. "You visited the same auto shop recently that serviced Alice's car before her accident," Ramirez says. "You asked the mechanic specifically about the brake work performed on her vehicle."

The walls of the room seem to close in. "I was curious," I say, the excuse pathetic even to my own ears. "After those videos started circulating, I wanted to know..."

"Wanted to know what?" Ramirez's voice has gone cold, professional. "If your husband had something to do with her death? Or if there was any way it could be traced back to you?"

"That's not—I didn't—" The words tangle and die in my throat.

"Mrs. Stone," Ramirez interrupts, leaning forward. "You're the only one who had reason to want Alice out of the picture."

The accusation lands like a physical blow. "What?"

"You worked at Stone Advertising when Alice was alive.

You noticed her husband before he saw you. You wanted to be with him already back then, didn't you?"

My head spins. "That's not true."

"You just said you saw him, but he didn't notice you till years later," Ramirez says. "You wanted him to see you. I have talked to several of your colleagues testifying to that. How you would blush when he walked in, how you would secretly look at him, tell people he was handsome, and so on."

"This is insane," I whisper.

"You wanted her life, didn't you?" Ramirez continues, his voice relentless. "And you got it. Her husband, her home, the family, the money, and a good position at the company."

"I didn't even know her!" The words burst from me, too loud in the formal quiet of the room. "How could I have wanted her dead when I never even met her?"

"Colleagues at Stone Advertising say otherwise," Ramirez counters. "They remember you attending the same functions, working on projects for her gallery."

"That's not possible." My voice shakes now. These are lies. Fabrications. But who would create them? And why?

Lily. She could have spread those rumors.

"I have nothing to hide," I say, the lie burning my tongue. "But I don't understand where these accusations are coming from. I never competed with Alice. I never even met her."

I did receive letters from her, though. After her death!

Ramirez gathers his notes, his expression neutral. "Sometimes people have selective memories when under stress," he says. "Perhaps you'll remember more details later. I'd like to speak with your husband's daughter now, if you'd permit it."

"Of course," I say while my heart drops. Lily. What is she going to tell him? Nothing good about me, that's for sure.

"Let me get her."

TWENTY-SIX

I call Lily's name and soon hear footsteps—not rushed but measured. Deliberate. I hear her before I see her, each step on the tiles a pronouncement. Then she appears.

Ramirez gestures to the armchair opposite where I sit. A single table lamp bathes the space between us in warm amber light that does nothing to dispel the chill radiating from Lily's presence. Ben walks in behind her and stands by the window, keeping his distance from me.

"Thank you for speaking with me, Lily," Ramirez says, his voice gentler than the one he used with me. "I know this must be confusing and upsetting. You are a minor, so I have asked your parents to be here too."

Lily nods, a perfect picture of teenage stoicism in the face of adult chaos. "It's okay. I want to help." Her gaze flicks between Ramirez and me, measuring, calculating. I recognize the look—I've seen it countless times when she's manipulating her father. Setting the stage for whatever performance she's about to give. Her eyes say it clearly: This one is not my parent and never will be.

"You've heard that we're investigating the possibility that

your mother's death might not have been an accident?" Ramirez asks, notepad ready.

"Yes." Lily's voice is steady, controlled. "My dad told me just now. I don't know what to think."

"That's understandable." Ramirez smiles reassuringly. "I'm hoping you might have noticed anything unusual. Any strange calls, texts, maybe someone watching the house?"

Lily hesitates, a perfectly timed pause that draws both our attention. "I'm not sure if it's related," she says carefully, "but Emma's been acting strange for weeks."

My shoulders tense. Here it comes.

"Strange how?" Ramirez prompts.

Lily turns those calculating eyes directly on me. "She's always asking about my mom," she says coolly. "What she was like, what she enjoyed, her habits. At first, I thought she was just trying to connect with me, but it became... intense. Obsessive."

"That's not true," I interject, the words bursting out before I can stop them. "I've asked normal questions anyone would ask about their predecessor."

Ramirez raises an eyebrow at my interruption but says nothing. Lily continues as if I hadn't spoken.

"A few days ago, I came home early from debate practice. The house was quiet, so I thought no one was home. But when I went upstairs, I found Emma in my parents' old bedroom. She was holding my mom's phone, trying to turn it on."

The floor seems to drop from beneath me. Ramirez's pen pauses above his notepad. "And you're certain it was your mom's?"

"Yes," Lily says with a small shrug. "I recognized it from when my mom was... still here. She had a brown Louis Vuitton cover. Most people can't afford one of those."

Ramirez turns to me, his expression unreadable. "Emma?"

My mind races, searching for an explanation that won't incriminate me further. If I admit to having the phone, I confirm Lily's account and reveal that I've been lying. If I deny it, Lily will simply insist she saw it, making me look even more suspicious.

"I found a phone in the vanity," I say carefully, only lying a little. I can't let them know about the storage unit and the things I found there. It will seem suspicious. "I wasn't sure whose it was."

"It was my mom's," Lily insists, her voice gaining an edge. "It had her name engraved on it. You were trying to open it. Not just 'finding' it."

Ramirez makes another note, his pen scratching loudly in the tense silence. "And what happened to the phone after that day?"

Lily's eyes narrow slightly. "I don't know. Emma must have hidden it somewhere. I looked for it later but couldn't find it."

The trap closes around me, steel jaws snapping shut. If the phone is found in my possession, it confirms Lily's story. If it's not found, it suggests I've destroyed evidence—evidence that might explain whether Alice was murdered.

"She's been acting weird in other ways too," Lily continues, warming to her role as the concerned, observant stepdaughter. "Staying up late on her computer. I've seen the light under her office door at three, four in the morning."

What? That's all lies! I never did that.

"That's not—" I begin, but Ramirez cuts me off with a raised hand.

"Let's hear Lily out first," he says, his tone making it clear he finds her account compelling. "Then you'll have a chance to respond."

Lily straightens, shoulders squaring. "There's something else," she says, her voice dropping to a near whisper. "I saw her searching through the basement last week. She had all these papers spread out with the Crystal River Bridge marked on a map. That's where my mom's accident happened."

Basement? We don't even have a basement. The house is built on a concrete slab—Florida's water table makes real basements impossible. I open my mouth to object, but Detective Ramirez raises his hand, silencing me before I can speak. The lie hangs in the air between us, impossible yet damning. A cold realization washes over me: Lily is deliberately fabricating evidence against me.

Ramirez continues taking notes, his expression giving nothing away. "Anything else you've noticed, Lily? Anything that might help us understand what's happening?"

Lily hesitates, glancing at me then back to Ramirez. A perfect display of reluctance, of someone who doesn't want to cause trouble but feels compelled to speak the truth.

"She asks a lot of questions about the accident," Lily says finally. "Details that weren't in the news. Like she's trying to piece something together. And she gets this look sometimes when she thinks no one's watching. Like she's waiting for something. Or worried about something."

The portrait she's painting is devastatingly effective: Emma the obsessed second wife, fixated on the first wife's death, possibly involved in her death, potentially dangerous.

"Thank you, Lily," Ramirez says, closing his notepad. "This has been very helpful."

Lily stands, smoothing her dark clothes, composed. She looks every inch Alice's daughter in this moment—poised, controlled, strategically vulnerable when necessary. As she turns to go, she pauses at the threshold, looking past Ramirez to fix her gaze on me.

"Detective," she whispers, just loud enough for both of us to hear, "I'm scared of what she might do."

The words hang in the air as Lily's footsteps recede on the marble floors, leaving us alone with Ramirez and the damning portrait she's painted. He studies me with new intensity, his earlier professional detachment replaced by something sharper, more focused.

"Would you like to respond to any of that, Mrs. Stone?" he asks quietly.

What can I possibly say? That, yes, I've been investigating Alice's death because I have received letters from her? That I found her phone and have been hiding it? That I've been meeting with my sister, who's been feeding information to a TikToker accusing Ben of murder? Every truth I could offer only makes me look more guilty in the scenario Lily has constructed.

"Lily has struggled ever since her mother died," I say finally, the words hollow even to my own ears. "And my interest in Alice's death is natural with everything we've been dealing with online."

Ramirez doesn't look convinced. "You've lied about the phone," he observes. " I'd like to see it."

"I don't have it. I threw it away. I didn't know it belonged to Alice. It was broken anyway and couldn't turn on."

The walls seem to close in around me. I am lying like crazy and fear he might see it on my face. I fear that the phone might contain something that might end up hurting Ben. I want to give it to Marcus first so he can see if he can get something out of it.

Ramirez rises from his chair, tucking his notebook into his jacket pocket. "We'll need to continue this conversation soon," he says, his tone deceptively casual. "For now, I suggest you remain in the area. And perhaps reconsider destroying anything that might be... relevant... to our investigation."

The warning hangs in the air between us. I'm a suspect now. In the corner of the room, Ben's head drops into his hands, his shoulders curved inward like a wounded animal.

As Ramirez leaves, I remain frozen in the armchair, the amber lamp light suddenly feeling less warm and more like a spotlight, exposing me to unseen watchers. I hear the elevator ding—Lily, no doubt, leaving, pleased with her performance. From Ben, there's silence. Absolute silence.

I am completely, utterly alone. And the evidence I've gathered to protect myself has become the very thing that might condemn me.

TWENTY-SEVEN

When we come home, I breathe in. Out. In again. My heart hammers against my ribs, a trapped bird seeking escape. Upstairs, a door opens then closes. Lily, moving through the house like a ghost. Or a predator. I can almost feel her satisfaction radiating through the ceiling.

Ben stands in front of me, face flushed, jaw tight. For a moment, he just stares at me, as if seeing a stranger in his living room.

"What the hell was that?" His voice is controlled, the surgeon's tone that betrays no emotion. But his eyes burn. I open my mouth to respond, but he's already moving, pacing the length of the living room, hands running through his hair, disheveling the perfect coif he maintains even at home.

"Ben—" I start, but he cuts me off with a chopping motion.

"Ramirez is my friend. He knows what I went through. And now he's treating me like a suspect? And you." He stops pacing, fixing me with that penetrating gaze that once made me feel seen but now makes me feel exposed. "What was that about her phone, Emma? What aren't you telling me?"

Decision time. The moment stretches, elastic and terrible. If

I continue hiding what I know, I become the suspicious wife with secrets, validating Lily's accusations. If I reveal everything, I risk Ben's rage—or worse, I might incriminate him, making him look like a suspect.

But Ramirez knows about the phone. Lily claims to have seen me with it. The lies I've told today will be exposed when Ramirez returns. My only hope now is to control the narrative, to be the one who brings the truth to light rather than having it dragged from me.

"Ben, I need to tell you something." My voice emerges as a whisper, fragile and uncertain.

He stills, watching me with narrowed eyes as I reach into my purse with trembling hands. The leather is butter soft beneath my fingers, expensive—a wedding gift from him. I wonder, fleetingly, if he gave Alice similar gifts before her death. Before whatever happened that night at Crystal River Bridge.

I pull out the stack of letters—cream-colored envelopes tied with a thin blue ribbon. My handwriting on the dates I've marked in the corner of each. Then the phone, with the cracked glass.

"These letters started arriving after our honeymoon." The words tumble out, unstoppable now that I've begun. "They're from Alice. Or... someone pretending to be her."

Ben freezes in place, his body going unnaturally still. Only his eyes move, fixing on the items in my hands as if they might bite him. The silence stretches between us, taut as a wire.

"What is it?" The word is barely audible, exhaled rather than spoken.

"Letters," I say, holding them out like an offering. "Addressed to me. About you. About your marriage. About what really happened the night she died." My hand shakes, the envelopes trembling visibly. "And her phone. The letters sort of led me to finding it, in a storage unit."

"Give those to me." Ben's voice has changed, hardened into something I don't recognize. He doesn't move, doesn't reach for them. Just stands there, commanding.

"I think we should give them to Ramirez," I say, surprised by the steadiness in my voice. "Whoever is writing them is trying to break us apart."

"Give. Them. To. Me." Each word is sharp, precise, a scalpel cutting through the air between us.

I clutch the evidence closer to my chest. "Ben, please. Let's just talk about this. About what they say. About why someone would send these to me."

"Why didn't you tell me?" He takes a step forward, then another. "How long have you been hiding these?"

"The first letter came right when we got back from Tahiti. I didn't know what to think. I thought someone was playing a cruel joke. Then... and the videos started online..."

"And what, Emma?" Another step. The coffee table is all that separates us now. "You thought I killed her? Is that what you think? Is that why you've been investigating me behind my back? Ramirez told me you went to the auto shop. Was that to prove that I murdered her? So you and your sister could put it all over the internet?"

My throat constricts. "I didn't say that. I never believed the letters or the videos."

"You didn't have to." His face twists, features rearranging into something unfamiliar. "I see it in your eyes."

My heart hammers faster. He looks hurt, disappointed in me. "Ben, please. Let's just read them together. Let's figure this out."

His eyes flick to the letters in my hand, then back to my face. Something cold and calculating passes behind them, a shadow moving beneath ice. "Of course," he says, his voice suddenly gentle. "You're right. We should look at these together."

The look on his face makes my heart drop. I have hurt his feelings. I feel awful.

"Yes," I agree cautiously. "We're a team. That's why I am telling you about them."

He holds out his hand, palm up, expectant. "Let me see them."

I place the top letter in his outstretched hand, keeping the rest—and the phone—clutched against my chest. His fingers close around the envelope, and for a moment, we're connected by this physical link, this tangible piece of the mystery that's consuming us both.

"Let's go upstairs," he says, the perfect concerned husband once more. "We should discuss this privately, away from prying ears." His eyes flick toward the ceiling—toward Lily's room.

As Ben gestures for me to precede him up the stairs, I catch a glimpse of movement at the top of the staircase—a shadow withdrawing quickly into darkness. Lily. Watching. Always watching.

TWENTY-EIGHT

The bedroom door closes behind us with a soft click. Ben moves to the center of the room, the single letter still pinched between his fingers, his back to me. I hover near the door, clutching the remaining letters and the phone. The space between us stretches. Outside, rain begins to patter against the windows—a gentle sound at odds with the storm brewing inside.

"How many letters, Emma? How many did you receive?"

"This is the fourth."

He looks up sharply, his eyes narrowing. "The fourth? How many are there?"

"Four total." My grip tightens on the bundle in my arms. "They come every two to three days. Always in the same type of envelope."

Ben opens the envelope. He unfolds the single sheet of paper inside, his eyes scanning the contents. I watch his face transform—confusion to disbelief to something harder, colder. His cheeks flush dark red, a vein pulsing at his temple.

"This is sick," he whispers, then louder, "This is SICK." He crumples the letter in his fist. "Who would write this garbage?

Surely you know this is nonsense, don't you? It can't possibly be Alice—I saw her body for God's sake." He puts his head in his hands, his grief overwhelming him.

"Of course," I say. "That's why I kept them. To try to figure it out."

"By yourself?" He advances toward me. "Without telling me? Your husband?"

"I didn't know what to think, Ben." My back presses against the door. "The first letter just talked about your marriage to Alice. Details I didn't know. Then the second one mentioned the white orchids—how you brought them to her just like you bring them to me. The same words you used. 'When you know, you know.' It was creepy to me. I should have just thrown them out. I don't believe anything they say."

Ben's face contorts, and he sighs deeply, hurt painted all over him. "You should have brought these to me immediately." His voice drops dangerously low. "The moment you received the first one. That's what a loyal wife would do. A trusting wife."

"And what would a loyal husband do, Ben?" The words escape before I can stop them.

His hands clench into fists at his sides, knuckles whitening. "You have no idea what you're talking about. No idea what our marriage was like. What Alice was like."

"Then tell me," I challenge, adrenaline overriding caution. "Tell me why it says in the letters that you checked her phone and hid cameras to keep an eye on her. Why was she hiding money? Why are there hospital records of her coming in with bruises?"

"You're my wife," he says. "You're supposed to be on my side. Not believing anonymous letters over your own husband."

His face shifts again—the rage receding, replaced by something else, a hurt. "I'm sorry," he says, running a hand through his hair. "I'm just... this is a lot to process. My dead wife might have been murdered. My current wife has been hiding evidence. My daughter is being questioned by the police." His voice breaks slightly on the last sentence. "What kind of wife keeps secrets like this?" he asks, his tone gentler but the accusation still clear. "Did you think I wouldn't find out? Did you think Ramirez wouldn't eventually discover you've been hiding evidence?"

"I was afraid," I admit, the truth slipping out despite my resolve.

"Afraid of what?" He steps closer again. "Afraid of me? Is that it? You think I'm capable of hurting you? Of hurting Alice?"

"I don't know what to think any more," I say, fighting to keep my voice steady. "The letters suggest Alice was afraid of you. Now Ramirez says she might have been murdered, and you're burning with rage that I kept these from you rather than concerned about whether your dead wife was killed."

"Because it's absurd!" His shout bounces off the cream-colored walls, making me flinch. "These letters are a sick joke, and you've fallen for it. You've let someone manipulate you into suspecting me—your husband—of terrible things."

"I told you I don't believe them. Someone is trying to hurt us. To come between us, and maybe even send me to jail."

I don't say that I know who it is. It would kill him to know what his daughter has done to me. He runs both hands through his hair now, pulling at it in frustration. "I don't understand anything any more!"

For a moment, he sounds genuinely bewildered, genuinely hurt.

"All I know," he continues, voice dropping to an intense whisper, "is that my wife should trust me. Should come to me with concerns, not hide things and investigate me behind my back."

His eyes settle on the letters in my hand. "I need to see these, Emma. I need to know what lies they contain about me."

I meet his gaze, heart steady. I trust him completely. "All right," I say, and hand him the bundle without hesitation.

He offers me a small, grateful smile. "Thank you," he murmurs.

"Let's decide together what to do with them."

He reaches out and takes them gently. His hand brushes mine for an instant—a quiet promise that we're in this together. Rain drums against the windows. We cross the room toward the old fireplace. I used to think it was romantic; now it feels like the perfect place to lay these accusations to rest.

Ben kneels beside the hearth. From his pocket he retrieves a small silver lighter—the one he shares with Robert on their occasional cigar nights. He clicks it open, and a warm flame springs to life.

"These are lies," he says calmly, leaning forward. He touches the flame to the corner of the first letter, watching it curl and blacken.

I kneel at his side, my hand on his shoulder. "Then let's burn them," I agree, voice steady and sure. "Together."

As each letter flares orange and drifts to ash, I feel the weight of their accusations lifting. We feed them into the fire, one by one, Ben's strong, steady movements matched by my own. Neither of us hurries; neither of us hesitates. This is ours to do, side by side. Smoke curls upward in gray tendrils, the acrid smell of paper and ink filling the room. I rest my hand on Ben's back as the final letter vanishes. Only glowing embers remain in the grate.

He stands and brushes ash from his hands. "They wanted to turn us against each other," he says softly. He turns to me, eyes bright in the firelight. "But we saw through it."

I smile, and he tucks the lighter away.

In the dim hallway, a slight movement catches my eye. Lily stands just beyond the doorway, half in shadow, watching the aftermath. She doesn't speak—her face is unreadable, but I sense a spark of something in her expression. A plan forming, perhaps. A witness to our unity rather than our discord.

TWENTY-NINE

I stir the pasta sauce mechanically, wrist rotating in perfect circles while my mind spins faster. Two days since Ben and I burned the letters. Two hours since he left for an emergency surgery. The wooden spoon scrapes the bottom of the pot. Keep moving. It's all good. You and Ben are one unit. Lily can't get between you any more.

I hum as I reach for the oregano, feeling lighter than I have in weeks. Ben's smile over breakfast seemed genuine—the first real one since we burned those awful letters. Maybe Lily leaving for college in the fall will reset everything. The pantry door creaks as I push it wider, scanning the spice shelf. My fingertips brush something odd as I reach behind the tomato cans—a small ridge that doesn't belong. I trace it carefully, discovering what feels like a metal catch. My humming stops. I press it experimentally, then push against the wall. Nothing. I try pulling instead.

The wall swings inward with a soft groan as if the hinges haven't been oiled in years. A draft of cool, damp air touches my face. Stairs descend into darkness—wooden, narrow, steep. I remember Alice mentioning in letter number three that there was a basement underneath the house. A basement. In Florida, I thought. That's ridiculous. As if I didn't know that houses in Florida don't have basements, due to the high water table. But there it is after all. I'm shocked it actually exists.

I reach for the light switch beside the hidden door. I flip it. Nothing happens. Of course.

My phone is in my back pocket. I pull it out, turn on the flashlight function. The beam cuts through the darkness, illuminating dust motes swirling in the disturbed air. I should wait for Ben to leave for longer. Should call Rachel or Ramirez. Should do anything but descend those stairs alone.

But I'm already taking the first step down. Then the second.

The wooden stairs creak beneath my weight. Each sound feels amplified in the enclosed space, broadcasting my presence to anyone who might be listening. Seventeen steps. I count them like heartbeats as I descend into the Morrison Estate's secret. The air grows colder, mustier. Smells of damp concrete and something else.

At the bottom, my flashlight beam dances across the space, revealing a finished basement roughly the size of our living room. The walls are concrete, painted a dingy white decades ago. Metal shelving units line three walls, stacked with cardboard boxes. A desk sits against the fourth wall, beneath a single bare bulb hanging from the ceiling.

I try another light switch at the bottom of the stairs. Again, nothing happens. The only light comes from my phone, casting long, distorted shadows as I move deeper into the room.

The boxes have labels. Neat handwriting I recognize as Ben's. "Alice—Clothes." "Alice—Books." "Alice—Photos." The possessions of a dead woman, cataloged and stored away like museum artifacts.

I open the nearest box. Inside, neatly folded sweaters, blouses, dresses. The clothes of a woman my size, my coloring. The clothes of the woman I replaced.

My hands shake as I move to the next box. Jewelry. A silver bracelet. Pearl earrings. I pull out the bracelet and look at it in the light, startled by its beauty, before putting it back.

The third box contains photo albums. I flip one open with trembling fingers. Alice stares back at me—smiling, laughing, alive. The resemblance between us is unsettling. Brown hair, heart-shaped face, wide-set eyes. Different women, same type. Replaceable parts.

The desk draws me next. My flashlight beam reveals what looks like a letter-writing station. Cream-colored stationery—identical to the letters that now lie as ashes in our bedroom fireplace. Envelopes with my name and address already printed on them. A fountain pen rests in a holder, its nib stained with ink.

And there, stacked neatly in the corner of the desk: drafts.

My hands shake so violently I nearly drop my phone.

The writing isn't as good in these. Not as perfect. Not as swirly and pristine as Alice's handwriting.

I pick up the top sheet, the words swimming before my eyes.

Emma, when you find this letter, I'll already be gone. Not missing—gone. Dead.

Proof.

That Lily sent the letters.

My stomach heaves. I swallow hard against the acid rising in my throat.

In the drawer, more evidence. A sheet of paper with my daily schedule. Notes about which hours I'm at work, and when I'm alone in the house. A folder labeled "Emma—Instability Documentation." Inside, photos of me looking distraught, confused, afraid—all taken without my knowledge. Building a case. Creating a narrative.

Above me, a floorboard creaks. Footsteps. Someone moving across the kitchen floor directly over my head.

Ben's supposed to be at the hospital. Lily's supposed to be on a video call.

More footsteps. Deliberate. Moving toward the pantry.

I swing my flashlight toward the stairs, mind racing. Do I hide among the boxes? Make a run for it? Confront whoever is coming with the evidence I've found?

The footsteps stop directly above the hidden door.

My heart slams against my ribs as I hear the distinct sound of the pantry door opening wider. Then the soft click of the latch being released.

THIRTY

Ben's silhouette fills the doorway at the top of the stairs, a black cutout against the dim light from the kitchen. My breath catches in my throat as he descends one step, then another, his movements unhurried and confident.

"Ben? I'm so glad it's you," I say, relieved. I was afraid it was Lily. "You won't believe what I've found. Come see."

My phone's flashlight cuts through the darkness, casting grotesque shadows across his face as he continues his measured descent. His features are arranged in an expression of perfect calm—the same expression he wears entering a difficult surgery.

"What are you doing down here? Looking for something?" His voice is mild, conversational. As if finding me in his secret basement is a minor curiosity rather than a catastrophe.

"Why are you home already?" I ask. "I thought you had surgery?"

"I've been watching you."

"What do you mean?"

"I watched you go down the stairs and going through all this stuff."

"How long have you been watching me?" My voice emerges steadier than I expected. "And why?"

"The security system sends alerts to my phone when certain areas of the house are accessed." Ben reaches the bottom of the stairs, one hand trailing along the wall with casual familiarity. "Including a pantry with an unusual latch. I saw you on the camera."

"You have cameras?" I say, but we both know I already know this.

His smile is thin, indulgent. "Every doctor's home should have proper security, Emma. For the family's protection."

I take another step back, bumping against one of the shelving units. Boxes shift behind me. Alice's possessions. Alice's life. Cataloged and stored. Lily didn't do that.

Then it hits me.

"It was you, not Lily. You wrote the letters." I shine the light directly at the desk with its cream-colored stationery and drafts in his handwriting. "You pretended to be Alice. You've been gaslighting me."

Ben sighs, the sound heavy with disappointment. "I had hoped you would bring those letters to me immediately. That you would trust your husband enough to ask him about these disturbing messages." He takes another step toward me. "Instead, you hid them. Investigated me. Betrayed my trust."

A rush of cool air hits me as the door Ben walked through closes with a bang.

I can't believe what I'm hearing. I want to shake the truth away.

But it was him.

"You killed her, didn't you?" The words escape in a rush, pushed out by months of growing suspicion. "Why?"

His expression doesn't change, but something shifts in his eyes—a cooling, a hardening. "Alice was unstable. No one questioned her accident till your sister got involved with that character Patel. She interviewed me last year and told me she had proof: the SD card from Alice's necklace, the reports from the hospital. She did this to you. If only she had stayed away and kept what she knew to herself. I only did what I had to do. We could have been happy, Emma." Not a denial. Not even close to a denial.

"You tampered with her brakes." I'm piecing it together now, the evidence. "You gave her medications that made her confused, paranoid. Just like the pills you gave me. When she tried to leave you, you killed her and made it look like an accident. Why?" My final question comes out louder than I expected.

"She was going to take Lily away from me." The first crack in his calm, a flash of genuine emotion. "She was going to destroy everything I'd built. My reputation. My family. My life." He smooths his expression back to neutral with practiced ease. "I gave her every chance to be reasonable."

My skin crawls with each word. The casual way he confirms my worst fears. The clinical detachment with which he discusses ending his wife's life.

"And me?" I ask, though I already know the answer. "Are you... are you going to kill me?"

"No." He gestures toward the desk with its damning evidence. "I don't need to."

I try to edge sideways, working my way gradually toward the stairs. Ben mirrors my movement, cutting off my path without seeming hurried.

I clutch my phone tighter, the flashlight beam trembling across his face. "Ramirez will find all this. The letter drafts. Your handwriting."

"Will he?" Ben's smile returns, colder than before. "By tomorrow, this room will be empty. And what will be left? The increasingly erratic behavior of my troubled wife. Her obsession with my first wife's death. Her deteriorating mental state, documented by concerned family members. Ramirez knows all this. He's watched it. And he is my close friend, don't forget that." His gaze flicks meaningfully to the ceiling, to where Lily might be listening. "Such a tragedy in the making."

He set me up.

I think about how desperately he wanted the letters back.

He burnt them.

The evidence of his own treachery is gone.

What does this mean? All I know is I'm not safe here with him.

I lunge suddenly to the right, hoping to catch him out, to slip past him to the stairs. His hand shoots out, fingers closing around my wrist with that same controlled strength I've felt a hundred times before—when he guides me through crowded rooms, when he positions me for photographs, when he silently corrects my posture at dinner with his parents.

"Let go." I pull against his grip, panic rising in my throat.

"Emma." My name in his mouth sounds like a diagnosis. "You need help. You're not well."

"You're hurting me." It's barely true—his grip is tight but calibrated to restrain without bruising. Evidence management, even now.

"I would never hurt you." The practiced sincerity in his voice makes my skin crawl. "I just want what's best for you. For us."

I twist sharply, using a self-defense move Rachel insisted I learn after my divorce. The sudden movement catches Ben by surprise. His grip loosens just enough for me to wrench free, but the momentum sends me stumbling backward.

My phone slips from my grasp, clattering to the concrete floor between us. It lands face down, the flashlight beam shooting upward, illuminating our faces.

In that stark, unnatural light, I finally see Ben clearly. The mask of concern has fallen away completely, revealing something cold and calculating beneath. His features, handsome in normal light, transform into something monstrous in the harsh shadows. His eyes are black holes, his smile a slash across the lower half of his face.

"You can't leave, Emma." His voice drops to a whisper. "Not with what you know now."

The implications of his words freeze the blood in my veins. This isn't just about gaslighting any more. Not just about psychological control. This is about survival.

I glance at my phone on the floor between us.

"I loved you." The words taste like ash on my tongue. "I believed in you. Even when I found Alice's phone, I wanted there to be another explanation."

"There is." He takes a step closer, the light casting his shadow huge and distorted against the wall behind him. "Alice was mentally ill. Paranoid. She believed it was reality. And you've fallen into the same delusion."

His hand extends toward me again—not grabbing this time but offering. Palm up. An invitation. A last chance.

"Let me get you the help you need, Emma." His voice gentles, the skilled surgeon calming a frightened patient. "We can still fix this. Still be happy. I can help you get better."

My eyes dart to my phone on the floor, to the stairs beyond him, to the shadows where boxes contain the dismantled life of the woman who came before me. The woman who might have faced the same choice I do now.

Comply or die.

I guess I'd rather die.

I dive for the phone, my body moving before my brain can calculate the risk. My fingers close around it just as Ben lunges after me. We collide in a tangle of limbs, his weight nearly crushing me against the concrete floor. My thumb swipes desperately across the screen. Ben's hand clamps over mine, trying to pry the phone away, but I curl around it, protecting it with my body like a wounded animal protecting its young.

"Give it to me," he hisses, his doctor's composure fracturing into something raw and dangerous.

I twist beneath him, creating just enough space to tap on Ramirez's name in my recent calls. The phone begins to ring, the sound impossibly loud in the basement's close confines. Ben's fingers dig into my wrist, hard enough to leave marks now. He's abandoned caution, no longer concerned about leaving evidence.

"Emma, stop this." His voice drops to that doctor's tone again—authoritative, reasonable—even as his body pins me to the floor. "You're having an episode. Let me help you."

The call connects. "Detective Ramirez," comes the gruff voice, tinny through the speaker. "Hello? Emma, is that you?"

THIRTY-ONE

Ben's weight crushes me against the cold concrete floor as Ramirez's voice crackles through the speaker. My fingers grip the phone like a lifeline, but Ben is stronger. His face hovers inches from mine, a mask of controlled rage illuminated from below by the phone's glow. I open my mouth to scream for help, but before I can make a sound, he wrenches the phone from my grasp with a single violent twist.

"Lucas, hello." Ben's voice transforms instantly—smooth, steady, professional. The doctor's voice that has reassured countless parents before operating on their children. "Sorry about that. Emma's not well."

I thrash beneath him, desperate to reclaim the phone, to shout the truth to Ramirez. Ben shifts his weight, pinning me more effectively with his knee pressed into my stomach. The pressure steals my breath, silences me as effectively as a hand over my mouth.

"Everything all right over there?" Ramirez's voice sounds tinny through the speaker. Suspicious. Cautious.

"Just a misunderstanding." Ben presses harder with his knee. A warning. "Emma's been having a difficult time lately.

Confused. Finding things in the house that trigger paranoid episodes."

I claw at his arm, my nails leaving white tracks that quickly redden. Evidence. Proof. Ben doesn't even flinch, just catches my wrist with his free hand and pins it to the floor beside my head. His eyes never leave mine—cold, calculating, watching for my next move while he spins lies into Ramirez's ear.

"I'm actually glad she called you, Lucas." Ben's voice drops to a confidential tone, friend to friend. "I've been meaning to reach out. I'm concerned about Emma's mental state. She's been fixating on Alice, convinced there's some conspiracy."

"Put Emma on the phone," Ramirez demands, his voice sharp even through the small speaker.

Ben's smile doesn't reach his eyes as he holds the phone closer to my face. "Of course. She's right here."

The pressure on my stomach eases just enough for me to draw breath. Hope flares—a chance to tell Ramirez what's happening, what I've found, that I'm not crazy but in danger. Ben's eyes narrow, a silent threat clear in their depths. I see his thumb hovering over the mute button.

"He—" I start, but Ben cuts me off, pressing his knee into my diaphragm again.

"She's having trouble speaking clearly right now," Ben interrupts, pulling the phone back. "Panic attack. Extremely agitated. I found her in our storage area, going through boxes of Alice's things. When I confronted her, she became hysterical."

My lungs burn from lack of air. Black spots dance at the edges of my vision. I twist my head to the side, gasping as Ben eases the pressure just enough to keep me conscious. The concrete floor is cold against my cheek. Dust clings to my eyelashes, making my eyes water.

"I heard a struggle," Ramirez says, his voice carrying an edge of authority now. "Emma called me. Not you."

Ben sighs—the put-upon, patient husband dealing with a

difficult situation. "She's been calling people at all hours, Lucas. Making accusations. Last week it was my father. Yesterday, Lily's debate coach." Each lie flows smoothly, building on the foundation he's been laying for weeks. "I've been trying to manage it privately, but it's getting worse. They even had to send her home from work and told her to take a sabbatical."

From my position on the floor, I can see the staircase leading up to the kitchen. Freedom, just fifteen steps away. But Ben's body blocks the path, his weight immovable as stone.

"Emma?" Ramirez again, his voice more insistent. "Are you there?"

Ben holds the phone closer again, his eyes boring into mine. A silent instruction. Say what I want you to say, or else. I swallow hard, mind racing. If I tell the truth, Ramirez might not believe me—not with the groundwork Ben has laid portraying me as unstable. If I play along, I might get another chance later.

"I'm—" My voice comes out raspy, weak. "I'm okay."

"You don't sound okay," Ramirez presses.

"She's been crying," Ben interjects smoothly. "Finding Alice's things upset her. I should have cleared them out years ago, but..." He lets his voice trail off, the grieving widower still haunted by his past.

"Emma, did you call me by accident?" Ramirez asks directly.

Ben's eyes harden. His thumb caresses the end call button, a reminder of how quickly he can cut off my lifeline.

"N-no," I manage, fighting for a plan. For words that might signal Ramirez without triggering Ben. "I need—I need help."

"See?" Ben's voice remains calm, but his fingers dig painfully into my wrist. "This is what I've been dealing with. She thinks my daughter wrote some letters to her pretending to be from my ex-wife. That's how insane this has become. She's convinced she needs police protection. From a seventeen-year-old." He forces a sad laugh. "From my daughter."

"Emma, are you in danger?" Ramirez asks, cutting through Ben's performance.

Ben's eyes lock with mine, daring me to contradict him. His thumb slides partially over the end call button.

"I—" The words stick in my throat. One wrong move and he'll disconnect my only hope. "I found things. In the basement. Evidence."

"She means Alice's things," Ben says quickly. "She's been going through them obsessively."

"Lucas," I try again, desperation making my voice stronger. "The letters—"

"She thinks my daughter wrote letters to her pretending to be Alice," Ben interrupts, his doctor's voice perfectly calibrated to convey concern rather than anger. "But there are no letters. They're all part of her delusion. I've consulted with a colleague. The symptoms align with acute stress disorder, possibly developing into—"

"We're coming over," Ramirez cuts him off. "Keep Emma calm until we get there."

"That's not necessary," Ben says, but the line has already gone dead.

The mask drops instantly. Ben's face contorts with rage as he flings the phone across the room. It hits a metal shelf with a crack, then clatters to the floor, screen dark.

"Now look what you've done," he hisses, releasing my wrist to grab my shoulders, fingers digging painfully into my flesh. "You stupid, ungrateful bitch."

And there it is. The respected doctor turning into raging monster in seconds.

"They're coming," I whisper, clinging to that single thread of hope. "Ramirez is coming."

Ben laughs, the sound harsh in the basement's confines. "Good. Perfect, actually." He rises suddenly, releasing me. "This is exactly what we need to complete your psychological evaluation. Your obsession with Alice, wanting her life. It all paints a disturbing picture."

I scramble backward, putting distance between us, my back pressing against the cold concrete wall. He makes no move to stop me. Instead, he straightens his shirt, smooths his hair. The monster recedes, replaced by Dr. Benjamin Stone, respected pediatric surgeon, concerned husband.

"When Ramirez arrives," he says, voice calm again, "he'll find exactly what I described. A disturbed woman who's been obsessing over her husband's dead wife. Who's been hiding evidence to fuel her delusions." His smile is terrible in its confidence. "Evidence that, strangely enough, has your fingerprints all over it."

The realization hits me like a physical blow. Every box I touched. The phone. The evidence I thought would save me has become the noose around my neck. "You wrote those letters so I would look for the phone, didn't you? And her jewelry? So they would have my fingerprints all over them? You wanted me to try and get the SD card from Rachel? That's why you mentioned it? I was nothing but a puppet in your hands?"

Ben steps casually toward the staircase, his body blocking my escape route. He glances at his watch, then at the stack of draft letters on the workbench. With methodical movements, he begins feeding them into the paper shredder, wincing at each mechanical grind.

"Careless," he mutters to himself. "Should have destroyed these weeks ago." His eyes find mine, clinical and assessing. "How did you even find this place? I've kept this basement locked for years." He checks his watch again. "Doesn't matter now. The police will be here in twelve minutes. Just enough time for you to decide what version of events you'll share with them."

Behind him, the narrow wooden stairs lead up to light, to potential safety. But to reach them, I would have to get past

Ben. And there's nowhere to run in this house that he hasn't already mapped, planned for, controlled.

Ben's momentary glance at his watch is all I need. A half second of distraction, his focus shifting from me to time. I launch myself forward, every muscle coiled with desperation, aiming not for the center of the stairs but for the narrow gap between his body and the railing. My shoulder slams against his hip, throwing him off balance just enough. His hand grasps at my shirt but catches only air as I scramble past him, taking the wooden steps two at a time, my feet barely touching the treads as terror propels me upward.

"Emma!" His roar follows me up the stairs. Footsteps thunder behind me, too close, getting closer.

I burst through the pantry door into the kitchen, bright light momentarily blinding me after the basement's dimness. The smell hits me first—burning pasta sauce, water boiling over, steam rising in angry clouds from the stove. The mundane dinner preparations from a lifetime ago, when I was still just a wife with suspicions, not a woman running for her life.

No time to think. Move.

I slam the pantry door behind me, fumbling for the lock, but there isn't one—just a simple latch that won't keep him out for more than seconds. My eyes dart around the kitchen, seeking weapons, exits, anything that might help. The knife block sits on the counter near the sink. I lunge for it, my hands shaking so violently I knock it sideways. Knives clatter across the granite, several falling to the floor with metallic clangs that sound impossibly loud in the kitchen's pristine silence.

The pasta pot boils over again, angry bubbles hissing as they hit the burner. I reach out instinctively to turn it off, my mind still processing the absurd domesticity of the action even as I hear Ben crashing against the pantry door. My hand catches the edge of the scalding metal pot. Pain sears through my palm, sharp and clarifying. I jerk back with a gasp, cradling my burned hand against my chest.

Focus, Emma. Focus.

The largest knife has fallen to the floor. I snatch it up, the handle cool and solid in my uninjured hand. Six inches of German steel. A wedding gift from Margaret. ("Every wife should have proper kitchen tools." Her cultured voice echoes in my memory. She didn't know how right she was.)

Behind me, the pantry door shudders under Ben's weight. It won't hold. Nothing in this house was designed to keep him out.

My gaze catches on the refrigerator—stainless steel perfection covered with photographs held by magnetic frames. Ben and me on our wedding day, his arm around my waist, my smile radiant with hope and trust. Ben with Lily at her debate championship, both of them beaming with identical proud smiles. The three of us at Christmas, arranged in perfect familial harmony before the fireplace.

The photos mock me now. The careful curation of normal life, of family happiness. The perfect facade hiding the monster beneath. Was there ever a moment when his love was real? Or was I always just a replacement part, selected in case of emergency, to take the fall, groomed to fit the role before being discarded?

The pantry door flies open. I spin around, knife raised, as Ben steps into the kitchen. He freezes, eyes locking on the blade in my hand.

"Emma." His voice shifts again—gentle, soothing, the voice he uses with frightened children before surgery. "Put that down. You're going to hurt yourself."

"Stay back." My voice shakes, but the knife doesn't. My burned hand throbs with each heartbeat.

His eyes track my movements as he takes another careful step forward, hands raised in a gesture of peace that doesn't match the predatory calculation in his gaze. "Think about what you're doing. How this looks."

"I know exactly how this looks." I edge sideways, trying to keep the island between us. "A woman defending herself from the man who killed his first wife."

"Listen to yourself." He shakes his head, the picture of reasonable concern. "This is exactly what I was telling Ramirez. The paranoid delusions. The fixation on Alice."

In the distance, sirens wail—growing louder, closer. Ramirez, coming because he heard something wrong in our call. But what will he see when he arrives? A respected doctor dealing with his unstable wife? Or a woman uncovering the truth about a murderer?

"The evidence is in the basement." I adjust my grip on the knife, pain shooting through my burned palm. "The letters you wrote pretending to be Alice. Your handwriting on the drafts."

"You mean the evidence you've been collecting? Hiding? Touching?" Ben takes another step around the island, cutting off my path to the hallway. "Your fingerprints are all over those items, Emma."

The sirens grow louder. Two minutes away, maybe less.

"Ramirez will see through you." But even as I say it, doubt creeps in. The seeds Ben has planted—my supposed instability, my obsession with Alice, the evidence that links me rather than him to her death. The way Lily watched me today, along with her calculated testimony. The staged conflicts at work. The groundwork laid so carefully.

"Ramirez is my friend," Ben reminds me, taking another step closer. "Has been for twenty years. He knows about your increasingly erratic behavior. Your fixation on Alice's death. The way you've been isolating yourself, acting paranoid."

The perfect kitchen surrounds us—gleaming surfaces, state-of-the-art appliances, everything in its designated place.

Another step. Ben is only feet away now, his body blocking

the most direct path to the front door. Behind me, the sliding glass doors lead to the patio, the pool, the high fence that surrounds our property. No escape that way.

The sirens cut off abruptly. They're here. In our driveway. Boots on pavement. Car doors slamming.

"Last chance, Emma." Ben's voice drops to a whisper. "Put down the knife. Tell Ramirez you're sorry for the confusion. That you've been under stress. That you need help." His eyes hold mine, intense and unblinking. "If you do that, we can still fix this. Still be a family."

The same words he must have spoken to Alice before the end. The same false choice—surrender or destruction.

Heavy footsteps approach the front door. A fist pounds against wood. "Police! Open up!"

Ben's eyes never leave mine as he calls out, voice perfectly steady: "Come in! Thank you for getting here so quickly."

The knife feels impossibly heavy in my hand. If I keep holding it when Ramirez enters, I become the threat, the unstable wife with a weapon. If I put it down, I'm defenseless against whatever Ben has planned.

Ben reads the calculation in my eyes. A smile touches the corner of his mouth—not warm, not kind, but triumphant. He knows he's won this round.

"Think of Lily," he whispers, a final twist of the knife. "What this will do to her if you continue with these delusions."

The door opens and footsteps emerge. I have seconds to decide. Fight with a weapon and confirm Ben's narrative about my instability or surrender and pray that Ramirez will see through Ben's performance.

The burned skin on my palm screams with pain, a physical echo of the betrayal burning through my chest. I make my choice.

* * *

"Put down the knife."

I glance at my hand in surprise and put the knife on the counter, slowly, carefully. The pasta water is still boiling violently, overflowing again. I never turned it off. I reach for it.

"Keep your hands where I can see them," snaps one of the uniforms.

I freeze, and my heart starts hammering against my ribs.

Ben's eyes follow the movement, a flash of triumph crossing his features before he masks it with concern. He strides toward the front door, shoulders squared, the perfect husband rushing to greet the police he called to help his troubled wife. I stay frozen in the kitchen, knife within reach, burned hand throbbing in time with my racing heart.

"Detective Ramirez, thank God you're here." Ben's voice carries, relief and tension perfectly balanced. "I'm worried she might hurt herself."

Heavy footsteps approach. Ramirez comes closer, his expression grim, eyes scanning the room and fixing on me. Two uniformed officers flank him, hands resting on their holstered weapons. Behind them, Ben hovers, his face a masterpiece of concern.

Lucas takes a step forward. His muddy shoes leave light footprints on the tiles. Evidence contamination, my mind notes absurdly. "Emma Stone, you are under arrest for the murder of Alice Stone."

"Me? No. That's—that's impossible." My voice rises, thin and desperate. "You have the wrong person. It's not me you want to arrest."

"New evidence has come to light this evening," Ramirez says. "The man who towed Alice's car found an object lodged underneath the brake pedal of the car. A metal object, a shim. It was handed to us yesterday, and today we received the lab results. Your fingerprints were all over it."

I stare at him, then remember. The shim. It was in the box,

the one I found in the storage room. Did I pick it up? Yes, I did. Would they ever believe me? No. What do I do? Panic sets in, and I feel my hands get clammy. The room tilts beneath my feet. "That's impossible. I never met Alice. I never came near her car."

"The mechanic identified you from a photo lineup this morning," Ramirez continues, his voice flat. "We went and talked to him after we found out about the shim. The mechanic recognized you, said you came in recently and asked about the brakes on Alice's car."

My mind is swirling. All those things I touched in the boxes and in the storage unit. They have my fingerprints all over them. The phone, the necklace. But worst is the shim. The very thing that must have blocked her brakes when trying to stop her car.

The murder weapon. The smoking gun. With my fingerprints on it. I went there because of the letters. Ben's letters. He planned all of this.

Ben steps forward, his performance impeccable. "I didn't want to believe it," he says, voice cracking with emotion. "But when Lily told me she found Emma with Alice's phone, I started looking for answers." He runs a hand through his hair, the picture of a man grappling with terrible revelations. "I found the box with the shim and the jewelry and Alice's will in the back of her closet and handed it in to Lucas. I wanted to know. And now I do."

"That's not possible," I whisper, but my protest sounds fake even to my own ears. "Ben planted that evidence. He wrote those letters. He made me go find all those things so I would touch them. He set this all up."

"She also has Alice's phone," Ben adds, looking at Ramirez with pained eyes. "I never found it, though, but it should be here somewhere, maybe her purse. I saw her holding it two days ago. She showed it to me upstairs and wouldn't give it to me when I asked her to. And when I confronted her about it in the basement, she tried to attack me." Ben pulls up his sleeve, revealing a dark bruise forming on his forearm along with the scratches I gave him while escaping up the stairs.

Ramirez nods to the officers. "Mrs. Stone, place your hands behind your back, please."

"No." I back away, panic rising in my throat. "This is insane. He's framing me! He led me to those things, helped me find them so I could touch them and leave fingerprints. He did this. He sent the letters leading me to those things!"

"What letters?" Ramirez asks.

I open my mouth to speak, but no words come out. The letters are nothing more than ashes now upstairs in the fireplace.

I have no proof. I have nothing.

The officers advance, their expressions impassive. One reaches for his handcuffs.

"You have to believe me," I plead, looking directly at Ramirez. "Ben killed Alice. He's been plotting this for a long time. The letters, the phone, everything was planted to make me look unstable. To set me up if I ever figured out what he did."

"Emma's been struggling with reality for some time now," Ben says, his voice dropping into clinical territory. "Initially presenting with paranoid ideation focused on my first wife, progressing to delusions of persecution and conspiracy. The pattern is consistent with delusional disorder, possibly exacerbated by extreme stress."

The perfect diagnosis. The perfect medical explanation from the perfect doctor.

"I'm not delusional!" My voice rises, desperate. "Look at his handwriting on the letter drafts in the basement."

"We'll examine all the evidence," Ramirez assures me, but his tone suggests he's already made up his mind. He nods to the officers again. "Proceed."

Cold metal closes around my wrists with a definitive click. The handcuffs bite into skin, pain layering upon pain from my fight with Ben. Unfortunately for me, I don't bruise easily, so again I have no proof of what he did to me. You can't see anything on my skin while his is scratched into bloody streaks. The officer recites my rights in a monotone, words washing over me in a meaningless stream as the reality of my situation crystallizes with terrible clarity.

I've been outmaneuvered at every turn. Every piece of evidence I found has been twisted to incriminate me instead of Ben. Every suspicion I had has been reframed as delusion. Every action I took to protect myself has become proof of my instability.

"This isn't happening," I whisper as the officers take position on either side of me. "This can't be happening."

Ben approaches, stopping just out of reach. The perfect distance for a man concerned about his unpredictable wife. "I'll get you the help you need," he promises, his voice carrying just the right note of heartbroken determination. "The best doctors. The best care."

As the officers guide me toward the foyer, a movement at the top of the stairs catches my eye. Lily stands there, one hand gripping the banister, the other covering her mouth. Her face is pale with what looks like shock, eyes wide as she watches the scene below.

Our eyes meet across the distance—stepdaughter and stepmother, adversaries in Ben's twisted game. For a moment, something flickers across her features—not triumph or satisfaction as I expected, but something more complex. Confusion? Doubt? Fear?

"Dad?" Her voice is small, uncertain.

Ben turns, arms outstretched toward his daughter. "It's okay, Lily. Everything's going to be okay now."

She descends a few steps, eyes still locked with mine. "Is Emma... she really...?"

"We'll talk about it later," Ben says, voice gentle but firm. The voice that brooks no argument.

The officers move me toward the door. I keep my eyes on Lily, searching for any sign that she sees through her father's performance, that she might question the narrative he's constructed. Her hand slides from the banister to twist the edge of her sweater—a nervous gesture I've seen before when she's uncertain.

"She didn't do anything wrong," Lily says suddenly, her voice stronger. "She was just looking for—"

"Lily." Ben's voice cuts through her words, sharp as a scalpel. "This is not the time."

The flash of fear that crosses her face is achingly familiar—the same fear I've felt, the same fear Alice must have known. The fear of contradicting Ben Stone.

"Ramirez," I say as they push me through the doorway, making one last desperate attempt. "The phone is in my bedside table upstairs. Please. Maybe it will contain the answers."

Ben's hand settles on Ramirez's shoulder, colleague to colleague, friend to friend. "We'll find whatever she's hidden," he assures him. "And get to the bottom of this."

The last thing I see as they lead me to the waiting police car is Lily's face, framed underneath the streetlamp beside her father. Her expression is unreadable now, mask firmly back in place. But her eyes follow me, and in them, I catch something that might be understanding—or might be fear for what happens when you cross Benjamin Stone.

The police car door closes with a final, definitive thud. Through the window, I watch my home—my prison—recede. Somewhere inside those walls, Alice's words wait to be found. Somewhere, the truth exists. But will anyone believe it coming from the unstable second Mrs. Stone?

NOW

THIRTY-TWO

The handcuffs bite into my wrists as I shift in the hard wooden chair, the orange jumpsuit scratching against my skin like sandpaper. Two months in county jail, and I still haven't adjusted to the constant restraints, the watchful eyes, the assumption of guilt that clings to me. The courtroom buzzes with whispered conversations that fall silent when the prosecutor rises, a slim folder in his hands.

"Your Honor, the state would like to enter into evidence Exhibit 14C." The prosecutor—Sikes, with his perfectly tailored suit and calculated pauses—holds up the phone. "This belongs to Alice Stone, found in the defendant's possession."

The judge nods, and a court officer carries the phone to her.

My public defender shifts beside me, papers rustling. Sam Torres, overworked and underprepared, assigned to me when Ben's accusations drained my bank accounts and froze my assets. Torres means well, but he's drowning in this case, outmatched by the state's resources and Ben's influence.

"This phone," Sikes continues, approaching the jury box, "belonged to Alice Stone and wasn't with her when she was pulled out of the water." He pauses, letting the words sink in. "Tell me, how do you come to be in possession of a person's phone after they've died? And why didn't Alice have it with her in her car when she drove into the water? What kind of woman—person—in this day and age doesn't have their phone with them at all times? Unless someone took it from her. So she couldn't call for help. Unless this someone planned on killing her, and destroying the phone afterwards? Unless it was her murderer who took it?"

My stomach knots. The twisting of truth is so complete, so perfect, I almost admire the artistry of Ben's frame. Almost.

"Objection," Torres mumbles, half rising. "Speculation."

"Sustained," the judge replies, but the damage is done. The seed planted in twelve minds.

I scan the courtroom, seeking any friendly face. Rachel sits directly behind me, her presence my only constant these past months. Her pen scratches furiously against her notepad, documenting every word, every inconsistency. She's been my lifeline, my advocate when everyone else abandoned me.

At the back of the courtroom, Ramirez leans against the wall, arms crossed over his chest. His expression is troubled, brow furrowed as he watches the proceedings.

"The state would also like to enter into evidence Exhibit 15A," Sikes says, gesturing to his assistant, who sets up a laptop and projector. "Internet search records retrieved from the defendant's devices."

The screen flickers to life on the courtroom wall. My search history from months ago: "brake line failures," "car accidents water edge," "untraceable poisons."

"As you can see"—Sikes points to timestamps—"the defendant methodically researched methods that would appear accidental. Then she finally found an example from Indiana where a husband tried to kill his wife by placing a shim underneath her brakes and that caused her to have a terrible accident, she narrowly survived. As you can see, Mrs. Stone has been reading about this event for a long time."

Torres scribbles something, slides it toward me: *Did you make these searches?*

I shake my head vehemently. No. Never. Another piece of Ben's elaborate puzzle. He could have used my laptop when I wasn't looking. He could easily have created this trail to make me look guilty.

Behind me, Rachel tears a page from her notebook, folds it precisely, passes it forward to Torres. He unfolds it, scans the contents, his eyebrows rising slightly. Hope flickers, then dies as he shakes his head minutely at Rachel. Whatever she's found, it's not enough.

"The state will demonstrate," Sikes says, moving to a new exhibit, "that Emma Stone Caldwell had both motive and opportunity to tamper with Alice Stone's vehicle. As a former employee of Stone Advertising, she was often near her husband, Dr. Stone, and fell in love with him. We have many testimonies to this from people working at the agency where Mrs. Stone Caldwell shared her feelings with them. She was jealous of Alice and wanted her husband, and her life. She knew she could never compete with Alice, the mother of Dr. Stone's only child, so she had to get rid of her."

My nails dig into my palms. This is all so twisted. I never competed with Alice. Never even met her. Yes, I had an eye for Benjamin when I saw him. I thought he was attractive, but I never made a move, never even tried to. He was a married man. Even after she died, I kept my distance. He was the one who finally approached me. But no one knows this except him and me.

"Your Honor," Torres interjects, "these employment statements are secondhand witnesses. They couldn't possibly have known what my client felt. Their authenticity is questionable at best."

"Your Honor," Sikes counters smoothly, "several employees from Stone Advertising can testify to this. She was, and I quote one of them, 'smitten with Dr. Stone from the moment she laid her eyes on him'."

The judge peers at Torres over her glasses. "I'll allow it, Counselor. We will hear from these witnesses later."

Torres deflates slightly. "Yes, Your Honor."

I watch Ramirez shift his weight, checking his phone, then slipping out of the courtroom.

Sikes moves to his final blow. "Your Honor, the state would like to present Exhibit 22B: the forensic analysis of fingerprints found on the shim that was located inside of Alice Stone's car, blocking the use of her brakes at the moment of the accident."

A new slide appears on the projector. A technical report with highlighted sections.

"The analysis confirms that the defendant's fingerprints appear on seventy-eight percent of the shim's surface." Sikes turns to face the jury directly. "And these were the only fingerprints found on this metal device. Fingerprints that could only be there if the defendant handled this and placed it underneath Alice Stone's brakes to cause an accident. The shim was found by the man towing the car out of the water, but it disappeared the next day as he was about to turn it over to the police. We will hear his testimony to this later on during this trial. But since her fingerprints are the only ones on its surface, we must conclude that she is the one who made it disappear, probably to get rid of any evidence leading to her."

My world collapses inward. Of course my fingerprints are on it. I touched it when I found the box that I thought Alice was leading me to. Ben knew I would. Counted on it. Every piece of evidence I thought would save me has been meticulously transformed into proof of my guilt. And he paid off the towing company. Gave them a huge donation to keep quiet about it.

Torres looks defeated beside me, shuffling papers without

purpose. Behind me, Rachel's pen has stopped its furious scratching. The courtroom seems to expand and contract with my breathing, faces blurring except for one—the forensic expert now taking the stand, ready to explain in scientific detail how my fingerprints prove my guilt.

I close my eyes briefly, the weight of Ben's perfect frame crushing me. He predicted every move I would make. Led me down each path like a master chess player, always twelve steps ahead. I never stood a chance.

When I open my eyes again, I notice something unexpected. Ramirez has returned, slipping quietly back into his spot at the rear of the courtroom. His expression has changed—something sharper, more focused in his gaze as it moves between the prosecutor, the evidence, and me.

For a moment, our eyes meet across the crowded room. He doesn't look away. Doesn't offer reassurance or condemnation. Just watches, his detective's mind visibly working behind that impassive face.

It's not much. Barely a spark in the darkness. But right now, it's all I have.

THIRTY-THREE

The consultation room is barely bigger than my jail cell—just a metal table bolted to the floor, two plastic chairs, and walls the color of old chewing gum. No windows. The guard locks the door behind us with a metallic click that makes me flinch, but for the first time today, I can breathe. No jury studying my every expression. No prosecutor twisting my life into a crime novel. No Ben, watching from the gallery with that perfect mask of concern. Just Rachel, her eyes red-rimmed from lack of sleep, sliding into the chair across from me.

"You're doing great," she says immediately, reaching across to squeeze my hands. Her fingers are warm against mine, which seem permanently cold these days. "Torres is useless, but we're building something."

I don't bother arguing with her assessment of my public defender. We both know he's drowning in this case. Rachel gave the police the SD card, but it doesn't show a lot, except for recordings of Alice doing normal things. There are a few recordings of them fighting, but what couple doesn't do that? It hardly proves he murdered her. I wonder why it scared Ben so much. He probably thought there was something on it that was damning to him.

"Did you see the fingerprint analysis? They have me all over that shim, Rachel. All over."

"Of course they do." She pulls a thick folder from her bag. "You found it. That's not proof you placed it in the car." She flips open the folder, revealing stacks of annotated papers, sticky notes protruding from every edge. My sister the advocate, in her element. "I've been pulling sixteen-hour days on this. And Emma, I've found things."

The urgency in her voice makes me lean forward. "What things?"

"Ben's past. His patterns." She extracts a paper with a timeline sketched in her handwriting. "I've tracked down three women from his med school days. None would go on record—they're still terrified of him—but they all described the same behavior."

My hands stop their nervous fidgeting. "What behavior?"

"The love-bombing phase. Expensive flowers. Morning coffee in bed. The 'when you know, you know' line he fed you." Rachel taps each bullet point on her notes. "Then isolation—subtle at first. Concerns about certain friends. Scheduling conflicts with family events. Always with a plausible explanation."

My stomach tightens. The pattern is so familiar it makes me nauseated. "That's exactly what he did with me."

I think about how I spent the first twenty minutes of Rachel's first visit apologizing—for the mess, for the orange jumpsuit, for not believing her warnings. Now she sits across from me like we've never been apart.

Rachel nods grimly. "Then the gaslighting. One woman—I'll call her J—said she would find her car keys in places she never left them. Credit card charges for restaurants she didn't remember visiting. Ben would express concern about her memory, suggest she see a neurologist. He even scheduled the appointment for her."

"Did she go?"

"Yes. Tests came back normal, of course. But Ben had already planted seeds with her family about her 'concerning memory issues.' When she tried to tell them about the strange things happening, they dismissed it." Rachel's eyes flash with anger. "By the time she broke things off, she was questioning her own sanity. Fifteen years later, and she still checks her doors are locked three times before going to bed."

I rub my wrists where the handcuffs have left permanent red marks. This may be true, but it doesn't prove my innocence. And we both know it. "Did any of them report him?"

"One tried. Campus police took a report about items missing from her apartment. Two days later, the items reappeared. She was warned about filing false reports." Rachel reaches into her folder again. "There's more. I've hired a PI—"

"Rachel, you can't afford—"

"Don't worry about that." She waves off my concern. "The PI's been tracking down former Harbor Heights neighbors and colleagues who knew Alice. People not connected to the Stone family money or influence."

Hope flickers, fragile as a candle flame. "And?"

"Three neighbors reported hearing arguments. One saw Alice with a bruise she tried to hide with makeup. And a former coworker at the gallery—not currently employed there—remembers Alice becoming increasingly withdrawn in the months before her death. Said she jumped at loud noises, checked her phone constantly."

Classic signs of abuse. Rachel's told me this. I still can't believe I trusted Ben over my own sister. She was right. She did meet Alice. She sees men like him all the time at the shelter. I should have believed her. But what good does this do me now?

"Will they testify?" My voice cracks on the question.

Rachel's expression tightens. "We're working on it. The PI is building trust, gathering statements. It's delicate."

I lean back, the brief flame of hope guttering. "It won't be enough. Not against the evidence they have." I lower my voice, though we're alone. "And Lily's testimony tomorrow will seal it. She's been building the case against me for months, Rachel. The troubled stepmother, obsessed with her father's first wife."

"We don't know what Lily will say," Rachel counters, but I can see the worry behind her reassurance.

"I do. I've lived with her. She hates me. She's her father's daughter." The words taste bitter. Despite everything, I still feel protective of Lily—another victim in Ben's perfect, poisonous family.

Rachel leans forward, gripping my hands tighter. "Listen to me. There's a pattern here, and patterns can be proven. That's not coincidence. You were just trying to find the truth."

"But everything is being used against me," I remind her. "They're saying that I engineered this whole thing and then tried to frame Ben."

"Which makes no sense," Rachel insists. "Why would you frame him, then keep the evidence that incriminates you? Torres should be hammering that logical inconsistency."

We both know why he isn't. Torres is outmatched, overwhelmed, possibly intimidated by going against the Stone family.

"I keep thinking about that basement," I whisper. "Everything was there, Rachel. Letter drafts in Ben's handwriting. If Ramirez had just found it before Ben cleared it out..."

"We're still pushing for another search warrant," Rachel says. "The PI found a contractor who renovated the Morrison Estate ten years ago. He remembers installing a hidden door in the pantry. Said Ben supervised the work personally, wouldn't allow photos or detailed plans."

A thread of possibility, thin as spider silk. I cling to it anyway.

"Time's up." The guard's voice cuts through the door before it opens.

Rachel gathers her papers quickly, stuffing them back into her folder. "I'll be there for Lily's testimony tomorrow," she promises. "Every step of the way."

As she stands to leave, she grips my shoulder, leaning close to my ear. "We'll find a way to expose him, Emma. The truth has to come out."

I nod, not trusting my voice. The truth. Such a simple concept, now buried beneath layers of Ben's careful manipulation.

As the guard leads me back toward the courtroom, I try to hold onto Rachel's certainty, her determination. But all I can think about is Lily taking the stand tomorrow, the final piece in Ben's perfect frame.

The holding cell is gray on gray on gray—concrete floor, concrete walls, metal bench bolted to concrete. No windows. Just a small, reinforced glass panel in the door that turns the corridor lights into slivers of false hope. I sit with my back against the wall, eyes closed. The sound of the door unlocking jerks me alert. Guards don't come this late unless something's wrong. The door swings open, and Detective Ramirez steps inside, his expression unreadable as the guard locks us in together.

"Mrs. Stone... Emma." He remains by the door, hands shoved deep in his pockets, shoulders tight beneath his rumpled jacket. He's aged since my arrest—new lines around his eyes, a slight stoop to his posture. The weight of the case? Or something else?

"Detective." My voice sounds rusty, unused. After a full day of silence in the courtroom, speaking feels strange. "Come to get another confession?"

His mouth twitches, not quite a smile. "I'm not here officially."

This gets my attention. I straighten, wincing as my back protests against the hard wall. "Then why are you here?"

Ramirez shifts his weight, glances at the door, then takes three steps into the cell. Still standing, but closer now. "Something about this case doesn't add up."

The words hang in the stale air between us. I study his face, looking for the trap, the trick, the next piece of Ben's elaborate game. "You're the one who arrested me."

"Based on evidence," he says, his voice dropping lower. "Evidence that looked solid at the time."

"And now?" I hardly dare to hope, but something has clearly changed for him to be here, off the record, after hours.

Ramirez drags a hand down his face. "Now I've spent two months going over every piece of this case. And there are... inconsistencies."

I say nothing, waiting. Let him talk. I don't want to get my hopes up.

"The letters you received," he continues after a moment. "The ones supposedly from Alice. You claimed Ben wrote them."

"He did. I found drafts in his handwriting in that hidden basement room."

"We found no trace of them or the room when we searched the house." Ramirez's tone isn't accusatory, just stating facts.

"Because it's a hidden entrance. I told you that during my initial interview." The frustration rises again, that helpless feeling of shouting truth into a void.

Ramirez nods slowly. "Here's one thing that's bothering me. Those letters mentioned Mack's Auto Shop specifically. If Ben wrote them to frame you, how would he know you'd go investigate the shop? Why plant that specific seed?"

The question catches me off guard. I've wondered the same thing countless times during sleepless nights in my cell. "I don't know. Maybe he mentioned it in conversation first, primed me to be interested. Or maybe he just knew I was curious enough to follow any lead."

He doesn't confirm or deny, just shifts to another question. "Tell me about finding the hidden room. Everything you remember."

I close my eyes, recalling that day with perfect clarity. "I was making dinner. Pasta. Ben was supposedly at the hospital for an emergency surgery. Lily was upstairs on a video call with her grandparents." The details matter, I realize. The specificity. "I noticed a seam in the pantry wall behind the spices that didn't match the rest of the paneling. Found a latch hidden behind a shelf of canned tomatoes."

Ramirez is taking mental notes, his gaze focused. "And inside?"

"Stairs leading to a finished basement. The walls were lined with shelving units full of boxes. All labeled in Ben's handwriting—'Alice—Clothes,' 'Alice—Books,' 'Alice—Photos.' There was a desk against one wall with cream-colored stationery identical to the letters I'd been receiving. And drafts, Detective. Drafts in Ben's handwriting, practicing Alice's voice."

"You touched these items?"

"Yes. I picked things up. I was in shock, trying to understand what I was seeing."

"Leaving your fingerprints," he murmurs, more to himself than to me.

"Exactly as he planned."

The memory of that moment when I was arrested—being stripped, searched—still burns.

"What else was in the room?" he presses.

"A folder labeled 'Emma—Instability Documentation.' Photos of me looking upset, confused, afraid—all taken without my knowledge. My daily schedule. Notes about when I was alone in the house." I swallow hard against the rising nausea. "He was building a case, Detective. Creating a narrative. Making sure no one would believe me. I figured he knew that the TikToker Mira Patel and her helpers were building a case against him, that they were closing in on him, and he needed a plan to get out of it. He needed a scapegoat. Me."

Ramirez is silent for a long moment, processing. When he speaks again, his voice has changed—less the detective interviewing a suspect, more the human being grappling with an uncomfortable truth.

"I've requested the original brake components from Alice's car for re-examination."

My heart skips. "They still exist?"

"Preserved in evidence storage. Standard procedure for vehicular fatalities, even those ruled accidental." He shifts his weight again.

The pieces click together in my mind like a terrible puzzle. Ben must have known Alice spoke to Rachel. He would have calculated that the police could find the necklace, access the SD card without needing a password. A perfect trail of evidence leading straight to him—the actual killer. That's when he began planning his way out, to make everything point to me. Hope flutters in my chest, fragile and frightening. "Why now? Why are you doing this?"

Ramirez meets my eyes directly for the first time. "I've known Ben for years. Attended his wedding to Alice. Coached Lily's soccer team for a season. I believed him when he identified Alice's body. Believed him when he expressed concern about your mental state."

I wait, sensing there's more.

"But I've also seen how evidence can be manipulated." His voice drops even lower. "How a careful person can construct a narrative that fits the facts while distorting the truth."

"You think that's what Ben did?"

"I think," he says carefully, "that a man willing to report his wife as mentally unstable might be capable of other deceptions." He checks his watch. "I need to go. The guard will be back soon for his rounds."

As he moves toward the door, I find my voice again. "Detective. If you find something—evidence that supports my story—will it be enough?"

Ramirez pauses, hand raised to signal the guard. "Truth has weight, Mrs. Stone. Even against money and power." He doesn't smile, doesn't offer false reassurance. "But truth needs evidence. And right now, all the evidence points to you."

As the door closes behind him, I remain on the hard bench, staring at the space he occupied. Not quite hope—I've learned better than to truly hope—but something adjacent to it. A small crack in the perfect frame Ben constructed. A single detective with enough doubt to keep looking.

It's not much. But right now, it's everything.

THIRTY-FOUR

They're moving me to another consultation room when I see her. Sitting alone in the witness-prep room, the door cracked open just enough for me to glimpse her profile as the guards pause to confer about something in hushed tones. I shouldn't look. Shouldn't care. She's the final nail in the coffin Ben has built for me. But I can't help myself. This girl who slept under my roof, who studied at the kitchen table while I cooked dinner, who watched me with calculating eyes so like her father's—she's still just a child caught in Ben's web, even if she doesn't know it.

The courthouse hallway buzzes with muted activity—lawyers in dark suits clutching coffee cups, clerks hurrying with stacks of files, families of defendants and victims sitting on hard benches with hollow eyes. No one pays attention to me in my orange jumpsuit and handcuffs, another faceless defendant being shuffled between rooms. The guards continue their whispered conversation about weekend plans. Twenty seconds of stillness. Twenty seconds to observe.

Lily looks smaller than I remember. Her shoulders curve inward beneath a prim black blazer that must be new—Ben making sure his daughter presents the perfect image of a grieving, traumatized child. Her dark hair falls forward, shielding part of her face as she stares at the floor, fingers working nervously at the edge of her phone case. Picking, picking, picking at the rubber bumper. A habit I've seen before, when she's anxious about a debate competition.

The prosecutor's voice drifts through the gap, but I can't make them out. Then, clearer: "—her obsession with your mother—" and "—need you to describe her erratic behavior—"

Lily's head lifts slightly at these phrases. I can't see her full expression, just the edge of her profile, but something in the set of her jaw is different. She's quiet. She seems uncertain.

She says something in response, her voice too low to catch. The prosecutor's tone sharpens, becoming more insistent. Lily's shoulders hunch further.

One of my guards checks his watch, signaling to the other that our impromptu pause has gone on too long. In seconds, they'll move me along, and this fragile moment of connection—if it can be called that—will end. I drink in the details greedily: Lily's right foot tapping a nervous rhythm against the carpet, her thumbnail now between her teeth, her school backpack slumped beside her chair as if she came directly from class.

"—just stick to what we practiced—" The prosecutor again, his tone softening to something almost paternal. Manipulative. The voice Ben uses when he wants something.

A new voice joins the hallway chorus—my public defender, Torres, speaking in low tones to someone just out of my line of sight. "—answers growing more hesitant each time we run through it—" and "—could work in our favor if she cracks on the stand—"

Torres hasn't seen me yet, doesn't realize I can hear him discussing Lily's preparation. There's something hungry in his tone, the desperation of a drowning man spotting a potential lifeline. If Lily falters in her testimony, if she contradicts the narrative Ben has crafted so carefully...

But hope is dangerous. I've learned that lesson well these past months. Hope makes you vulnerable, blinds you to the traps being laid. Lily has been her father's perfect ally from the beginning, watching me, reporting back, helping construct the image of the unstable, obsessed stepmother. Why would she change course now, at the moment of their triumph?

And yet.

Something in her posture nags at me. The slump of her shoulders. The restless movement of her hands. This isn't the confident, calculating Lily who watched me with cold eyes across the dinner table. This is a child being asked to bear the weight of adult decisions.

I think of Lily's face when I told her about the internship—how, for just a moment, genuine excitement replaced her usual coldness. And that afternoon in the kitchen when she laughed at my terrible pun about avocados, then quickly composed herself, as if remembering she wasn't supposed to like me. Those tiny cracks in her perfect Stone veneer, revealing the lonely, wounded girl beneath.

Did she believe Ben's lies about me? Or has she known the truth all along, forced to play her role in his elaborate performance?

The prosecutor's voice rises again, clearer now as someone shifts position inside the room, widening the gap in the doorway. "—need you to be absolutely clear about finding her with your mother's phone—"

Lily lifts her head fully now, and I can see her face in profile. Her eyes are red-rimmed, her bottom lip caught between her teeth. There's a tension in her expression I recognize—the look she gets when she's being pushed to do something that conflicts with her internal sense of right.

"I know what I saw," she says, her voice carrying just

enough for me to catch it. Not defiant. Not compliant. Ambiguous.

The prosecutor says something else, too low to hear. Lily doesn't respond, just takes a deep breath that lifts her shoulders and then drops them heavily. Her fingers stop their nervous movement, growing still as she seems to come to some decision. She straightens her back slightly, a physical gathering of resolve.

"Let's go." The guard's hand on my elbow breaks the moment. "Your attorney's waiting."

As they guide me down the hallway, I cast one final glance toward the prep room. Lily has stood up, gathering her backpack. For a split second, she looks toward the doorway—toward me—though I can't tell whether she actually sees me or simply senses being watched. Our eyes meet, or seem to, across the distance.

Then the moment breaks. The guards turn me around a corner, and Lily vanishes from sight. But the image stays with me—her straight back, her bitten lip, the look of someone preparing to step into a courtroom and speak words that will change lives forever.

Including her own.

* * *

The courtroom falls silent as Lily approaches the witness stand. She looks impossibly young in her skirt with a white shirt and black blazer. Ben's perfect daughter, the grieving child whose testimony will seal my fate. My hands tremble in my lap as she's sworn in, her voice barely audible as she promises to tell the truth, the whole truth, nothing but the truth. I wonder if she knows what truth even is any more, after living in Ben's carefully constructed reality. I wonder if any of us do.

Lily doesn't look at me as she settles into the witness chair. Doesn't look at Ben either, though I see his encouraging nod from the gallery's front row. Her eyes fix somewhere in the middle distance, focused on nothing, or perhaps on some internal battleground I can't see.

The prosecutor approaches, all sympathetic smiles and gentle tones. "Lily, I know this is difficult. We appreciate your courage in being here today."

She nods mechanically, hands folded in her lap like a schoolgirl at prayer.

"Can you tell the court about your relationship with the defendant, Emma Stone Caldwell?"

Lily clears her throat. "She's married to my father. My stepmother."

"And when did you first notice her strange behavior regarding your mother, Alice?"

Torres shifts beside me, straightening papers unnecessarily. This is it—the testimony that will destroy any remaining doubt about my guilt. I brace myself, fingernails digging half-moons into my palms.

"It started a few weeks after they got married." Lily's voice grows slightly stronger. "She asked questions about my mom. What she was like. What she enjoyed doing. Her habits."

"Did these questions seem normal to you? The kind any new stepmother might ask?"

Lily hesitates, the first crack in her rehearsed responses. "At first, yes. But they became... more frequent. More specific."

"Can you give us an example?"

Another hesitation, longer this time. "She asked about my mom's routines. Her medications. Whether she and my dad argued."

The prosecutor nods encouragingly. "And did you ever find Emma going through your mother's belongings?"

This is the critical point—the moment Lily claimed to have caught me with Alice's phone. The cornerstone of Ben's frame. I can't breathe as I wait for her answer.

"She..." Lily's voice falters. She glances down at her hands, now twisted together in her lap. "She was interested in my mom. Asking questions."

Not the answer the prosecutor expected. He blinks, recalibrates. "Lily, do you recall telling your father that you found Emma with your mother's phone?"

Lily's shoulders tense visibly. "I told him that, yes."

"Because that's what you saw, correct?"

The courtroom seems to hold its collective breath. Lily's eyes flick to Ben for the first time—a quick, nervous glance that I recognize from a hundred dinner conversations. Seeking approval. Seeking direction.

"Lily?" the prosecutor prompts when her silence stretches too long.

"Yes," she says finally. "That's what I told him."

The careful phrasing isn't lost on the prosecutor. He frowns slightly, approaches the stand. "Let me be more direct. Did you see Emma with your mother's phone?"

Lily's gaze drops to her hands again. "I saw her with a phone, yes. It looked a lot like my mom's."

Behind me, I hear Rachel's sharp intake of breath. The prosecutor's expression tightens almost imperceptibly.

"Let's move on," he says, regrouping. "Did Emma ever express hatred toward your mother? Ever say she was glad Alice was gone?"

"No." This comes quickly, firmly. "She never said anything like that."

The prosecutor's frown deepens. This is not the testimony he prepared, not the final nail in my coffin he promised the jury in his opening statement.

"Did you ever witness Emma threaten your father? Show aggression toward him?"

Lily's eyes flick up again, this time toward me. Our gazes lock across the courtroom. Something passes between us—not quite understanding, but recognition. Two people caught in Ben's web, one still tangled, one beginning to break free.

"No." Another firm denial. "Emma was never aggressive."

The prosecutor's frustration is palpable now. He glances toward Ben, whose face has gone carefully blank. The perfect mask slipping just enough to reveal the calculation beneath.

"Lily," the prosecutor says, his tone hardening slightly, "let me remind you that you're under oath. Your previous statements to the police described Emma as 'increasingly unstable' and 'obsessed' with your mother's death. Were those statements accurate?"

Lily's hands tremble visibly. She looks at Ben again, longer this time. Then at me. Then down at her trembling hands.

"I..." Her voice cracks. She takes a deep breath, steadying herself. When she looks up, something has changed in her expression—a resolution, a clearing. "I need to tell the truth."

The words fall into the silent courtroom like stones into still water, sending ripples of tension through the gallery. The prosecutor freezes, pen hovering above his notepad.

"Lily," he says carefully, "you are telling the truth. You're under oath."

"No." Her voice grows stronger, steadier. "I've been telling my father's truth. Not mine."

A murmur sweeps through the courtroom like wind through dry leaves. The judge leans forward. Ben's posture stiffens, his expression hardening into something I recognize with visceral fear—the look that preceded his worst moments of rage.

"Your Honor," the prosecutor says quickly, "may we approach?"

But Lily isn't finished. "My father told me what to say. About Emma. About my mother's phone. About everything." Her words tumble out faster now, as if she fears being stopped. "He made me practice my statements. Said it was to protect our family. But I need to tell what really happened."

The gallery erupts in whispers. The judge bangs her gavel once, twice. "Order! Counsel, approach the bench immediately."

As Sikes and Torres hurry forward, I sit frozen in disbelief. Lily's eyes meet mine again across the courtroom chaos—terrified but somehow lighter, as if a great weight has lifted from her slight shoulders.

In the back of the courtroom, movement catches my eye. Ramirez is standing, phone to his ear, speaking urgently. Our eyes meet briefly before he slips out the side door, his expression transformed by purposeful intensity.

Torres returns to our table, leaning close to whisper in my ear. "The judge has called a recess. Lily's going to be questioned in chambers with a child advocate present." His voice contains something I haven't heard before—hope. "This changes everything, Emma."

As court officers move to escort Lily from the stand, she stands straighter, taller. Ben rises from his seat, one hand outstretched toward his daughter. "Lily," he calls, his voice carrying that perfect note of fatherly concern. "Sweetheart, you're confused. Let me help you."

Lily steps back, away from his reach. "No, Dad." Two simple words, spoken with quiet certainty. "Not any more."

The bailiff leads her away through a side door as Ben sinks back into his seat, mask finally slipping to reveal naked fury beneath. He doesn't look at me, but I feel his rage radiating across the courtroom like heat from a fire.

Rachel squeezes my shoulder from behind. "Ramirez just left to request a search warrant," she whispers. "Based on Lily's statement about being coached. He's going back to the house."

Back to the Morrison Estate. Back to the pantry with its hidden door. Back to whatever evidence Ben might have missed in his haste to clear out his secret room.

As the guards come to lead me back to holding, I feel something crack open inside my chest—not quite hope, not after so many disappointments, but possibility. Lily broke free from Ben's control. Spoke her truth despite his manipulation, despite his power over her.

The truth has a voice now. And maybe, just maybe, it will be loud enough to drown out Ben's perfect lies.

THIRTY-FIVE

I sit at the defense table, my heart hammering against my ribs as the courtroom buzzes with whispers. The wooden chair creaks beneath me as I shift my weight, hands clasped so tightly my knuckles have gone white. Third day of trial. Third chance at truth. My mouth is dry, tongue like sandpaper against my teeth. I haven't slept. Haven't eaten. Exist in a suspended state between hope and terror after yesterday's bombshell from Lily.

Torres leans toward me, his breath smelling of coffee and mint. "Lily has agreed to testify again," he whispers, excitement making his voice crack. "Full testimony this time. No chambers. No child advocate restricting questions."

I stare at him, disbelieving. "They're letting her?"

"Judge ruled she's competent to testify. And since she's the one who requested to continue..." His eyes dart to the prosecution table where Sikes sits reviewing notes, back rigid with confidence he doesn't deserve. "They think she's just confused. That they can redirect her, get her back on script."

Across the room, Ben sits perfectly still in his tailored suit with Robert and Margaret flanking him like grim sentinels. His eyes never leave the door where witnesses enter. Waiting for his daughter. Planning his next move.

The bailiff's voice cuts through the murmurs. "All rise. The Honorable Judge Eliza Montgomery presiding."

We stand. My legs shake. The judge enters, face unreadable as stone as she takes her seat and nods for us to do the same.

"Are counsel prepared to continue?" she asks, gaze sweeping from Torres to Sikes.

"Yes, Your Honor." Sikes's voice drips with assurance. "The state requests to continue direct examination of Lily Stone."

The judge nods. "Bailiff, please bring in the witness."

A hush falls over the courtroom as the side door opens. Lily enters. She wears a simple blue dress, hair pulled back with a headband. Seventeen going on thirty in her careful, measured steps. Her eyes fix straight ahead, deliberately avoiding the place where her father sits. Deliberately avoiding me.

"Remember," Torres whispers, "she requested this. Whatever comes next, she's choosing to be here."

Lily reaches the witness stand. The bailiff administers the oath again, and her "I do" is barely audible, a ghost of sound in the tense silence.

Sikes approaches, all practiced sympathy. "Miss Stone, thank you for returning today. I know this is difficult."

Lily nods, hands folded in her lap.

"Yesterday, you made some statements that contradicted your prior testimony to the police. Have you had time to reflect on those statements?"

"Yes." Her voice is small but steady.

"And would you like to clarify anything about your previous testimony?"

Torres tenses beside me, pen poised over his legal pad. Here it is. The moment Sikes tries to pull her back into Ben's narrative.

"I want to tell the whole truth." Lily's eyes lift, scanning the courtroom before landing on her father. The first direct look since she entered. Something passes between them—challenge from her, threat from him.

She turns away first, gaze dropping to her hands. "I need to explain my relationship with Emma."

Sikes frowns slightly, but nods. "Please do."

"When my father married Emma, I hated her." The words come out flat, emotionless. "Not because she did anything wrong. Because she wasn't my mom."

I feel a pang in my chest, sharp and sudden. Despite everything, her pain still reaches me.

"I tried to make her life difficult," Lily continues. "I sabotaged things around the house and blamed her. I reported private conversations to my dad out of context. I looked for ways to make her seem unstable. I even did stuff at her work, at my grandparents' agency, to make her look bad. Spread rumors and removed important papers and changed numbers on her computer before an important presentation."

Sikes's expression tightens. This isn't the testimony he expected. "Miss Stone, are you saying you lied in your police statements?"

"Not completely. I just... twisted things." Her voice wavers slightly. "When Emma started finding things—my mom's phone especially—I told my dad right away. I thought she was the problem. I thought if I could prove it, things would go back to how they were before. Just me and Dad."

The jury shifts in their seats, several members leaning forward.

"So you admit to manipulating situations to make Emma appear unstable?" Sikes asks, his tone sharpening as he realizes he's losing control of his star witness.

"Yes." Lily meets his gaze directly. "But then I saw something that changed everything."

The courtroom falls silent. Even the usual shuffling of

papers and clearing of throats ceases. Everyone holds their breath, waiting.

"What did you see, Lily?" Torres calls out, unable to contain himself.

"Objection!" Sikes snaps. "Counsel is not conducting cross-examination."

"Sustained." The judge fixes Torres with a stern look. "Mr. Torres, wait your turn."

Lily continues before Sikes can form his next question. "I recorded a video of them. Of Emma and my dad. In the basement."

My pulse jumps, thudding so loudly in my ears I almost can't hear Sikes's next words.

"A video? When was this taken?"

"The night Emma was arrested." Lily's hands twist together in her lap. "I've been recording things for weeks. To catch Emma doing something wrong. To prove to Dad she was bad for us."

A tremor runs through me. Weeks of surveillance. Weeks of a child watching, recording, waiting to catch me in some imagined transgression. But instead, she caught her father.

"I used my phone," Lily continues, her voice dropping. "To record them."

Sikes paces now, thrown off balance by this revelation. "And what exactly did these recordings capture?"

"My dad." Lily's voice cracks, tears welling in her eyes. "Saying things. Doing things. Things that proved Emma was telling the truth all along."

I can't breathe. Can't move. The room seems to tilt around me as Lily's words sink in. Evidence. Real, concrete evidence beyond testimony and conjecture. Something Ben couldn't manipulate or destroy.

"I thought Emma was the problem." Lily's voice breaks completely now, tears spilling down her cheeks. "I wanted to prove it to Dad. But the recordings showed me who the real monster was."

The gallery erupts in whispers. The judge doesn't bang her gavel, equally stunned by this turn.

Ben's face transforms before my eyes. The perfect mask of concerned father crumbles, revealing something cold and calculating beneath. His jaw tightens, eyes narrowing to slits as he stares at his daughter. Not with hurt or betrayal—with fury. With the same expression he wore in the basement that night when I discovered his secrets.

The look of a man who has just lost control of his perfect frame.

The courtroom technician wheels in a monitor on a metal cart, the wheels squeaking against the polished floor. The sound slices through the silence that followed Lily's revelation. I can't take my eyes off her—this child who holds my fate in her hands, who watched and recorded while her father systematically destroyed my life. Torres grips my arm, a silent warning to maintain composure as the technician connects cables methodically. Black cords snake across the floor like harbingers of truth about to be unleashed.

Lily watches the setup, her shoulders rigid under her blue dress. "I have the videos on my phone," she says, her voice steadier now. "I backed them up to my private cloud account too. Dad doesn't know about it. The first one I will show you was when my dad burned some letters in their bedroom fireplace." Lily's eyes flick to Ben, then away. "The second was the night Emma was arrested. I heard shouting from the basement and walked down the stairwell, recording them."

Torres is on his feet before Sikes can continue. "Your Honor, the defense requests permission to play these recordings for the court immediately. They contain exculpatory evidence directly relevant to these proceedings."

"Objection!" Sikes nearly shouts. "These recordings haven't been authenticated or submitted during discovery. We have no way to verify they haven't been altered."

The judge turns to Lily. "Miss Stone, have you edited or altered these recordings in any way?"

"No, Your Honor." Lily's voice is clear, confident for the first time. "They're the original files with timestamps. I can show the metadata."

The judge considers for a long moment, fingers steepled beneath her chin. "Given the extraordinary circumstances and the defendant's constitutional right to present exculpatory evidence, I'll allow the recordings to be played." She fixes Sikes with a stern look. "The prosecution will have full opportunity to challenge their authenticity afterward."

Sikes sinks back into his chair, jaw tight with barely contained fury. Beside him, his assistant whispers frantically in his ear.

The technician approaches Lily for her phone. She unplugs it from a portable charger in her pocket and unlocks it with trembling fingers. "It's in my secured folder," she explains, navigating to the files. "The first one is labeled 'EB1' and the second is 'EB2'."

Torres moves closer to the witness stand. "Lily, what do those labels mean?"

"Evidence against Ben, one and two." Her voice is small again. "I started labeling them that after... after I realized what they showed."

The technician connects her phone to the monitor. The large screen remains black as he tests the connection. Each second stretches into eternity as I grip the edge of the table, my nails digging into the wood. This is it. Proof. Vindication. If the videos show what Lily claims...

"We're ready, Your Honor," the technician announces.

The judge nods. "Proceed with the first recording."

The lights dim slightly. The screen flickers to life, showing a bedroom view from an odd angle—looking inside through a cracked-open door. It's our bedroom. The master suite at the Morrison Estate. My breath catches in my throat as two figures come into view—Ben and me, standing near the fireplace.

I'm holding papers to my chest. Ben's face is twisted with rage. The audio is surprisingly clear.

"Emma, give me those letters." Ben's voice fills the courtroom, precise and cold. "Give them to me."

The courtroom is utterly silent as we watch the scene unfold. I feel exposed, raw, seeing myself displayed so publicly in a private moment. But there's validation too—proof that I didn't imagine or fabricate this moment. That it happened exactly as I described to Ramirez. The letters were real.

The video continues for another minute.

Torres steps forward. "Please play the second recording."

The screen remains dark for a moment, then flickers back to life. A different angle now—looking down the basement stairs, capturing the concrete floor below and part of a desk. The timestamp shows 7:23 p.m. the night of my arrest. The basement. The secret room Ben claimed never existed.

Two figures enter the frame—Ben descending the stairs, me backing away from him across the concrete floor. The lighting is poor, but Ben's voice cuts through the darkness with crystal clarity.

"What are you doing down here? Looking for something?" he asks, casual and menacing at once.

And then it comes—the moment that changes everything. Ben's damning confession, clear as a bell.

Murmurs ripple through the courtroom. The judge doesn't silence them, her own expression frozen in shock.

The recording continues, capturing every word of Ben's

admission. His casual description of the "contingency plan" to frame me if it became necessary.

Then the final nail: "Alice made choices. So have you."

As the video continues playing our physical struggle, Ben rises from his seat across the courtroom. "This is a fabrication!" he shouts, pointing at the screen. "That's not me! Those aren't my words!"

"Order!" The judge slams her gavel. "Dr. Stone, sit down immediately!"

But Ben is beyond control now, his perfect mask shattered completely. "My daughter has been manipulated! This recording has been doctored!"

"Bailiff!" The judge calls, banging her gavel again.

On screen, the recording captures my desperate attempt to escape up the basement stairs, Ben's pursuit, his hand grabbing my wrist with clinical precision. "You need help, Emma. You're not well."

The courtroom erupts in chaos as Ben continues shouting objections. Through the commotion, I see Detective Ramirez moving from the back of the room, his purposeful stride carrying him toward Ben. His hand moves to his belt, where his handcuffs hang in silent promise.

The video reaches its climax—Ben's cold statement as he pins me to the basement floor: "You can't leave, Emma. Not with what you know now."

The screen goes black, but the confession echoes in the stunned silence that follows. One heartbeat. Two. Then chaos erupts like a dam breaking. Ben lunges to his feet, face contorted beyond recognition. No longer the composed surgeon, the grieving widower, the concerned father. Just raw, exposed rage as he lunges toward the witness stand.

"You ungrateful little—" The words tear from his throat, savage and unfinished as two court officers move efficiently, intercepting him before he can reach Lily.

She flinches but doesn't run, watching her father struggle against the officers' grip with wide, wounded eyes. The girl who spent years worshipping him, molding herself to his expectations, now witnessing the monster beneath the mask in full public view.

"Order! Order in my court!" The judge's gavel pounds a frantic rhythm, barely audible above the gallery's uproar. Reporters scramble toward the doors, phones clutched in white-knuckled grips. The jury stares, transfixed by the spectacle of Benjamin Stone's unraveling.

Ben thrashes against restraint, surgeon's hands curled into claws. "She's lying! The recording is fake! This is a conspiracy against me!"

Each desperate claim lands with hollow impotence against the weight of his recorded confession. Robert and Margaret have retreated to the far end of their bench, faces ashen with shock or perhaps—finally—recognition of their son's true nature.

Ramirez reaches Ben's side, handcuffs already unclipped from his belt. His movements are deliberate, almost ceremonial, as he steps between the court officers.

"Benjamin Stone," he announces, voice carrying through the chaos with official finality, "you're under arrest for the murder of Alice Graham Stone and attempted framing of Emma Caldwell."

My legs weaken beneath me. Torres grips my elbow, steadying me as I sink back into my chair.

"You have the right to remain silent," Ramirez continues, the familiar cadence of Miranda rights flowing easily. "Anything you say can and will be used against you in a court of law."

Ben's struggles cease as the cold metal closes around his wrists with a definitive click. The sound cuts through the pandemonium small but final. The same sound I heard the night he framed me, now binding him instead.

"This is ridiculous," Ben hisses, but the confident command has drained from his voice, replaced by something high and desperate. "Lucas. It's me. You know me. I save children's lives. Buddy. You can't—"

"You have the right to an attorney," Ramirez continues, unmoved. "If you cannot afford an attorney, one will be provided for you."

I watch Ben's transformation with a strange detachment, as if observing a surgical procedure from behind glass. The precise, controlled man who terrorized me for months crumbles by increments. His shoulders slump. His jaw works silently, forming arguments that find no voice. The mask he's worn so perfectly falls away completely, revealing the terrified core beneath.

Tears stream down my face, hot and uncontrolled. Not from fear or pain this time, but release. Vindication. The unburdening of truth finally revealed. Torres squeezes my shoulder, his own eyes bright with emotion.

"We did it," he whispers, voice thick. "You did it, Emma. You held on long enough for the truth to come out."

Across the courtroom, Rachel pushes through the crowd toward me, her face transformed by fierce joy. She reaches over the barrier, grabbing my hand with crushing strength. "I told you," she says, her voice breaking. "I told you the truth would come out."

The judge's gavel crashes down again. "This court is in recess," she announces, voice cutting through the diminishing chaos. "Counsel for both sides, in my chambers immediately."

At these words, Lily finally moves, stepping down from the witness stand with careful, measured steps. Her face holds grief and relief in equal measure—the complicated emotion of doing the right thing at tremendous personal cost. Our eyes meet briefly across the chaos. No words pass between us, just a moment of recognition. Two women broken by the same man, finding strength to stand against him.

"I'm sorry," she mouths, though whether to me or to herself, I can't tell.

The judge rises, and the bailiff calls for all to stand. I push myself upright on trembling legs, watching as Ramirez guides Ben toward the side door that leads to holding cells. Ben's head swivels back toward the courtroom as they reach the threshold.

Our eyes lock across the distance. His burn with naked hatred, all pretense of love or concern incinerated in the flames of his exposure. But beneath the rage, I see something else. Fear. The same fear Alice must have felt in her final moments. The fear I lived with for months as he systematically destroyed my sense of reality.

I hold his gaze, refusing to look away this time. Not backing down. Not doubting myself. The truth stands between us now, immovable and final.

Then he's gone, the door closing behind him with a heavy thud that resonates through my bones. Two months in custody. Two months of being called delusional, unstable, obsessed. Two months of carefully constructed lies presented as evidence against me. So well-constructed I almost believed them myself.

And now, in the span of twenty minutes, vindication.

My legs give way as the adrenaline drains from my system. I collapse back into my chair, body trembling with aftershocks of fear and relief. Torres is beside me, one hand on my arm, saying something I can't process through the rushing in my ears. Rachel pushes past the barrier, ignoring the bailiff's protest, to wrap her arms around my shoulders.

"It's over," she says against my hair, her voice fierce and tender at once. "It's over, Emma. Case is dismissed. You're free."

Free. The word floats through my consciousness, foreign and familiar at once. I've spent so long fighting to prove my innocence, to expose Ben's crimes, that I've forgotten what freedom feels like. The absence of fear. The presence of truth.

As the courtroom slowly empties around us, I remain seated, allowing the reality to settle into my bones. Benjamin Stone, respected surgeon and pillar of the community, is being processed into the same system he engineered for me. The same cells. The same jumpsuit. The same presumption of guilt.

My body still trembles, but something has shifted inside me. The constant vigilance, the desperate need to be believed—it eases by small degrees, muscles unclenching one by one. I am not completely whole. May never be after what he's done. But I am believed. I am vindicated.

And most importantly, I am free.

THIRTY-SIX

The Spanish-style house appears in my windshield—coral stucco walls and terracotta roof tiles gleaming in morning light. Our house. Not Ben's. I pull into the driveway, tires crunching on fresh gravel. Three months since the trial ended, two weeks since we moved in, and I still feel a jolt of disbelief each time I approach this place.

I kill the engine and sit for a moment, breathing in the quiet. Palm fronds sway against a cloudless sky. A mockingbird trills from the orange tree by the front door. Normal sounds. Safe sounds.

The front door sticks slightly—something I need to fix but secretly love. A small imperfection in a house we chose together. I push it open and step into light. So much light. Windows everywhere, no heavy drapes to block the sun, no dark corners where secrets hide. The open floor plan stretches before me—kitchen flowing into dining area flowing into living room. No maze of hallways. No hidden rooms behind pantry shelves.

Unpacked boxes line the entryway, labeled in my decisive handwriting. "KITCHEN—EVERYDAY." "LIVING ROOM

—BOOKS." "LILY—ART SUPPLIES." The moving truck left yesterday, carrying away furniture from my old apartment, things I'd stored when marrying Ben, thinking one day I might sell them. Nothing from the Morrison Estate except a few photos of Alice. We both decided we needed clean slates.

I run my fingers along the kitchen counter—cool quartz, specked with blue. Not the black granite Ben insisted showed fewer stains. My touch lingers on the fruit bowl Lily and I bought at a beach market last weekend. Oranges and apples tumble together, bright against white ceramic.

"Mine," I whisper, the word still unfamiliar on my tongue after months of having nothing. No home. No possessions. Not even my name, reduced to "the defendant" in court transcripts.

Footsteps thunder down the stairs—quick, light, unburdened. Lily appears, backpack slung over one shoulder, leather therapy journal clutched in her other hand. Her hair is pulled into a messy bun, strands escaping around her face. She's wearing ripped jeans and a faded band T-shirt that would have horrified Margaret. Three months ago, she wouldn't have dared.

"Morning," she says, and her smile reaches her eyes. That's new too. Before, her smiles were calculated performances, perfect curves that never warmed her gaze. "I made coffee."

"My hero." I move toward the pot, inhaling the rich scent. Another small freedom—choosing our own coffee instead of the precise brand Ben insisted was the only acceptable option. "I went downtown and got us fresh donuts. Thought we deserved it."

"Yum!"

Lily drops her backpack on a kitchen stool. Her movements are different now—looser, less measured. She no longer calculates each gesture for maximum effect. "Don't forget we have therapy today," she reminds me, grabbing a glass from the cabinet.

I nod, watching her pour orange juice. "Four o'clock. I've got it on my calendar."

"Cool." She takes a long drink, then reaches for a donut. "Dr. Foster wants to talk about the college tour next week. She thinks it's a good sign I'm planning that far ahead."

Dr. Foster—Lily's therapist. Not the psychiatrist Ben had selected to document my "instability," but a gentle-voiced woman specializing in trauma recovery. Twice weekly sessions for Lily. Once weekly for me. Monthly joint sessions where we navigate our complicated shared history.

"It is a good sign," I agree, pouring coffee into a mug painted with sunflowers—another market find. "Stanford has an amazing photography program."

Lily's face brightens at the mention of her newest passion. She turns toward the living room wall where we've hung her recent projects—abstract photographs and mixed media pieces from art therapy. Splashes of color and shadow, fragmented images that Dr. Foster says reveal remarkable progress in processing trauma. I see it too—the early pieces all darkness and jagged edges, the newer ones allowing light to break through.

"Mr. Harmon says my portfolio is getting stronger," she says, referring to her art teacher. "He thinks I should submit to that youth exhibition in Tampa."

"You should." I sip my coffee, marveling at this conversation. Six months ago, we communicated in careful barbs and silent accusations. Now we discuss art exhibitions and college tours over morning coffee.

Lily bites into her donut, checking her phone. "I'm giving Zoe a ride to school today. I should get going." She shoulders her backpack, grabs her journal. "See you at therapy."

"See you then," I say, watching her head toward the door. She pauses by the wall of photographs, adjusting one frame that hangs slightly crooked. A small, unconscious gesture that speaks volumes—caring for this space, claiming it as her own.

The door closes behind her, and I check my watch. 8:17. I need to hurry if I'm going to make my 9 a.m. meeting at Stone Advertising. The irony doesn't escape me—returning to work for the family whose son destroyed my life. But Robert's apology came with a promotion and a corner office, his way of making amends while saving the company's reputation. The devil you know, Rachel said when I accepted. Sometimes she's right.

I drain my coffee, rinse the mug, set it in the dish drainer. Simple tasks that ground me in the present. I gather my portfolio and keys, take one last look around the sunlit kitchen. No ghosts here. No memories lurking in shadows. Just morning light on clean counters, the lingering scent of coffee, a half-empty box of donuts.

Just home.

The corner office feels earned, not gifted. Not a consolation prize. Not Robert's attempt to bury a scandal. Sunlight spills through floor-to-ceiling windows, illuminating walls bare of the motivational quotes Robert always insisted every executive should display. My walls hold only client work and Lily's recent photographs—stark urban landscapes that capture beauty in broken things. My desk faces the door, not the window. I need to see who's coming. Some habits die harder than others.

Digital awards line the credenza behind me—three Gold ADDYs from last quarter's campaigns, a Clio for the homeless youth initiative, a Silver Pencil for the prescription drug awareness series. Tangible proof of worth. Evidence that my mind still works despite Ben's attempt to convince the world otherwise. The nameplate on my desk reads "Emma Caldwell, Creative Director"—my own name, not Stone. Another reclamation.

Robert appears in the doorway, silver hair immaculate as

always, but his posture different—less imperial, more cautious. The trial changed him too. Forced him to face what his son became under his watchful eye.

"Morning, Emma." He doesn't enter without permission any more. Another change.

"Robert." I nod, closing the document on my screen. "How was the charity gala?"

"Predictable." He shifts his weight, hands clasped behind his back. "The Hartman campaign numbers came in."

This catches my attention. Hartman Pharmaceuticals—my first major project after returning, the one I fought for despite concerns about my "fragile state." The one Robert reluctantly greenlit after I presented a concept so compelling even Margaret admitted its brilliance.

"And?" I keep my voice neutral, professional. Not betraying how much this matters.

Robert slides a folder across my desk. "Best quarter they've had in five years. The board is thrilled." He pauses, something like respect flickering across his features. "You were right about the approach."

I flip through the report, satisfaction warming my chest. Market share up seventeen percent. Brand recognition increased across all demographics. Social media engagement tripled. Numbers don't lie, don't gaslight, don't manipulate. Numbers are just truth.

"We're expanding the campaign next quarter," Robert continues. "National rollout. The client specifically requested you lead the team."

Six months ago, I would have gushed gratitude, desperate for validation. Now I simply nod. "I'll review the numbers and schedule a strategy session for next week."

Robert lingers, uncomfortable with this new dynamic—me not falling over myself to please him, him not holding all the power. "Margaret asked if you and Lily might join us for dinner next month. When you're ready."

The invitation hangs between us. Margaret—who testified as a character witness for her son until the videos played, who collapsed in the gallery as his confession echoed through the courtroom, who hasn't spoken his name since. Margaret, who lost everything and nothing at once.

"I'll check with Lily," I say, noncommittal. "She's setting her own boundaries these days."

"Of course." Robert nods, accepting this new reality where a seventeen-year-old's wishes matter. "Just... let us know."

He retreats, leaving the folder open before me. I trace the upward trajectory of the graph with my finger, remembering how close I came to losing this—my career, my freedom, my sanity. Ben's frame was so perfect, so meticulous. If not for Lily's sneaking around recording everything, I'd be serving twenty years while he performed surgeries and accepted humanitarian awards.

My phone buzzes, pulling me from the dark path. A text from Lily:

Don't forget to meet me outside right before 4 p.m.

I smile, typing quickly:

I wouldn't.

I add a heart emoji—something I wouldn't have dared months ago when our relationship balanced on razor wire.

Outside my office, the creative department hums with energy. Art directors huddled over tablets. Copywriters debating headline options. Account managers striding purposefully between meetings. I used to throw myself into this vortex, working fourteen-hour days, sacrificing sleep and health for the next great concept, the next nod of approval from Robert.

Not any more.

My calendar is color-coded now. Yellow blocks for client meetings. Blue for creative development. Green for therapy—individual and joint sessions with Lily. Red for non-negotiable personal time. The system keeps me anchored when old habits surface—the urge to prove my worth through martyrdom, to seek validation through exhaustion.

I turn back to my computer, reviewing presentation slides for tomorrow's pitch. My work is better now—sharper, more honest. Trauma stripped away pretense, left me with clarity I never had before. I see through marketing bullshit faster, cut to authentic stories that resonate because they're true.

At 3:30, my phone chimes with a calendar alert. Time to wrap up for therapy. The old Emma would have silenced it, pushed through, prioritized client needs over personal ones. The new Emma saves her work, closes unnecessary tabs, drafts a concise email to the creative team with tomorrow's objectives.

My office door remains open—another departure from Ben's influence. He kept doors closed, conversations private, created information silos that prevented anyone from seeing the complete picture. I've dismantled those barriers. Transparency as rebellion against a life built on secrets.

"Heading out early?" Sarah, my new assistant, appears with a stack of contracts needing signatures.

"Therapy day," I explain, signing each document with quick, decisive strokes. No apologies, no justifications. Just fact.

"Got it." She gathers the signed papers. "The Mercer team called. They want to move up Thursday's presentation."

"Tell them we're firm on Thursday. Moving it compromises our process." The words come easily now. No anxious need to accommodate every client whim, to bend myself into shapes that hurt.

I pack my laptop and portfolio into my bag, check my watch. Plenty of time. Dr. Foster's office sits halfway between here and our home—a triangulation of healing points in our new geography.

The elevator descends smoothly, mirrored walls reflecting a woman I'm still getting reacquainted with. Hair cut to shoulder length—free of the long style Ben preferred. Clothes chosen for comfort and confidence, not to meet someone else's specification. Eyes clear, direct, no longer darting to gauge reactions or seek approval.

In the lobby, interns and account coordinators hurry past, nodding respectfully. They know my story—everyone does. The trial made national news, Ben's confession played on every network and all social media platforms. "SURGEON KILLER EXPOSED BY DAUGHTER'S SECRET RECORDINGS." "GASLIGHTING HUSBAND FRAMED WIFE FOR MURDER."

I push through the revolving door into afternoon sunlight. The parking garage sits across the street, cars gleaming under fluorescent lights. I walk with purpose, keys already in hand—another safety habit that may never fade.

My watch reads exactly 3:40 p.m. On schedule. In control. The elevator lifts me to my parking level, doors opening on the black sedan I bought after the trial. No shared vehicles. Nothing connected to the past. Just mine.

I slide behind the wheel, set my bag on the passenger seat, take a moment to breathe. Three months ago, I sat in a courtroom watching my life reassemble from shattered pieces. Three months of rebuilding, reclaiming, remembering who I was before Ben attempted to erase me.

Not whole yet. Not completely healed. But present. Real. Moving forward one precisely scheduled appointment at a time.

THIRTY-SEVEN

Golden hour paints our driveway in honey light, the Spanish-style house warm against deepening blue sky. I turn off the ignition, watching shadow patterns from the palm trees slide across the hood of my car. Such a normal moment. Returning home after the therapy session. Planning dinner. Thinking about tomorrow's presentation. The ordinary rhythms we've fought so hard to establish these past months. Lily's already out of her car, heading inside with her backpack and journal, moving with the easy confidence of someone on familiar territory.

"I'll start the rice," she calls over her shoulder, fishing house keys from her pocket. Another small miracle—Lily cooking, taking initiative, claiming space in our home without calculation or agenda.

"Thanks. I'll grab the mail." I step out into late-afternoon warmth, inhaling the scent of jasmine from the vine we planted along the fence line. Our fence. Our jasmine. Our choice.

The mailbox stands at the end of the driveway—simple black metal on a wooden post. Nothing like the ornate monstrosity at the Morrison Estate with its custom Stone family crest. I flip it open, extracting the usual stack—bills, magazines, flyers for local businesses. The routine task no longer fills me with dread. No more mysterious notes slipped between legitimate mail. No more psychological warfare disguised as correspondence.

Until now.

My fingers freeze on a cream-colored envelope nestled between the electric bill and a home decor catalog. No return address. Just my name—*Emma Caldwell*—written in flowing script I'd recognize anywhere. The distinctive loop of the *E*. The precise angle of the *C*. Handwriting I studied in all those letters. Handwriting that provided the first clues to Ben's deception when I wouldn't listen.

Alice's handwriting.

My pulse hammers against my temples as I stare at the envelope. Impossible. Alice is dead. Ben killed her in cold blood. We know this now.

Yet here is her handwriting, undeniable, on cream stationery nearly identical to the letters that led me down the rabbit hole of Ben's deception.

I turn the envelope over, examining every detail with the heightened awareness of someone who's survived elaborate manipulation. The postmark is from Tampa, dated two days ago. The stamp perfectly straight. No distinctive marks or smudges that might suggest hasty handling.

My gaze lifts to our house—warm light spilling from windows, Lily visible through the kitchen archway unpacking groceries we bought on our way home. Our refrigerator covered with her photographs and my meeting schedule. The life we've carefully rebuilt from the wreckage Ben left behind.

Do I open this? Do I invite whatever chaos this letter contains into our healing sanctuary? Dr. Foster's voice echoes in my memory from last week's session: *Recovery isn't linear. Expect triggers. Expect setbacks. They don't erase your progress.*

But this isn't just a trigger. This is active disruption.

Someone—not Alice, it can't be Alice—using her handwriting to reach into our new life and pull us backward. Ben? Impossible. He's in maximum security, denied all communication beyond his lawyers. Robert or Margaret? They've kept respectful distance, allowing Lily to set the pace of reconnection. Someone else entirely, with unknown motives?

Through the window, I watch Lily measuring rice into the cooker, headphones on, swaying slightly to music only she can hear. The normalcy of the scene squeezes my heart. We fought so hard for this. Do I risk it all by acknowledging this intrusion?

But secrets fester. I learned that lesson through blood and tears. Hiding this letter, pretending it doesn't exist, that's the first step back into darkness. Into doubt. Into the gaslighting labyrinth I barely escaped.

My hands tremble slightly as I slide my finger under the seal, the paper cutting into my skin. A paper cut—small, sharp pain that draws a drop of blood. I smear it with my thumb, leaving a faint rust-colored print on the envelope's corner.

Inside is a single sheet of paper, folded in thirds. The same cream stationery. I open it slowly, my breath catching as I see more of that familiar handwriting filling the page. The first line leaps out, printed in slightly larger letters than the rest:

Dear Emma, Some secrets refuse to stay buried...

My blood turns to ice water in my veins. I scan the rest of the page, phrases jumping out in horrible, disjointed fragments:

...not who you think I am...
...Ben was right about one thing...
...Lily doesn't know the whole truth...
...meet me if you want answers...

At the bottom, an address in Crystal River—the same town

where Alice supposedly drove off the bridge. There's a date and time: tomorrow, 8 p.m.

I fold the letter with numb fingers, sliding it back into the envelope. My mind races through possibilities, each more disturbing than the last. Someone mimicking Alice's handwriting to lure me into danger. Some cruel game designed to shatter our healing. Or the most impossible, unthinkable option —that Alice Stone somehow survived the accident that Ben confessed to orchestrating.

But I saw the autopsy photos during trial prep. Saw the DNA confirmation. Watched the exhumation. Alice is dead. She has to be dead.

The front door opens, Lily's voice calling out: "Emma? Are we doing chicken or tofu with the stir-fry?"

Such an ordinary question. Such a normal concern. The life we've built one dinner decision at a time.

"Let's do tofu," I call back, my voice steadier than I feel. "I'll be right there."

I stand in our driveway, suspended between the peace we've earned and the chaos this letter threatens to unleash. The golden hour light fades to blue dusk around me, shadows deepening across our yard. Somewhere in Crystal River, someone with Alice's handwriting is waiting. Someone with secrets that "refuse to stay buried."

Tomorrow at 8 p.m., I'll have to decide which is more dangerous, facing this new threat or ignoring it. Continuing our careful healing or risking everything for answers. The letter burns in my pocket, its first line echoing in my mind as I walk toward our front door, toward Lily, toward the fragile normalcy we've so painfully constructed.

Dear Emma, Some secrets refuse to stay buried...

Well, maybe they should stay buried, I think to myself then throw the letter in the trash can before grabbing Lily's hand in mine and closing the door behind me.

A LETTER FROM WILLOW

Dear reader,

Thank you for purchasing *To His New Wife*. If you did enjoy it and want to keep up to date with all my latest releases, just sign up at the following link. Your email address will never be shared and you can unsubscribe at any time.

www.bookouture.com/willow-rose

I hope you loved the story, and if you did, I would be very grateful if you could write a review. I had a lot of fun writing this story, and it's all very fictional. The only thing I have taken from real life is the story of the shim. It actually happened. A husband in Cleveland tried to murder his wife by placing a shim in it so the car couldn't stop. Luckily, she just crashed into a building and is still alive. He is now serving eight years in jail. You can read more about that story here if you like:

https://www.cleveland19.com/story/24929377/prison-for-man-who-tried-to-kill-wife-by-tampering-with-her-car/

As always, I appreciate your support and reviews.

Take care,

Willow

KEEP IN TOUCH WITH WILLOW

www.willow-rose.net

- facebook.com/willowredrose
- x.com/madamwillowrose
- instagram.com/willowroseauthor
- bookbub.com/authors/willow-rose

PUBLISHING TEAM

Turning a manuscript into a book requires the efforts of many people. The publishing team at Bookouture would like to acknowledge everyone who contributed to this publication.

Audio
Alba Proko

Commercial
Lauren Morrissette
Hannah Richmond
Imogen Allport

Cover design
Eileen Carey

Data and analysis
Mark Alder
Mohamed Bussuri

Editorial
Jennifer Hunt
Charlotte Hegley

Copyeditor
Janette Currie

Proofreader
Lynne Walker

Marketing
Alex Crow
Melanie Price
Cíara Rosney
Martyna Młynarska

Operations and distribution
Marina Valles
Joe Morris

Production
Hannah Snetsinger
Mandy Kullar
Nadia Michael
Charlotte Hegley

Publicity
Kim Nash
Noelle Holten
Jess Readett
Sarah Hardy

Rights and contracts
Peta Nightingale
Richard King
Saidah Graham

RAISING READERS
Books Build Bright Futures

Dear Reader,

We'd love your attention for one more page to tell you about the crisis in children's reading, and what we can all do.

Studies have shown that reading for fun is the **single biggest predictor of a child's future life chances** – more than family circumstance, parents' educational background or income. It improves academic results, mental health, wealth, communication skills, ambition and happiness.

The number of children reading for fun is in rapid decline. Young people have a lot of competition for their time, and a worryingly high number do not have a single book at home.

Hachette works extensively with schools, libraries and literacy charities, but here are some ways we can all raise more readers:

- Reading to children for just 10 minutes a day makes a difference
- Don't give up if children aren't regular readers – there will be books for them!

- Visit bookshops and libraries to get recommendations
- Encourage them to listen to audiobooks
- Support school libraries
- Give books as gifts

There's a lot more information about how to encourage children to read on our websites: **www.RaisingReaders.co.uk** and **www.JoinRaisingReaders.com**.

Thank you for reading.

Made in United States
North Haven, CT
27 March 2026